"Can we talk, Commander?"

He shook his head. "Monday. Right now I'm playing pool. And you're leaving."

"Oh, really? Is that an order?" There was just enough impertinence in her voice to let him know she had no intention of following it.

"Consider it a suggestion."

Tabby apparently decided to try a new tack. "Wanna play?" she asked, nodding toward the pool table.

He picked up his cue stick and handed her another. "No shop talk," he said before letting go.

"I wouldn't dream of it." She opened her eyes wide with feigned innocence.

"Yeah, right." That innocent act didn't cut it with him, and neither did the femme fatale. She could hang around all night, use every feminine wile she possessed, and she still wouldn't change his mind. But why not enjoy the company?

He should have run when he had the chance.

ABOUT THE AUTHOR

When a high-school aptitude test said she was suited to work in either a library or the clergy, Rogenna Brewer joined the navy. After boot camp, her first assignment was at Naval Air Station Midway Island. She started in the CO's office but ended up in the chaplain's, where her duties included operating the base library. Other duty stations followed, though she never actually left U.S. territory.

Eventually she met and married a sailor and admits to being jealous of his travels. "My husband's visited seventeen countries and was stationed aboard the USS *Enterprise* for the filming of two major motion pictures, *Top Gun* and *The Hunt for Red October*.

After her stint in the navy, she became a bookseller and a reviewer. But she's always wanted to be a writer.

Rogenna would love to hear from her readers. You can write her at P.O. Box 9806, Denver, CO 80209; e-mail her at Rogenna@aol.com or visit her web site at http://members.aol.com/Rogenna

SEAL It
With a Kiss
Rogenna Brewer

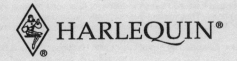

HARLEQUIN®

TORONTO • NEW YORK • LONDON
AMSTERDAM • PARIS • SYDNEY • HAMBURG
STOCKHOLM • ATHENS • TOKYO • MILAN • MADRID
PRAGUE • WARSAW • BUDAPEST • AUCKLAND

ISBN 0-373-70833-5

SEAL IT WITH A KISS

For my mother who believed,
For my husband, from the "Show Me" state,
For my three sons just because,
For my critique group/partners for their support...

I love you all.

Special thanks to my self-appointed research assistant,
Tina Novinski, for the countless little things you do.
Also to Deb Kastner for being able to read my mind.
And to Kathy Holzapfel for being just an e-mail away.

CHAPTER ONE

THE COMMANDER CONTINUED his relentless pacing behind the desk as he read her file. ''At ease,'' he ordered without looking up.

He seemed reluctant to give even that much. It wasn't his tone, resonant and deeply masculine, or his words that gave Lieutenant Tabitha Chapel the insight. It was what Commander Marc Miller left unsaid.

''Yes, sir.'' Tabby removed her cover, tucking the hat to her forearm. Her feet throbbed in new shoes. There wasn't a single pesky thread flagging her dress white uniform; she'd clipped them all down to the seam, wanting to make a good first impression. From the look on his face she was making anything but.

Then again she'd known this wasn't going to be easy.

Staring straight ahead, she studied Miller as he moved in and out of her peripheral vision. The man was younger than expected for a Commanding Officer, midthirties possibly. A frown furrowed otherwise handsome features, drawing dark brows slightly above a strong angular nose while his mouth held a firm line. She suspected a smile was rare. In any case, there were no laugh lines around his eyes.

For Tabby laugh lines on a man were a *must*.

But she wasn't here looking for a man. She was here reporting in for temporary duty, TDY in military terms.

He stopped pacing and cleared his throat. "I said at ease." Looking up from the file, he snapped it shut and leveled his baby blues at her. "That means relax."

She knew what it meant! She just didn't know *how* to relax while the man held her future in his hands.

"Yes, sir," she repeated, forcing herself to slacken her stance. Now that she had his undivided attention she was acutely aware of the sharp intelligence shining in his eyes.

Eyes that missed nothing.

He tossed the folder to the desktop and moved around in front of it. Hitching up a pant leg of his khaki uniform, he perched on the corner and gave her the once-over. "Tell me why you're here, Lieutenant."

"I believe the orders are self-explanatory, sir." It was all there in black and white. He must have read them at least a dozen times.

She was here to conduct a feasibility study on incorporating women into SEAL Training. Navy SEALs were part of the U.S. Special Operations Command. Miller was a prime example of their physical conditioning.

His well-muscled biceps strained the stitching of three-quarter sleeves as he folded tanned arms across a broad chest. "I didn't ask what your orders were. I asked why *you,* Tabitha Lilith Chapel-Prince were reporting in to *my* command."

Tabby tilted her chin. She understood perfectly. He was asking why *she,* a female, was reporting in to *his* all-male command. Because she had a lot more brass behind her than he did. At least she hoped she did.

"Then, sir, I'm afraid I don't understand your question."

"I don't buy that. According to your service record, five years ago you graduated first in your class at Annapolis. Is the Naval Academy lowering its standards to accommodate female Midshipmen?"

"No!" she snapped, immediately regretting her outburst. If he was trying to get a rise out of her, he'd gotten one. "No, sir," she corrected.

"I'm not impressed, Lieutenant. There are only three things that impress me. Honesty is one of them."

Did the top brass in Washington know about this guy? He belonged on a recruiting poster, finger pointing, the words I Want You in bold black letters with Old Glory flying in the background.

"I'm here because I was ordered here TDY," she said, a touch too haughtily for addressing a senior officer. Commander or not, she wasn't going to back down. And this man would likely turn out to be her worst enemy, if he wasn't already.

"I see." His tone told her he did see, too much.

"My apologies, sir. I was out of line."

"You can drop the Academy polish. We're a little less formal around here. The name's Marc, but Commander will do if you're uncomfortable using it."

"Yes, sir—Commander," Tabby corrected when his gaze narrowed.

"You're in serious need of an attitude adjustment, Lieutenant. An insult is an insult no matter how pretty the package."

He could have meant the insincerity of her words. But she suspected the insult was the fact her boss, Rear Admiral Gromley—the Chief of Naval Personnel—had sent her and not a man to do the job.

And why not? Gromley was a woman. The highest ranking woman in the Navy. More importantly, she supported Tabby's agenda.

He straightened. Tabby's gaze drifted upward with his movement. At five-feet-ten, an even six feet in pumps, she rarely had to look up to anyone.

"I'm trying to initiate dialogue here," he continued.

"I volunteered, Commander. Because the study is my idea." She maintained direct eye contact, noting the flash of surprise before he set his shuttered expression back in place.

"I see," he repeated in that all-knowing tone of his. He retreated behind his desk and opened her service record again. As if he'd missed some obvious answer earlier, he searched for it now, flipping through the pages.

She felt the pinch of her toes with increasing discomfort as he delayed the inevitable. "Commander—'' she broke protocol by speaking first ''—I'm waiting for you to throw me out.''

''And I would do that, why?'' He looked up.

''Because you don't want me here.''

''True enough. I don't want you here. But I'll work out that issue *up* the chain of command. I don't make a habit of eating junior officers for breakfast.''

He let her file fall closed and crossed his arms again. They stood facing each other on opposite sides of the desk and opposite sides of an issue equally important to both of them.

If he intended to go over her head, he had the rank and authority to do so. But Rear Admiral Gromley was her staunch ally on this project. And Tabby had a few tricks up her tailored uniform sleeve.

She wasn't going anywhere.

At least not until the study was complete. So he could very well wind up eating her for breakfast. Though he looked like a meat and potatoes man, she'd bet he'd make an exception for junior officers who crossed the line he chose to draw. And she *was* going to cross it. The prospect that he'd chew her up and spit her out wasn't the least bit appealing. But Miller would find her as tough as old boot leather.

''Chapel's your maiden name?'' he asked, derailing her train of thought.

''My mother's. But I prefer it.''

''Are you related to Captain Tad Prince, retired Navy?''

''He's my father.''

He acknowledged her answer with a curt nod. "I knew your father. Once upon a time…"

That didn't come as a surprise. Everyone who was anyone in the Navy knew her father. It was one of the reasons she used her mother's maiden name. Her father had retired from the Commander's very position fifteen years ago. It wasn't hard to imagine their career paths crossing.

She'd read Miller's bio. He was that rare breed the Navy called *Mustang*. He'd gone through SEAL Training as a nineteen-year-old Seaman. While serving his enlistment, he'd earned his bachelor's degree through applied studies and night school. Then he'd attended Officer Candidate School and received his commission at age twenty-three.

Miller hadn't missed a beat by not getting a conventional college education. He didn't seem like the Ivy League type anyway, too rough around the edges. And he definitely wasn't Academy material.

He pushed her file across the desk. "Hand carry this back to Personnel."

Tabby picked up the folder, wondering exactly what information he'd gleaned from it. She'd have to find a way to access his service record. The sketchy bio hadn't given her much to go on. Now that she'd met him, she wanted to know as much as possible about the man. She waited, expecting him to dismiss her.

"Are you staying at the BOQ?"

"Yes." She'd checked into the Bachelor Officers' Quarters that morning.

"Don't get too settled, Lieutenant. I'll have your

new orders cut by Monday. By this time next week you'll find yourself right back in D.C.''

She wondered if he was naturally optimistic, considering military paperwork and the fact that it was already past midweek. Or was the man just confident he had that much pull? She'd bet it was confidence. And she'd bet he was wrong. In fact, she was banking on it.

''Until Monday? What time do you want me here in the morning?''

''As far as I'm concerned you're on liberty. Take a couple days to see California compliments of Uncle Sam. Report back to me Monday at 0700.''

''If it's just the same—''

''Dismissed, Lieutenant.''

''Yes, sir.'' No use arguing with a superior officer. She'd just show up tomorrow and let him deal with her then. She couldn't be written up for disobeying a direct order when it contradicted a standing order from a higher authority.

A vacation on Uncle Sam indeed! She had a mission.

She held out her hand to shake his, then dropped it awkwardly when he didn't return the courtesy. His hand remained tucked in his folded arms. Accepting the insult for what it was, Tabby turned to leave.

Let him take it up the chain. She'd just be caught in the push-pull of Navy politics for a while. She'd gotten used to that as an admiral's aide in Washington, D.C. She didn't expect to leave it behind in Coronado, California.

''And, Lieutenant...''

Tabby halted in her trek across the room. ''Sir?''

"When you get here on Monday, I expect the hem of your skirt to be three inches below your knees." He looked pointedly at her exposed knee-caps.

To hell with protocol!

"Naval regulations state three inches above *or* below the knee, Commander," she snapped. "I prefer three inches above." She continued toward the door.

"*Miller* Regs say three inches below. By Monday." He cleared his throat. "One more thing…"

Tabby gripped the doorknob, waiting for him to hurl his next directive.

"Welcome aboard SEAL Training."

Marc caught the chin tilt as she left his inner office and smiled to himself. He followed the feminine sway of skirt to the door. Casually resting his shoulder against the jamb, he watched her go.

The lady knew how to make an exit.

"Attention on deck," Jeff "the Preacher" Perry called out, jumping to his feet.

The Lieutenant marched past reception and continued clicking her high-heeled way down the tiled passageway until she disappeared around the corner.

Marc shifted his gaze to the yeoman outfitted in green fatigues. "At ease, Preach," he said, dispensing with the usual formalities between an officer and his men. "She's out of the picture."

"Did you get a look at those legs?" Perry slipped into his creaky desk chair and leaned back. "What I wouldn't give to have them wrapped around me any night of the week!"

Since Petty Officer Second Class Perry rated women according to the day of the week on which he'd date them, Saturday being the highest and Sunday reserved for virgins, *any* day of the week was a pretty high compliment indeed.

Marc shook off the question and the accompanying comment with a shake of his head. Of course he'd gotten a look at the Lieutenant's legs.

He couldn't stop looking.

That was the problem. And the reason he'd buried his nose in her service record. So he wouldn't be *caught* looking. He preferred uniform skirts three inches above the knee, too.

"Pull out the Uniform Regs on hemlines before you head out to the gym," he instructed.

"Hemlines. You got it." Swiveling his chair around with a squeal, Perry faced a row of Navy manuals lining the credenza behind his desk.

"Better make that a copy of everything you can find on female uniforms," Marc added.

"Gonna give her a hard time, Commander?" With a cocky grin, the young enlisted man opened the requested manual.

"That's exactly what I'm going to give her."

"I could think of a better way to do it."

So could he. But he'd never admit it.

"Add a copy of the section on grooming standards," Marc said. "Could be she needs to lose an inch from the length of her hair."

Shaking his blond head, the petty officer moved to the Xerox machine along the far wall.

Marc pushed away from the door to sit on the yeoman's desk. He planned to run Ms. Spit and Polish through a little impromptu inspection before he sent her packing on Monday. There had to be something about her appearance he could pick on.

No woman was *that* close to perfect.

Filled with restless energy, he picked up a pencil and tapped it against his palm. "Would you say the Lieutenant was a blonde or a redhead?" He affected a disinterested tone.

"She's what you call one of them strawberry blondes," Perry informed him. "Here." He handed Marc the copies.

Marc stopped tapping and set the pencil aside. "Huh, whaddayaknow." There was actually a hair color called strawberry. That would also describe the faint scent still lingering in the air.

Papers in hand, he pushed off the yeoman's desk and headed back to his own office. Come Monday, he'd show Lieutenant Tabitha Chapel exactly who she was dealing with. Once he did, she wouldn't be able to leave Coronado fast enough. They didn't call him a hard-ass for nothing.

If she'd shined up her brass, he'd shine up his.

"Preach, get me Admiral Dann on the horn." She had the Chief of Naval Personnel in her pocket. But he had the Chief of SEALs in his.

Marc closed his office door behind him. He glanced briefly at the pages in hand, then tossed them to the In box on his desk. More paperwork to shuffle. He'd end up a lard ass instead of a hard-ass if this didn't stop.

Rounding the piece of furniture he called home, he picked up his copy of Lieutenant Chapel's orders.

Women SEALs? No way!

"Not in this man's Navy." Slapping the orders

back to the blotter, he sat down. Why did he have the feeling trouble was spelled "Tabitha" with a capital *T?*

Granted it was only a feasibility study. But with a study on how to incorporate women into SEAL Training could the directive making it so be that far behind?

He had to nip it in the bud here and now.

SEALs were the Navy's elite Special Warfare Commandos of SEa, Air, and Land. He was the man in charge of training them, really of handpicking them, since only a small percentage of candidates made it through the fifth week of training, called *Hell Week.* If women were allowed in, he'd be the man standing between them and the coveted Trident Insignia.

"Why me?" Marc groaned, but only because nobody could hear him. He wasn't the type to indulge in self-pity, at least not when it was counterproductive and he recognized it as such.

He'd been CO for less than a fiscal quarter with barely one class of SEAL wannabes behind him. His Commander's cluster was so new he wasn't even getting the 0-5 pay yet. But Marc knew he could handle anything one determined junior officer could throw at him.

She was what? All of twenty-five or so? No, twenty-seven. Twenty-eight next month. He'd noted her birth date in her service record. He was thirty-four, seven years and a world of experience older.

He dug into his In box without much enthusiasm. There were a few things he needed to get done before heading to the gym for his daily workout. He checked his wristwatch and discovered it was later than he thought.

Who was he kidding? He wouldn't get any work done this morning. Marc tossed the papers back to the overflowing box. Physical activity was exactly what he needed right now. Otherwise he'd spend the rest of the day thinking about strawberries, long legs and green cat eyes.

He didn't understand the effect she had on him. It wasn't like he'd never seen a woman in uniform. But right now he was as randy as any Seaman on his first shore leave.

He'd obviously been celibate far too long. But his days of thumbing through a little black book were over. It had been three years. And even if it meant three more, he intended to abstain for as long as it took to prove he was in control of his baser instincts. He'd prove himself better than his paternity.

Though he had to agree with Perry—the Lieutenant deserved an any-night-of-the-week rating. She'd offered her hand, and he'd been afraid to reach out and clasp it. One touch just wouldn't have satisfied him.

Maybe he'd skip the workout and head straight for the cold shower. Whatever name she called herself, Tabitha Lilith Chapel-Prince was the Toad Prince's daughter. If he dared touch, he imagined the retired Navy SEAL would have something to say about it.

"Commander?" Perry knocked and poked his head in.

"Yeah?" Marc looked up glad for the interruption.

"The Admiral's secretary said he's out of the office this week and next. She faxed this over." Perry approached with a sheet of paper in his outstretched hand. "We're on his agenda for Monday at 0900. Under feasibility study."

Marc grabbed the fax. There was indeed a meeting scheduled for 0900 at The Naval Special Warfare Center, Coronado, California. In his office.

Typed in bold black letters were the names of the attending officers: Admiral Mitchell Dann, Commander Marc Miller, and Lieutenant Tabitha Chapel.

"Damn!" Jerking open the file drawer to his left, Marc felt his way to the back where he kept a bag of Tootsie Pops. Pulling one out, he unwrapped it, then stuck the sucker in his mouth.

Even after fifteen years as a nonsmoker, he still craved the oral gratification of cigarettes when he was frustrated.

1134 Thursday
BACHELOR OFFICERS' QUARTERS,
Coronado, CA

"WELCOME ABOARD SEAL Training," Tabby mimicked, plopping down on the bunk in her BOQ room. She eased off first one white leather pump, then the other. Letting the second shoe drop to the floor, she rubbed her aching tootsies. "And by the way, Chapel, don't let the door hit you on the way out."

She offered a mock salute to her closed door. "Aye, aye, Commander. I'll be sure to let down those hems as set forth in Miller Regs, too." Her words were as sarcastic as she could make them.

The man was a chauvinist hiding behind Mr. Politically Correct. And to think she'd worn new shoes just to impress him. Impress him, ha! She'd had to walk all the way back to Personnel with her file. That's how *un*impressed he was. She'd known from the start he wasn't going to accept her presence. Unless she made him.

Tabby unbuttoned her uniform jacket and slumped back against the pillow, letting the tension drain from her body in a satisfied sigh. *At least she was here.*

She'd gotten her foot in the door. And she was one step closer to her life's ambition, becoming the first female Navy SEAL. Her mouth curved into a smile.

She couldn't shy away from the fact SEALs could become involved in combat, though their speciality was more clandestine. Those covert operations intrigued her, but it was their rescue missions that had captured her imagination. Was there anything nobler than service to others?

At the risk of one's own life?

"Greater love hath no woman than this, that she lay down her life for another," she paraphrased an old Sunday School lesson to the best of her recollection. Man, woman, it was all the same.

She'd been brought up to believe girls and boys were equal. That is, until she'd told her father she wanted to follow in his footsteps. Tabby's smile became strained.

He'd dismissed the idea immediately. She hadn't.

From that day forward she'd wanted to unlock the mystery of being part of a SEAL Team. Why would a father who encouraged his daughter to do any-thing, be anything, discourage her from a particular job?

Because of the element of danger inherent to *that* job? Maybe. He had the scarred face to prove it. But he'd expected both her brothers to join the SEALs. And she knew he'd been disappointed when Zach and Bowie had chosen different paths for their Naval careers. He'd ignored the fact there was still one member of the family to carry on his legacy. Could she help it if she was the wrong sex? That was his fault, too.

Despite his lack of faith, she loved him enough to try and was just stubborn enough to succeed. Tabby believed she could do anything she set her mind to. Though it seemed her father's belief in her had limits.

For the moment however, her father wasn't the problem, at least not until he found out what she was up to.

She had all her ducks in a row. And all her ad-mirals, too. In order to invade the exclusive "boys' club," she'd chosen her strategy carefully. After years of planning, only Commander Marc Miller stood in her way.

And he'd find her a worthy opponent. In fact, she looked forward to matching wits with him. She'd seen the challenge in his cornflower-blue eyes. And she was ready to meet it.

Actually now that she thought about it, his eyes were the deeper shade of morning glories. She won-dered what the man would think of her comparing his eyes to flowers. As macho as he was, it would probably be a direct hit to his ego!

Maybe she'd just have to tell him.

She practiced in a throaty whisper. "Marc, your eyes are the color of morning glories." With just the right amount of sensuality her voice was guaranteed to make a grown man drop to his knees. Especially the tough ones like Miller. She could tell by their single encounter he was tough. And controlled.

Grudgingly, she admired his control. Secretly, she wanted to break it just enough to see what lay beneath the veneer of Commanding Officer.

Staring at the ceiling, she recalled his hard chiseled cheeks, firm jaw and set lips. His hair was dark and military short. It reminded her of mink and looked just as soft.

It was probably the only soft thing about him. He was a typical SEAL. And yet, she knew intuitively there was nothing typical about him.

"Marc," she repeated the name he'd invited her to use. *The name's Marc, but Commander will do if you're uncomfortable using it.* "Commander," she said firmly, pushing up from the bed.

She had some unpacking to do.

Not only that, she had to break out her sewing kit for a tape measure. She wanted to make sure all her uniform skirts were exactly three inches *above* the knee. If she intended to fight Miller Regs, she'd better make sure she met the Navy standard.

0700 Friday
NAVAL SPECIAL WARFARE CENTER,
Coronado, CA

At precisely 0700 Friday morning, Tabby once again entered the cinder block building that served as SEAL Training Headquarters. The place seemed deserted. Her footfalls echoed down the tiled passageway. Even the yeoman's desk outside the Commander's office stood vacant with the chair missing.

"Don't tell me they all sleep in," she muttered, looking around for signs of life. Generally the Navy day started early. And she'd assumed the SEALs would be here.

The smell of fresh-brewed coffee led her to Miller's door. It figured. He seemed like the type. *All paperwork and no play made the Commander a dull boy.* He probably read Navy manuals in his spare time. When would that be? Between workouts?

She knocked and heard the muffled command. "Enter."

This was even harder than yesterday. Because today she knew who she was dealing with.

Taking a deep breath, Tabby checked her gig line, making sure her belt buckle was aligned with the placket of her khaki shirt. Then she opened the door.

Twenty-eight heads turned in her direction. All male. Her eyes went directly to the man in the center. She refused to look away first, and their gazes locked in a battle with no victor.

"Have a seat, Lieutenant," he said in invitation. He sat on the corner of his desk, just like yesterday. "We're in the middle of our morning briefing."

She slipped into the room, stepping around one man and scooting past another before she could shut the door. There was standing room only in Miller's spacious office. A quick-thinking enlisted man jumped from his seat and offered it to her. Tabby recognized him as the Commander's yeoman and waved him off, preferring to stand.

She took an inconspicuous spot at the back of the crowd. A difficult accomplishment with all eyes on her. From the looks on their faces, they knew who she was and why she was here.

Marc shifted his gaze away from the interruption and focused on the sea of frowning faces. "Where were we?" He knew damn well where he'd left off. And so did his men. Tension from what would remain unsaid, for now, supercharged the air.

He couldn't believe she had the nerve to walk in three days early. Though she tried, she failed to blend in with the mix of uniformed officers and enlisted men. He didn't know how he kept a straight face. What really got him was the fact she'd found a way around his hemline directive.

She wore pants!

Irony made life interesting. And Lieutenant Chapel apparently understood irony.

"It seems we were talking about you, Lieutenant."

"Sticks and stones..." she spouted, making some of the less restrained younger men chuckle.

Covering his own smile, Marc cleared his throat. "Rest assured we won't be breaking any bones or resort to name calling."

"I'm outta here." Lieutenant Leighton popped to his feet. Glowering in Tabitha Chapel's direction, Hugh Leighton crushed his empty coffee cup and tossed it to the wastebasket on his way toward the door.

''Sit,'' Marc ordered the others threatening to follow the example of the Texan tagged ''Houston.'' ''Hugh, that includes you.''

Hugh turned to meet his glare. ''Marc—''

''Now!'' He rarely raised his voice when he issued an order to one of the instructors. SEALs operated on a system of mutual respect. Officers and enlisted men alike were treated as equals. But there was a pecking order. And he was at the top. Hugh apparently needed a reminder.

Dragging his feet, Leighton shuffled back to his seat like a petulant schoolboy. Marc couldn't blame him for that bit of defiance. Hugh felt threatened. They all did.

Because of a single, solitary female. Everything they were as men suddenly meant nothing, less than nothing, if women were allowed to join their ranks.

They were men. They were elite. They were Navy SEALs.

The job required balls, not beauty.

Hugh made it to his seat, and Marc turned his attention to the senior enlisted man. ''Master Chief, go ahead with announcements.''

Command Master Chief Jack Murphy stood. Adjusting his reading glasses, he unfolded a piece of paper and read, ''The following personnel need to meet their jump quals…''

Throughout the reading, Lieutenant Chapel remained mute. Marc crooked his finger in her direction. He wanted her close. Close enough to keep an eye on her.

She eased her way through the crowd. Several appreciative male gazes followed.

He patted the desktop beside him. "Sit," he instructed. She propped herself against the desk in a stance that mimicked his. Leaning over, he whispered, "Nice pants."

Her mouth curved knowingly. Even smug she had a beautiful smile. Maybe he wanted her close. But he'd be better off if she was three thousand miles away.

Marc shifted his attention to where it belonged.

"Don't forget," Murphy continued. "Tonight is the retirement party for Master Chief Howard Thomas of SEAL Team One, 1900 at Manny's Dive. The first keg is on the Chiefs' Association. But we need two more designated drivers. Volunteers can see me after the briefing." Finished, he signaled Marc with a nod.

"Dismissed." Marc excused the men.

Hugh sprinted from the room. The rest swarmed the door behind the Texan, taking several chairs with them.

Lieutenant Chapel pushed to her feet.

"Not you." He stalled her departure by touching her forearm, noting the softness beneath his callused fingertips. She looked pointedly at his hand, and he dropped it. He was out of line.

The last man out closed the door, leaving the two of them alone. Suddenly the room felt too small, the space between them too narrow, his shirt collar too tight.

She tucked a strand of that unusual color hair behind her ear and stared at him with luminous eyes.

He channeled all his energy into what he wanted

to say. "I thought I'd made it clear I didn't want to see your face around here until Monday."

So why couldn't he take his eyes off her?

"About Monday, Commander. There's something you should know—"

"I got wind of the meeting, Lieutenant." Marc reached behind him and picked up his coffee mug. Taking a sip, he held back a grimace and swallowed the bitter lukewarm mud. She wasn't going to catch him off guard again. "Dismissed."

CHAPTER TWO

2130 Friday
MANNY'S DIVE,
Coronado, CA

"I DON'T EVEN WANT to think about her, let alone talk about her," Marc said, lining up his next shot. Friday nights were for kicking back with the guys. "Six ball, corner pocket." He gestured with his cue stick. At Manny's he could play a little pool, throw back a few brews and be himself.

Tonight's retirement party packed the place with instructors and Team One SEALs. It was the perfect atmosphere to forget about a certain strawberry blond Lieutenant.

So why couldn't he?

"You're the one who brought up the subject." Brad leaned against an old-fashioned jukebox blasting a new-fangled beat. Stick in one hand, beer bottle in the other, the man toasted his observation.

Bending over the table, Marc cast him a reproachful glare. Commander Brad "the Torch" Bailey, his best friend since Basic Underwater Demolition/SEAL Training, and his equal in all things except pool, wasn't about to let him get away with anything. Especially not an outright lie.

He *had* been the one to bring up the subject of Lieutenant Tabitha Chapel. He couldn't get past the fact a woman with that much feminine appeal wanted to be a Navy SEAL.

She hadn't said as much, but it was the only possible explanation. The study was her idea. But what, if anything, did it have to do with her old man? Did Prince even know what his little girl was up to?

Tapping the cue ball, Marc sent it to the cushion with a thunk. Rebounding off the side, the white ball smacked the six ball with the sweet crack of ivory on ivory, sending it neatly into the corner pocket.

"Nice shot," Brad praised. "All I said was I heard she's hot. Is she, or isn't she?"

Straightening, Marc moved around the table. "You're married."

"Married doesn't mean buried." Brad smiled and waved across the bar at his wife. Carol waved back, patiently occupying a corner booth while they played their game.

Marc shook his head. Coming from any other man the comment would have sounded arrogant. Coming from Brad, it sounded endearing. He knew his friend took a lot of ribbing for bringing his wife to the SEALs' off-base hangout. But the newlyweds were inseparable.

To most SEALs married *meant* buried. And freedom meant everything. Marc envied his friend's lack of freedom. Except, in his opinion, Brad would be wiser to leave his wife at home.

Manny's Dive was exactly that, a dockside hole-in-the-wall. A place for hardworking, hard-playing men to unwind. With the exception of gun groupies and barflies, you didn't walk in the place unless you were a Navy SEAL. Otherwise, you were quickly shown the door.

Occasionally a band of sailors or marines would come to test their mettle against the Navy's finest and the night would end in a brawl.

"Eight ball," Marc called his shot.

"Well?" Brad prompted.

Marc affected interest in chalking the felt tip of his stick before he answered. "She's easy on the eye," he admitted, setting the cube aside. "And a pain in the butt. My butt! Until I get her back to D.C. and out of my hair." He positioned himself at the table. "Side pocket."

"So you're interested?"

"She's—"

"Whoa!"

Marc lifted his gaze. The stick skipped, sending the cue ball into a harmless spin. He'd been about to say, *off limits.*

Straightening, he hit his head on the low hanging lamp above the pool table and winced. But it wasn't from the pain in his head.

His pain in the *butt* had just walked in the door.

Real or imagined there was a second of silence that told him they weren't the only ones who'd noticed a she-cat on the prowl. Even the jukebox paused between songs. Static hummed, then another CD dropped in place and the singer crooned a familiar love song just for her.

The comments started, spoiling the imagery.

"That her?" Looking from Marc back to the door, Brad let loose a low, easy whistle.

"That's her," Marc confirmed, trading places. Picking up his beer from the bumper, he watched as she managed to make her way through the press of male bodies with that cocky self-assurance that marked her step.

Wearing a bomber jacket and jump boots, she was otherwise dressed in civilian clothes. Tight jeans hugged the flare of her hips. A pink knit top traced the outline of her breasts. Strawberry girl looked ripe for the picking.

If she'd come looking for company, she'd find it. If she'd come looking for him, he'd better run.

She turned and stared directly at him. His mouth went dry and he was glad for the beer in his hand. Marc took a long draw to quench his thirst. His eyes remained on her despite the bottle impeding his otherwise perfect vision.

Tabby locked on that familiar blue gaze. Just the man she wanted to see. She acknowledged him with a nod he didn't bother to return.

Well, at least she knew he was here.

The retirement party provided a good excuse. Master Chief Thomas was an old friend of her father's and she needed to pay her respects. She looked around, but didn't see him. Her gaze kept wandering back to the one man intent on ignoring her.

Dismissing the Commander's rudeness with a frown, she leaned across the polished bar. "Miller Light." The significance of "Miller" registered only after it was too late to change her mind.

The bartender spun his wheelchair, deftly filling her order. A platform behind the bar put them on equal ground. "What else, sweetheart?" he asked, handing her the bottle.

"Nothing, thanks."

"Name's Manny, like the sign outside. If you need anything, just holler." The middle-aged owner had a generous sprinkle of salt coloring his thick beard and overlong hair. "In case you're the curious type, only two of my three legs are out of commission." He waggled his brows suggestively.

She'd never met a handicapped lecher before. In a single sentence the man told her everything she *never* wanted to know about him.

Shifting her black leather backpack, she pulled out her billfold. "What do I owe you?"

"Put it away, sweetheart," Manny instructed. "Your money's no good here. Let one of the boys get it."

Every sailor within five feet opened his wallet. Tabby shook her head at the offers. She could have thrown her cash down on the bar, but she knew how this game was played. So she tucked her money away and picked the biggest, baddest, safest guy in the place.

"Put it on Marc Miller's tab."

Wallets disappeared with murmurs of apology.

Manny's bushy brows rose above beady eyes. "About what I said—"

"Forget it."

"I didn't know you were with Miller."

She wasn't. But she smiled and let the assumption stand. It didn't hurt that Commander Miller had the rank to back up his attitude, and hers. And because she was his subordinate, to him, she was strictly off limits.

Picking up her beer, she made her way to the pool tables, approaching Miller from behind. His broad shoulders filled the chambray shirt he wore tucked into belted stonewashed jeans.

She hesitated before accepting that this was the same man who wore a commander's cluster. The Navy was a twenty-four-hour-a-day job. But tonight, the *image* of officer didn't fit. Not like that shirt and those jeans anyway.

"Tell me something," he said, without turning around. "Are you here looking for trouble? Or are you just going to let it find you?" Retrieving the colored balls from the chute in pairs, he rolled them toward the man at the opposite end. But there was no mistaking the fact he was talking to her.

"I'm here looking for you."

He set down the next batch of balls carefully and turned to face her. Leaning back against the cushioned bumper, he folded his arms. "You shouldn't be here."

"Well, I am," she said, putting her beer down beside him.

"This isn't the kind of place *nice girls* wander into."

"Oh really? What kind of *girls* do?"

"The lost and the lonely."

As sad as that sounded, it pretty much summed up the few she'd seen. *But not her.* "Well, I'm not lost or lonely."

"I know," he said, shifting his gaze to take in the room. "And you just made me the envy of every man in the place. Now, why are you looking for me?''

His words sent a thrill through Tabby. ''I thought we needed to talk. *Out* of uniform.''

''If I wasn't a nice guy, I'd take you up on that offer, Tabitha.''

Heat burst over her cheeks like a warning flare. ''You know I meant civilian clothes.''

''A-hem.''

She turned at the sound of a man clearing his throat.

''Before anyone takes off their clothes, I want an introduction.'' He looked expectantly at Miller who ignored the request. ''Brad Bailey,'' he introduced himself, filling the silence with a broad grin as he extended his hand. ''CO, SEAL Team One and Marc's swim buddy since BUDS training.''

His handshake was firm but friendly, and she smiled into warm chocolate eyes. His build was slighter than Marc's. And though Brad's brown hair receded from his forehead, she guessed them to be about the same age.

''Tabitha Chapel.''

''I know. Marc's been telling me all about you.''

They'd been talking about her? It couldn't be anything good. But at least he wasn't dismissing her. ''Call me Tabby.''

''Brad, I think I hear Carol calling,'' Marc interjected.

Tabby didn't hear a thing.

''What? Oh, right.'' Brad nodded. ''Don't go away. I'll be right back.'' He winked at her and flashed Miller a thumbs-up.

"Where were we?" Miller raked a hand through his hair.

"Talking?" she suggested.

The frown furrowing his forehead deepened. "I'm off duty."

"Since when is conversation considered duty?"

He shifted, knocking the bottle at his side. Her hand darted out, and they caught the tilting bottle together.

"Nice catch," he complimented, without letting go. His mouth quirked at the corner, and Tabby got the feeling he was holding back a thousand-kilowatt grin that would light up even the darkest and loneliest night.

"Martial arts." The explanation escaped on a husky note. "I mean, it helps the reflexes." Flustered, she overcompensated by babbling.

Slipping her hand from beneath his, she slid her palm along the wet condensation dripping down the long neck bottle. The warmth and wetness of their brief physical contact ended with her heart racing and her stomach roiling.

"I read that in your file." He held out her beer. "I'm not impressed."

That didn't surprise her. Nothing about her appeared to. And he was probably a fourth degree black belt anyway. Careful not to touch him again, she took the offered bottle.

This whole thing seemed to be blowing up in her face. She'd intended to catch him somewhere they could both talk. She was more uncomfortable around him here than she'd ever been in his office.

But in his office, in uniform, communication was a one-way street.

Refusing to get off track, she started over. "Can we sit and talk?"

"You had your chance yesterday."

"I just thought—"

"Monday morning." He crossed his arms. "Right now I'm playing pool. And you're leaving."

"Oh, really?" The man was in denial. The study would happen. And the sooner he accepted that, the sooner she could get started. And the sooner she could achieve her objective. "Is that an order, *Marc?*" She used his given name, adding enough impertinence to let him know she had no intention of following it. Even if it was.

"Consider it a suggestion."

Tabby pulled a couple of bills from her jacket pocket and tossed them to the green felt top. Let him think she was leaving. "I owe you two bucks."

He raised a dark brow.

"You bought my beer," she clarified, lifting the bottle.

"I won't take your money."

Seeing her chance, she tilted her head toward the triangle of waiting balls. "Play you for it?"

Marc shook his head. Not in answer to her question, but because she didn't give up, and he was about to give in. If only to prove a point. "Winner buys. *Loser* takes the cash."

"You're on."

He picked up his discarded cue stick and handed her another. "No shop talk," he said before letting go.

"I wouldn't dream of it." She opened her eyes wide with feigned innocence.

"Yeah, right." She may not be *lost*. And she may not be *lonely*. But Tabitha Chapel was way out of her league. That innocent act didn't cut it with him and neither did the femme fatale. She could hang around all night, use every feminine wile she possessed, and still wouldn't change his mind. He would *not* endorse a study on how to incorporate women into his world. But why not enjoy the company?

Setting aside her beer and stick, she shrugged out of her pack and jacket, stashing them under the table.

Without the oversize bomber jacket, her curves were even more pronounced. Seeing her bare arms, he recalled the softness of her skin. Not the tough hide of a seasoned SEAL.

He should have run when he had the chance.

"Ladies first." He gestured toward the table. "Your break."

"Such chivalry. I guess that means you think you're pretty good." She moved to the top of the table.

"That's exactly what it means."

"Then you'd better show me. 'Cause otherwise I'm buying." She made a playful poke at his gut with the butt end of her stick.

Contracting his stomach muscles, he grunted.

"Who are you kidding?" she admonished without the least bit of sympathy. "That six-pack's no beer belly."

Snorting at the offhand compliment, he leaned

back against the jukebox with his beer to enjoy the view.

Tabby stole a glance over her shoulder, struck by the contrast between the on duty and off duty officer. He seemed comfortable. Relaxed.

Maybe it was the atmosphere.

She forced herself to concentrate on the game, sinking two solid balls on the break and pocketing a third before losing her turn. "I'm better than you thought I'd be." She stepped back to switch places.

"No." He held her gaze. "I knew you'd be good."

She looked away first, tucking herself safely into the corner. From there she admired his fluid movements as he circled the table, calculating each shot. When he grinned across the length of the pool table, she wondered how she'd ever missed the laugh lines. They were clearly visible in the light from the ceiling lamp.

Throughout the game, she managed to stay one shot ahead. But she didn't know if it was luck, or skill, or even some maneuvering on his part. She chose to believe they were equally matched. But she was so focused on their game that conversation was minimal.

Tabby missed her shot. "Don't look so smug," she scolded. "You haven't won yet." *Yet* was accurate because he sank the last balls easily.

"Looks like I'm buying."

"This time." Without the slightest hesitation, she pocketed the money. "But that's only because I know which battles are worth fighting."

He didn't look pleased. "You didn't let me win."

She lifted a shoulder in a slight shrug and laid her cue stick across the table. "No," she agreed with a Cheshire-cat-size grin implying she *did*.

"You're playing with my pride. You know that, don't you?"

Leaning against the cushioned bumper, she refused to acknowledge his dilemma. "I'll never tell." She sent the cue ball spinning across the felt top before looking up again. Her eyes met and held his. A man like Miller was *all* pride. That was the problem.

"I wouldn't get in the way of training," she pleaded. "You won't even notice I'm there."

His assessing gaze skimmed her from breasts to boots, then back up to her face. "Oh, I'll notice."

This time heat spread all the way up from her toes. If the blush had ever left her cheeks this evening, it was back now in Technicolor. She should've been insulted. Instead, her gaze followed a similar pattern over his body. From broad shoulders to low-heeled, low-cut boots, and back up to bedroom eyes. "I guess I'm just not as observant."

"Ouch." He winced.

"I'm back," Brad announced. "But I can go away again," he added, looking first at Miller, then her.

"No," Miller answered. "Our game's over."

The hidden meaning wasn't lost on her.

He reached under the table for her things. Grudgingly, she accepted them. She hadn't accomplished what she set out to do—convince him to give her a chance. So she gave it another try. "I don't suppose I could talk you into a dance?"

"No," he said coolly.

It was her turn to wince. "Aren't you the least bit curious?"

"About?" His tone held a note of caution.

"Why I came looking for you tonight?"

"I think it's going to start with 'pretty please' and end in a tantrum. And the result is still going to be the same. On Monday, you're headed back to D.C."

The man was too stubborn for his own good. "We'll see who winds up throwing a tantrum." Turning on her boot heels, she marched off.

Ignoring a slew of invitations, Tabby settled in at the closest unoccupied table. Far enough to ignore Miller, and close enough to irritate him. She hoped.

She only hung around the noisy, smoke-filled bar with its flashes of neon, because Miller wanted her to leave. The word "surrender" was not in her vocabulary. Not back in the fifth grade when the school bully showed no mercy in blackening both her eyes. And not now when an even bigger bully wanted her off his playground.

Tabby felt some small sense of satisfaction when Brad won the next two games. Nursing her beer, she watched them play pool for the better part of an hour. With a growing sense of restlessness she decided to look for Master Chief Thomas by way of the jukebox. Which took her right past Miller. Not that she wanted his attention. She just wanted him to know he didn't have hers. Not when it came to ordering her to leave anyway. Feeding the coin slot, she pressed the numbers for half a dozen selections, and her first choice kicked in.

Marc noticed the change in tempo from hard rock

to a slower, more seductive song. All night he'd stared down any man bold enough to rise to his feet, or even look in Tabitha's direction. Just standing there, she practically issued the whole bar an invitation.

He watched Hugh strut toward her.

"Game over," Marc said, throwing his cue stick to the felt top even though he was up by four balls. The only use he could think of for the pool table right now involved laying Tabitha back on it and would get him fifteen to twenty at hard labor. *Like sire, like son.*

That thought brought him up short.

Hugh was stationed in front of Tabitha, demanding her attention. "Dance?" He slurred the single word.

"The Lieutenant's dance card is full," Marc answered, stepping up behind her.

She turned to look at him, but Marc didn't break eye contact with Hugh.

She shouldn't be here. But she was.

Her orders made her his responsibility. At least that's how he saw it. He didn't even want to explore any other motives.

"That a fact?" Hugh asked.

"It is now." Rank and reputation made further words unnecessary. If he wanted Hugh to back down, the Texan would back down.

"My mistake," Hugh conceded. The slur disappeared. "Another time, Lieutenant." With one last look in her direction, Hugh swaggered off.

Marc turned his attention to Tabitha.

"Excuse me!" She arched a brow. "I *love* to dance—"

He latched on to her elbow. "So do I."

Snatching her arm back, she hissed under her breath, "That's not an invitation. And we're not together."

It was his turn to cock a brow. "I thought we were. Isn't that what you told Manny?"

"How—?"

"I read lips," he lied. He *knew* Manny.

She worried her lower lip with even white teeth, and another way of reading lips came to mind.

"Indulge me," he coaxed. "If you're going to tell people we're together, then you'll have to understand if I take exception to your dancing with other men." He leaned in to whisper his next words. "It's a guy thing."

Tabby heaved a frustrated sigh. She'd used him when it had suited her purpose. He had her there. And he knew it.

She allowed him to lead her to the dance floor.

A guy thing? Forget that she'd asked him earlier, it was a *girl* thing now. Crossing her arms, she offered a saccharine sweet smile. After all he couldn't force her to dance. "I have some say in this."

He didn't say a word, but simply held out his hand.

Her throat tightened. Her resolve crumbled with one look in his morning glory eyes. She loved to dance. And she'd had no intention of dancing with Leighton. But when had she completely lost control of the situation?

As the next slow song started, she slipped her

hand in his. He drew her into his arms. Strong arms. Secure arms.

With barely a whisper between them, he led her to the rhythm. It wasn't every day she got to dance with a man tall enough for her to rest her head on his shoulder. She was tentative at first, hoping he wouldn't notice the way her cheek brushed his collar.

Closing her eyes, she inhaled deeply. The sea, the air, the land, all clung to him, forming his own unique scent. Okay, so it could be deodorant by Mennen and soap by Zest. But he wore it well. His stubble-rough chin touched her forehead and she melted into his arms with the abrasive heat.

What was she doing? She was here to conduct a study on incorporating women into SEAL Training. Instead, she was studying the man determined to send her packing.

What purpose did that serve?

Another song started. Country singer Deana Carter belted out the words to "Strawberry Wine." His shoulder tensed beneath her resting hand. Tabby kneaded the corded muscle lightly with her fingertips, stealing a furtive glance upward.

The dim lighting softened his handsome features. Getting to know him did serve a purpose. She could discover his strengths and his weaknesses. She didn't dare cross the line from professional to personal. Not with him—her Commanding Officer.

But she could flirt awfully close to the edge.

"Marc…"

"Hmm?"

"Nothing," she said, capitulating.

"I apologize if I do. And I apologize if I don't," he murmured.

She cocked her head, curious about his comment.

He answered by pulling her closer. Their entwined fingers rested against his shoulder while his other hand settled at the small of her back. Her breasts flattened against his chest, and her thighs brushed his. The friction of their bodies swaying together left little to the imagination.

He was hard in all the right places. And getting harder in some.

A knowing smile curved her lips. "Apology accepted." She saw the tightly held control in his eyes. She wanted to be the one to make him let go. "Marc," she whispered, "has anyone ever told you your eyes are the color of morning glories?"

"We'd have to dance 'til dawn to find out." The low timbre of his voice caressed the shell of her ear, but the tone was light and playful.

Who was flirting with whom?

"You're teasing," she accused, suddenly uncomfortable with the direction of their conversation. She wanted the man to take her seriously, and he wouldn't do that as long as she kept sending the wrong signals.

She may be attracted to him, he may be attracted to her, but he could get in a whole lot of trouble if either of them acted on that attraction. The worst that could happen to her was a transfer out of his command.

Considering how hard she'd worked to get here that was the last thing she wanted.

The song ended abruptly and he spun her away,

relieving the tension between them. He pulled her back and dropped her into an exaggerated dip, holding it a moment too long. ''What's the Chief of SEALs doing here?'' he asked.

''Where?'' From her topsy-turvy view of the world, she spotted the uniformed officer headed in their direction. Fiftyish and distinguished with graying temples, he leaned heavily on his walking stick. Otherwise he looked every bit as fit as any Navy SEAL. ''Uncle Mitch!''

Marc jerked her back up. ''Uncle?''

CHAPTER THREE

"UNCLE!" MARC CHOKED out a second time, making the word sound like the childhood cry of surrender.

"Actually, he's my godfather," Tabitha admitted. "I just call him Uncle Mitch. When I'm not in uniform, of course."

"The Chief of SEALs is your godfather." He ground his teeth to keep from uttering a string of expletives.

Her godfather. His boss.

"I tried to tell you." Turning, she left him standing in the middle of the dance floor.

She hadn't tried very hard. Of course, he hadn't exactly been open to communication. At least not verbal communication. The body had a language all its own. And theirs had been talking all night.

He'd never been in the position of being attracted to a subordinate before. It didn't help that she had no business being under his command, or that it was temporary.

Besides, she'd still be the Chief of SEALs' goddaughter and Prince's daughter. Not to mention he'd sworn off *dancing* until the right woman came along. Tabitha Chapel was definitely not that woman.

"I'm glad you made it in early," she was saying when Marc joined the pair where they stood off to the side.

"I didn't have a choice. Somebody left D.C. ahead of schedule." The Admiral directed his penetrating stare at Tabitha.

Marc watched her squirm. *Somebody* didn't have her brass as polished as it appeared.

"Admiral." He extended his hand.

Shifting his walking stick, Admiral Mitchell Dann shook hands with a confidence befitting his rank. "Good to see you again, Miller."

"Likewise, sir."

"I see you've met my goddaughter." There was a subtle undertone to his words. He'd noticed them dancing, but was willing to overlook it *this* time.

"The Lieutenant was just explaining that connection."

"I'm surprised she mentioned it at all." The Admiral chuckled, wiping the slate of her transgressions clean. The man turned to his goddaughter. "So tell me, Tabby, how've you been keeping yourself busy?"

"Giving the Commander a hard time." Her words dared Marc to deny it.

"You could say that," he agreed carefully.

"Relax, you two." The Admiral looked from one to the other. "This is a social call. The uniform's just for travel. Which reminds me… Tabby, I have a FedEx for you from your parents. It came after you left." He signaled the very tall junior officer who'd arrived with him and stood at the ready, but was otherwise unobtrusive. "You two know my aide, Lieutenant Alan Ogden,'' he said as the other man joined them.

A hint of admiration gleamed in the giant's deep-set blue eyes. ''Ms. Chapel.''

''Thanks, Alan.'' She accepted the package apparently oblivious to the man's attraction and her own appeal.

''Oh, I know what this is.'' Tabitha tore open the envelope. ''Cruise tickets for Master Chief Thomas and his wife. I mentioned to my folks that I'd be coming to Coronado.''

It was the way she said it that got Marc's attention. Did they know why? How could she keep a secret like that from Prince with his connections? But if he knew, wouldn't a combat SEAL like the Toad stop his daughter from trying to follow in his footsteps?

''Excuse me,'' Tabitha said. ''I haven't paid my respects to the man of the hour.'' She bussed her godfather's cheek. ''Be right back.''

Marc stepped aside to let her pass.

But instead of continuing on, she stopped. ''We're not through yet.''

Though she'd lowered her voice, she came through loud and clear. Lieutenant Chapel would stop at *nothing* to get what she wanted.

Neither would he.

She moved to shoulder past him, but he grabbed her upper arm. Her lips parted in surprise, tempting him to kiss the look right off her face.

She was a odd mix of innocence and experience. And getting rid of her was becoming complicated.

He could handle complicated. But he was beginning to wonder if he could handle Tabitha Chapel.

He had to remind himself it was his butt on the line. One wrong move while she was under his command, and he could flush his career down the head. Superior officers did not kiss subordinates. Dancing could be considered questionable behavior, and their flirting definitely was. All the more reason to send her back where she belonged.

Until then, he'd put her in her place. "Thanks for the dance," he whispered, letting go.

She walked away without a comment.

The Admiral cleared his throat. "Mind telling me what that was all about?"

"A little two-step," Marc answered, holding his own under the older man's scrutiny. "I'd really like to know where you stand on this feasibility study."

"Rest assured, Miller, I'm in your corner. But…"

"But?"

"Get used to having Tabby around for a while." The Admiral glanced over his shoulder at his aide. "Why don't we discuss this in your office. Say, 0800 Monday."

TABBY LEANED OVER the sink in the deserted ladies' room, splashing cold water on her face. She'd found Master Chief Thomas surrounded by a group of chiefs and delivered the package. It had been years since she'd seen him. He'd complimented her on the way she'd grown up, then lectured her for what she was trying to accomplish by being here.

News traveled fast through the Navy SEAL network. It was only a matter of time before her father found out.

She'd stayed while the Master Chief and the others regaled her with sea stories. Most involved her father, known to SEALs as the Toad. Some included Miller.

In fact she learned Miller used to be a smoker—a chain-smoker with insomnia, according to the Master Chief. While going through SEAL Training, Miller had almost burned down the barracks, and the Toad had threatened to kick his butt if he ever caught him smoking again after lights out. Miller's nicotine addiction got the best of him, though, because he got caught again.

Only the brave or the stupid defied her father.

Tabby could picture it now, a teenage, buzz-cut version of Miller hiding the burning evidence in his mouth while he stood toe-to-toe with the Toad—eyes watering as he tried not to choke on smoke and give himself away. He probably burned a blister on the roof of his mouth putting out the ember. But her father had time on his side. *"I'm not leaving until you swallow,"* were the Toad's words, according to the tale.

But the story had a happy ending. Miller never touched a cigarette again.

So was she being brave or stupid in defying her father's wishes with this study? And if it came to a showdown between her and Miller which one of them would swallow their pride first?

She was the one hiding out in the ladies' room. Tabby let out a puff of air. Regrouping, not hiding.

She'd hoped to sell Miller on the idea of the study

before mentioning her connection to the Chief of SEALs. She knew how it looked. A high-profile father and a high-ranking godfather equaled privileged, and discounted the value of all her hard work. If only she actually had that kind of pull. She might have knocked off a year or two of overcoming objections.

It had taken climbing a mountain of bureaucratic red tape to get this far. And that wasn't the end of it. The cutoff age for SEAL Training was twenty-nine. She was fighting an uphill battle, and it wasn't just her sex dragging her down.

Who could blame her for using what little leverage she did have? Miller, that's who.

Thanks for the dance. She supposed from his perspective she had been leading him on from the moment they'd met. In more ways than one. She hadn't anticipated the attraction. But she should have come clean about Uncle Mitch right from the start. And she shouldn't have rubbed his nose in it after the fact.

"Real smart, Chapel. Push the man's buttons and just expect him to take it—"

"You must be Tabby."

Tabby lifted her startled gaze to the mirror and stared at the blonde's reflection. *Petite* said it all. The woman was everything Tabby wasn't, and wearing a form-fitting, black knit dress to boot.

"I'm Carol, Brad's wife."

The woman smiled, and Tabby smiled in return. "I guess you caught me talking to myself."

"You'll have to tell me exactly what buttons those were." Carol set her purse down on the vanity and rummaged through it. "You were talking about Marc, right? I know women who'd pay for that information." She pulled out a tube of lipstick and applied the bright pink color.

Tabby reached for a paper towel and propped a hip against the sink. Patting her face dry, she pretended to consider the possibility. "How much?"

"A lot." Carol laughed, then sobered. "And not nearly enough if you're interested in keeping him all to yourself." She dropped the lipstick back in her purse.

"I'm not." Tabby tossed the wadded paper into the trash. She only had one use for Miller. And that was to back up her study with his expertise. So why had she felt the need to antagonize the man?

"Too bad. He's really a nice guy."

That was the second time she'd heard that tonight. Nice wasn't exactly the word she'd use to describe Marc Miller. Nice butt. Nice bod.

But *nice?*

"Carol?" Brad burst into the ladies' room. "There you are. Oh, Tabby." He blushed the exact shade of pink as the candy-striped wallpaper. "Sorry."

"Looking for a little privacy?" Tabby gathered up her things. "I was just leaving."

"Not necessary," he answered, grinning.

"What's up?" Carol asked.

He took an apologetic peek at his pager. "Duty calls."

"Oh, no." Carol heaved a sigh. "Go, get out of my face so I can start missing you."

"Keep the car. I'll ride in with the guys." He planted a quick kiss on his wife's mouth, then left.

Carol was left holding the keys to the Bailey family car. "Such is the life of a Navy wife," she tried to sound stoic, even with tears streaming down her cheeks. "Hormones," she explained, wiping them away.

How many times had Tabby's mother gone through the same thing? Life with a Navy SEAL wasn't easy. A wife wasn't privy to even the smallest details of her husband's job. Like when he'd be leaving, and when he'd be back. *Where* remained another unanswered question.

Tabby didn't know whether to offer sympathy or break into a rendition of "Stand By Your Man." But when it became painfully obvious the other woman wanted privacy, Tabby excused herself.

The crowd thinned as Brad's team filed out. *What she wouldn't give to be going with them...*

Uncle Mitch sat at the bar, talking to Alan. Tabby squeezed her godfather's shoulder in passing to keep him seated. His knees were probably killing him by now, though he'd never admit it. Alan stood and moved down a stool so she could sit between them.

"Here you go." Setting a beer in front of her, Manny twisted off the cap. "With Miller's compliments." He nodded in the general direction.

Tabby turned and found the man in question sitting alone in a booth across the room. Why did the word *lonely* come to mind? According to Carol the man could have any woman he wanted. Not that she needed Carol to tell her that.

He saluted with his bottle and challenged with his

eyes. She lifted her bottle in return. They weren't through yet. Not until she was through with the feasibility study.

"Would you care to dance, Ms. Chapel?" Alan asked.

One of her favorite songs filled the air. "No thanks. I don't feel much like dancing."

At least, not with Alan.

MARC WATCHED TABITHA follow her godfather out the door. In jeans she tended to stride rather than swing, but he liked the view just the same.

With the departure of Team One the bar had cleared to half the patrons. Leighton and Perry played pool with the petty officer's Friday night girl. A boisterous group of chiefs and retirees occupied the back tables. And some guy at the bar looked like he'd have to pay to get lucky tonight if the woman draped all over him was any indication.

But the place hadn't seemed empty until now.

He remembered the Admiral's words. *Get used to having Tabby around for a while.* That was the problem. He could easily get used to it. Until Monday when the Admiral pulled rank, and the Lieutenant shoved the fact she was staying down his throat.

Carol emerged from the ladies' room looking lost and a little disheveled. She spotted him and headed toward his table.

Meeting her halfway, he noted her ashen complexion and led her back to the isolation of his corner booth. "Sit. You look awful." He signaled their server.

"Thanks. You sure know how to make a girl feel

better.'' She attempted a smile, but it remained as flat as the sarcasm. ''I'm just feeling a little woozy.''

''Too much to drink?''

She clicked her tongue. ''You know I don't drink.''

''If you're sick—''

''I'm not—''

''I can take you to the E.R.''

''Marc, would you please quit fussing. There's nothing wrong with me…it's morning sickness. I'm pregnant.'' She softened her last words. But they still hit with the force of a two-by-four to the gut.

''Congratulations.'' The sentiment was sincere enough. He knew how badly Carol wanted children. The fact that he didn't was the reason they weren't together and she was married to his best friend.

A gum-snapping bleach-blonde in short shorts and cropped T-shirt with a your-place-or-mine smile appeared at his elbow. ''What can I get ya'll?''

''Nothing for me, thanks,'' Carol said.

''Club soda and another Corona.''

''Sure thing.'' Kewpie Doll picked up his empty bottle and collected more on her way back to the bar.

''And crackers,'' Marc called after her, then turned his attention back to Carol. ''Soda and crackers will settle your stomach.''

Carol reached across the table and covered his hand with hers. ''Brad and I wanted to tell you together.''

''I'm okay with this, really.''

''I know you are.''

Marc had introduced his swim buddy to his high

school sweetheart last year when Brad had accompanied him to his fifteen-year class reunion. The rest, as they say, was history. Now the couple was adding branches to their family tree.

There'd been a time when Carol had been the girl of his dreams. But dreams faded and changed. And they didn't share the same ones anymore.

Drinks arrived, giving Marc a needed break from his thoughts.

''More peanuts was the best I could do.'' The barmaid leaned in, displaying ample endowments.

He dug out his wallet and threw the money on her tray, including a generous tip. She tossed him a wink and a book of matches in return before sauntering off with a follow-me shake of her generous hips.

Marc flipped open the matchbook and read the name—Connie—and the penciled digits. Closing it, he tapped the book every quarter turn. He needed a smoke.

''She's not your type,'' Carol commented.

''What's my type?''

''I like Tabby.''

Marc snorted. ''Definitely not my type.'' Not unless he was in self-destruct mode. Fraternizing with the Lieutenant could cost him his career. ''It's my own damn fault I lost the best thing that ever happened to me. And Brad would have every right to kick my butt if he heard me talking to you like this.''

''As if I'd believe you anyway.'' Carol squeezed his hand. ''I wasn't the one, Marc Miller, and you know it.''

True. But the clincher had been his refusal to even

consider children. And now it was too late to change his mind. A youthful decision cost him the chance of ever being a father. Never mind that his reason for it was still the same.

Damn but he needed a smoke.

His needs had been simple when he walked in the door. Play a little pool and relax. Now he wanted to get drunk, get laid, but mostly he just wanted a cigarette.

A man should never try and give up more than one bad habit in a lifetime. He was bound to fail.

Behind the bar, Manny rang the ship's bell. ''Last call.''

Marc checked his watch. There wasn't enough time left to get drunk. His gaze settled on Kewpie Doll Connie eyeing him from across the room, waiting for an answer to her invitation.

FROM THE PARKING LOT, Tabby waved goodbye to Uncle Mitch. Her ears were still ringing as the limousine drove out of sight. He'd given her a well-deserved dressing-down for this latest escapade. And it had taken forever to convince him she had a ride.

She still had hopes of hanging around long enough to persuade Miller to talk about the feasibility study. And if Carol hadn't already left maybe she'd catch a ride with her. The other woman had appeared to need some company.

Tabby stepped back into the bar, her eyes adjusting easily to the dim light. The first thing that caught her attention was all the open space. The second was the couple holding hands in the corner.

She made a hasty retreat back outside.

Standing alone in the near-empty lot, she tried to decide what to do next. The broken floodlight overhead left her in almost total darkness. Another illuminated only a small circle while kamikaze moths dove into the source. The same thing she'd been doing all night. And it looked as if she'd just gotten burned.

If she was honest with herself, she'd admit to staying for Miller's company. But it seemed he'd already found some. Brad and Marc were friends. Naturally Carol and Marc were too, right?

She wasn't going to assume anything else.

So unless she intended to hang out in the parking lot with her wayward thoughts, she needed to get going.

From behind, the crunch of glass and gravel beneath heavy bootsteps alerted her. Her heartbeat jump-started and she turned to face the sound.

Ogden stepped from the shadows.

Tabby put a hand to her heart. "Alan, you startled me."

His tag was Sleeping Giant. His lumbering gait made him appear slow, but she imagined his sheer size was all he needed to bring down the enemy. She knew he went everywhere with Uncle Mitch as his aide. That's why she'd assumed he was in the limo even though she hadn't actually seen through the tinted windows.

"Can I give you a ride back to base, Ms. Chapel…Tabby?" he asked politely in his slow Southern style, using her name now that they were alone. "I've rented a car."

"No. No." She shook her head. "I have a ride, thanks."

"Okay then… Good night."

"Good night, Alan." She waved him off with a twinge of guilt. The SEAL was always asking her out in D.C., and she was always turning him down. He was nice enough, even tall enough, but she just wasn't interested.

She waited until he drove off in a dark blue rental car. She didn't want to be caught in a lie that would get back to Uncle Mitch. While she considered her own two feet adequate transportation, her godfather might not.

Turning, Tabby slammed straight into Hugh. For the second time that night she felt like jumping out of her skin. She hadn't even heard him approach.

"Evenin'," he drawled, steadying her. Tipping his Stetson, he staggered away.

"Lieutenant Leighton," she called after him. "You shouldn't be driving."

He dangled his car keys and kept walking. "You're welcome to take me home, darlin'."

Tabby caught up with him and snatched the keys. "I'll get the Commander's yeoman to drive you." At least she thought she'd seen the young enlisted man playing pool. The thought of going back in the bar and running into Carol and Marc was a bit unnerving, but she couldn't let a man drive drunk. She took a quick look around the parking lot. Where were those designated drivers?

"But I want *you* to drive me." He stepped closer.

Close enough for her to smell his heated breath. It wasn't overpowering. In the dim light, his clear blue gaze remained unwavering. In her best *guess*-timation, he wasn't even intoxicated.

"I get your game, Leighton." She tossed the keys onto the trunk of a nearby car. Black and sporty, it looked like something the SEAL would drive.

"Come on, darlin'. I did have two beers."

"So did I." She moved away, keeping an eye on him.

"Then I should be driving you home." He retrieved his keys and inserted one into the door of a dark blue sedan similar to the one Ogden had rented.

"I'm quite capable, thanks. Besides, I'm not headed home." Just a BOQ room.

"I meant my home," he confessed with a grin as wide as the state of Texas. Hardly the same man who'd thrown the fit in the Commander's office.

"I know what you meant."

"You're breaking my heart," he said as she started walking off.

"It's not your heart I'm breaking, Cowboy."

His laughter sounded, then faded into the night.

Shifting the backpack on her shoulder, Tabby shoved her hands deep into her jacket pockets and headed toward the base. Her footfalls echoed on deserted concrete.

Crossing an alley, she almost ran down a transient who appeared out of nowhere pushing an overflowing grocery cart. The man cursed with vague mutterings when the stacked items threatened to topple.

Compliments of one lost game of eight ball, Tabby shoved the two bucks from her pocket at him and picked up her pace, nixing the idea of stopping to help with the cart. She was alone. And she wasn't looking for trouble. Though she was certainly bumping into a lot of people.

In the distance a cat yowled. A trash can crashed to the ground. She heard the purr of a fine-tuned engine. At this hour traffic was almost nonexistent. It didn't take long to realize the vehicle was following her.

Her heart raced. She stopped and turned to size up the sleek black Dodge Viper with tinted windows, sunroof and personalized plates. SNAKEATR.

Snake eater. Another name for Navy SEAL.

The passenger door opened. "Get in," Miller ordered.

His high-handed manner was enough to make her change her mind about talking tonight. Monday, when she had the Chief of SEALs to run interference would be soon enough. At least Ogden and Leighton had asked.

Tabby plotted her escape route. Headlights flashed across her path, cutting it off. A dark blue car pulled on to the street ahead of the Viper, then with squealing tires sped away.

"Get in," Miller repeated. "I'm driving you back to base."

"No thanks." She started walking, keeping her pace brisk.

Coasting up the street, he threatened through the open passenger door, "You don't want me to get out."

She stopped. He braked.

Heading over to the car, Tabby leaned in. "I'm perfectly capable of walking two miles. Thanks, but no thanks.'' She slammed the door and went back to the curb.

He got out. ''This isn't the best part of town.''

She turned to glare at him. ''I'll take my chances.''

''You don't mean that.'' He stared her down over the roof of the car. ''Here's your chance to convince me we need to study the *feasibility* of women SEALs.'' He strode around to the passenger side and opened it again.

Tabby sized up man and machine, his rough exterior a powerful contrast to the sleek sports car. It was tempting. He sounded sincere enough. He even looked sincere enough in the pale cast of the moonlit night. This *was* the opportunity she'd been waiting for.

Closing the distance between them, she squeezed into the low-slung seat. ''I'm surprised you didn't have a better offer tonight.'' Not to mention surprised by how relieved she felt.

''What makes you think I didn't?''

''You're giving me a ride, right?''

''Don't push it.''

It was her nature to push it.

He secured her door. Walking around behind the car, he paused to swipe his hand across the trunk. ''I can't believe it,'' he muttered, getting in behind the wheel and setting the car in motion. ''Somebody keyed my car.''

Oops. Tabby shrank into the butter-soft leather. Her stomach growled, drawing his attention.

''Hungry?'' he asked.

"A little," she confessed. It would be a while before she made a full confession.

Downshifting, he glanced in the rearview mirror, then at her before returning his attention to the road. "I'm just going to spell it out for you, Tabitha. Women have no place on the teams. This proposed study is a waste of your time. And mine."

She regarded his profile, giving his words more consideration than they deserved. The shadow of a beard etched his jaw. "Do you know how stubborn you sound?"

As stubborn as that beard.

The hairs were coarse, she remembered from their dance. Coarse enough to redden her cheek. Coarse enough to let a woman know she held a man.

"Stubborn is my middle name." He turned right and his gaze naturally followed. She looked away first.

Pursuing a dream doggedly was not a waste of time. Pursuing this man was.

Neon lights led to an all-night burger drive-through. "I'm still buying," he insisted, pulling up to the intercom. He acted as if the battle of the sexes had been decided with that one game of pool.

For him it probably had.

Right now she was waging an entire war trying to get him to see things her way when his eyes were shut tight.

"Gromley's behind me on this. And I've convinced Uncle Mitch the study has merit. But I need your expertise. I have the opportunity to prove on paper what I already know…. I can meet or exceed requirements for entry into the SEAL training program. I'm a competitive runner—''

''I know. This past year you ran your first Iron Man.'' He continued to peruse the menu, but she could just imagine his lofty expression.

''Let me guess. You read it in my file, and you're not impressed.''

He turned toward her. ''Aside from the obvious gender differences, the biggest physical difference between men and women is in upper body strength. The average SEAL can bench four hundred pounds.''

''I can bench press double my weight. It's the equivalent—''

''But not the same.'' His gaze shifted from her eyes to her mouth. ''Do you know what you want?''

All she'd ever wanted was to be a Navy SEAL. Except when he looked at her mouth that way. Then she wanted something even more elusive. ''Cheeseburger, fries, shake.''

His gaze remained fixed on her mouth.

The crackle of the speaker broke in. ''Can I supersize your order for you tonight?'' He supersized for them both.

Picking up their order at the window, he continued the short drive to the base while Tabby dug into the fries to curb at least one of her raging appetites.

''You're not planning on eating in my car?''

She stopped chewing and swallowed. ''I guess not…''

''I'm kidding.'' He chuckled. ''I promise not to tear into you if you get catsup on the leather upholstery.''

''You have a warped sense of humor.'' She didn't find it all that funny. Especially since she still had to tell him she'd scratched his prized possession with a careless toss.

He pulled up to the gatehouse. The sailor standing guard checked ID, then waved them through with a smart salute.

Marc navigated his way around the base. Turning into the BOQ parking lot, he pulled into an open spot up front.

''Thank you for the ride, Commander.''

She should have just said thanks for nothing. He was sure that's what she meant. She divvied up the food and gathered up her things.

''I...apologize if I misled you into accepting a ride. It was for your own safety.''

''And I'm sorry, too,'' she said, climbing out. ''I scratched your car fending off advances from one of your SEAL buddies.''

''Who the hell—''

She slammed the door.

Marc winced. How many times was she going to do that? And which SEAL? Hugh? Was she implying he should have picked her up sooner? Or was she telling him she could take care of herself? He'd never understand women.

He got out anyway. ''I'm walking you to your door.''

''I'm on the third floor.'' She dismissed his offer.

''No problem. I do stairs.''

The brick building surrounded a courtyard on three sides with stairs on the outside at either end. She headed for the stairs to the right. The open design had the look and feel of a cheap motel, typical of the many quarters he'd occupied throughout his career.

After his promotion to Commander, he'd rented a place on the beach. He could see himself finishing out his career in California, maybe even settling down here.

They reached the door to three-eighteen.

"Security check," he said, taking the key and unlocking the door. Once inside, he flipped on the light switch.

"That must get you into a lot of women's apartments." She stopped in the doorway, arms crossed, fast food bag dangling from one hand.

"I've never needed an excuse." Surveying the small room, he noted the white pictureless walls and the single bed. Typical transit barracks, reminding him she was just passing through. Which was exactly what he wanted.

From her post, she tapped her foot impatiently.

He picked up a family photo from the nightstand. Prince stared back at him with a get-out-now look on his scarred face. "The Toad's boots would be hard to fill," he commented, maybe to her, maybe to himself. He knew because every day he tried. Marc set the picture facedown.

Clicking her tongue, she moved away from the door. Dumping her load on the bed in passing, she set the picture upright again, but kept her distance. "I have my own boots, thank you very much."

The messages he'd been getting all night weren't because she wanted him. Instead, she wanted something from him. He was disappointed, but not surprised. Especially now that he'd made it clear she couldn't change his mind.

If he was the type, he could use that knowledge to take advantage of her. But he wasn't the type. He had no intention of wandering down the road of Commanding Officers who'd taken advantage of women in their command.

He walked over to the window to escape the uncomfortable realization he was being less than his professional best to even entertain the notion. Checking the lock, he popped the catch easily. "Have the manager replace this."

"I'm on the third floor. I sleep with it open."

"I'd come in from the roof. Drop a rope over the side. It'd take about two seconds. Have it fixed. And keep it closed." He leveled his gaze on her to let her know he was serious.

"Sure. Just in case someone decides to rappel down the side of the building."

"See you Monday, Lieutenant. Don't forget to lock up behind me." Letting himself out, Marc closed the door on all the possibilities, and all the impossibilities.

He'd done his duty. He'd seen her home safe and sound.

If only... If only what? She wasn't under his command? She wasn't Prince's daughter? She wasn't dead set on being a Navy SEAL? If only they'd gotten to dance a little longer.

He brushed aside those thoughts.

Relationships made it harder to concentrate on his career. The serious kind required effort. Effort he wasn't willing to expend. He'd proved that with

Carol. And the not so serious were a waste of time. He'd proved that with every other woman he'd ever been with.

Hustling down the three flights of stairs to his waiting car, he felt the hairs on the back of his neck rise. He spotted a dark blue sedan. The same make and model he'd seen circling the block when he'd stopped to pick up Tabitha. At the time he'd noted a rental sticker but hadn't got a good look at the plates.

Coincidence? He didn't believe in coincidence. The car ripped into reverse and burned rubber getting out of the parking lot.

He didn't know what the other driver had in mind. But after what Tabitha had said about the SEAL in the parking lot it looked like *he'd* be spending the night in his car.

Climbing behind the wheel, he opened the glove box and dug into his stash of Tootsie Pops, opting to ignore the cold fries. During his surveillance of the building, his gaze naturally drifted toward Tabitha's door.

Taking the book of matches from his pocket, Marc flipped it open, then closed. Picking up his cell phone, he punched in the base prefix, then gave the switchboard operator the number and counted rings. One...two...

She picked up. "Hello?"

"Talk to me, Tabitha."

"Marc?" The surprise in her voice was evident by the use of his given name.

"Yeah. Is it too late to call?" He checked his watch, 0249. He'd left her less than five minutes ago. But he didn't like the way he'd left things between them.

"I guess that depends. What do you want?"

To hear your voice. "Nothing. I just called to say good-night. And to let you know the morning glories are blooming."

"Good night," she said with finality, but he heard the soft laughter in her voice.

Relieved, he let her hang up first.

Marc tossed the matchbook into the trash.

Someday, maybe, he'd take Kewpie Doll Connie up on her offer. But tonight he craved strawberries.

0700 Saturday
BACHELOR OFFICERS' QUARTERS,
Coronado, CA

TABBY AWOKE BRIGHT and early for her run. Closing the door behind her, she pocketed the room key and used the balcony rail to begin stretches in the crisp March air. A black Dodge Viper pulling out of the parking lot caught her attention.

"I want some of what you've got, girlfriend."

Tabby's BOQ neighbor, Lieutenant Nydia Jones, Navy Nurse in transit, inserted her key into the keyhole of three twenty. The woman balanced a steaming cup of coffee and a paper bag in one hand with a Saturday morning newspaper tucked under her arm.

"Excuse me?"

"The man spends the night and you're up jogging first thing in the morning."

"He didn't—"

"Uh-huh." The woman raised both perfectly tweezed brows. "Lost track of time? I saw him bring you home." Nydia pushed into her room. "That's one fine hunka hunka burnin' love."

Tabby stared after the nurse.

She'd thought the phone call was a nice touch. But had Miller spent the night in his car? In the parking lot outside her room? A chill crept into the morning air. *Why?*

CHAPTER FOUR

0845 Monday: The Commander's Office
NAVAL SPECIAL WARFARE CENTER,
Coronado, CA

"LET ME GET THIS straight." Marc turned and faced the Admiral. "You approve of this study?"

"Yes." Admiral Dann shifted in the wing-backed chair. "Sit down, Miller. Your pacing makes me nervous."

Marc sank into the empty seat. The senior man deserved his attention and respect. But *why* was the Admiral giving Lieutenant Chapel the green light instead of putting a stop to all this nonsense?

Didn't the man perceive the threat? Ignore the implications and they'd wind up with BUD/S trainees doing push-ups on their knees. He blinked back the image of Tabitha on her knees in a way that had *nothing* to do with push-ups.

"Lieutenant Chapel's not objective enough to conduct this study. And quite frankly, sir, it looks like there's a conflict of interest on your part in letting her go through with this."

"I know what it looks like. Though things aren't always as they seem." The Admiral paused for a drink of coffee and Marc had the feeling the last words were directed at him. "I realize Lieutenant Chapel's recommendations are going to be biased. But Tabby's pushed paper for five years to get this far. She's crossed all her *t*'s and dotted all her *i*'s. I'm inclined to let her succeed or fail on her own."

Marc opened his mouth to comment, but the Admiral held up his hand and continued, "I don't like it any more than you do. Maybe not for the same reasons—I wouldn't want to see anything happen to her. I love her like my own. But this is the *new* Navy, an equal opportunity Navy and my hands are tied. Tabby feels up to the challenge, and Gromley has spearheaded this campaign through Congress.

"Now a congressional committee wants this study. Our only chance is to give them what they want. That doesn't mean I've gone soft. Or expect you to. I'd like you to do a counter-study. Address the issue from the SEAL perspective—cold hard facts that can be presented to the committee. It will put my mind at ease about what you call my conflicting interests, and Congress can compare the male and female points of view." He paused for effect. "Do you have a problem with that, Commander Miller?"

"No, sir." Though he didn't appreciate the additional paperwork, this was too important to shuffle to the bottom of the pile. His side would prevail.

"Good."

Two sharp raps drew Marc's attention.

"Commander—" Perry poked his head in "—Lieutenant Chapel is here, sir."

"You may want to keep this under your hat," Admiral Dann advised.

"That was my intention, sir." Marc turned his attention to his waiting yeoman. "Show the Lieutenant in."

Perry opened the door wider and stepped aside to admit the Lieutenant. She wore dress whites again. Skirt three inches *above* the knee. Legs sexy as hell and twice as distracting. That was another thing he'd take care of. If she stayed, she played by his rules.

"Have a seat, Lieutenant." He gestured toward the matching black leather couch, noting the fact she avoided direct eye contact. The rules had changed since Friday.

She released the last button on her jacket. Setting her laptop on the coffee table and her briefcase by her feet, she perched carefully on the edge of the seat, knees primly together. She caught him looking and tugged at the hem of her skirt, then checked her action and hiked it back up.

Not so cautious.

"Admiral." Genuine pleasure sparkled in her eyes. "Commander." Wariness replaced pleasure.

Though he thought they'd ended Friday with a truce, she must decided otherwise. It was just as well. The real battle had yet to begin.

Marc waved the petty officer out, then got right to the point. "The Admiral's explained your request, Lieutenant."

"And?"

"And, I'm open to the idea."

She looked from him to the Admiral. The older man offered a curt nod. She was clearly surprised. "What's the catch?"

"No catch." Marc's voice remained open and direct in spite of what could be considered a little white lie. His position hadn't changed. He didn't want her here. He didn't want her study to proceed. It was hard enough to pretend he did.

"Somehow I didn't expect you to be this easy."

"I haven't said yes, yet."

"What is it going to take to get you to say yes?"

The corner of his mouth quirked. "I'd like to see what I'm getting myself into first."

"I'd like to get started right away." Popping the catch on her briefcase, she produced handouts for each of them. "This is my proposal. There's a time-line on the last page." She gave them a minute to flip to it.

"One year? With six months spent in actual train-ing?" Marc questioned.

"It will give me a chance—"

"That's not acceptable." He dropped the cover sheet back in place and set the proposal aside. He didn't want to think about an extended period of time in her company.

"I'd have to agree with Miller, Tabby."

Her gaze darted between them. "I need to observe *at least* one training group. And participate with an-other. For practical application and comparison."

"I can assure you, Lieutenant, my instructors are equally *hard* on all trainees." He turned to the se-nior man. "Admiral, I can spare four weeks. Any-thing more would be disruptive."

"What? You're in downtime. There aren't even any trainees for me to observe. How am I sup-posed—"

"Lieutenant Chapel," Admiral Dann cautioned.

She clamped her mouth shut.

Marc leaned forward. ''Because we're in down-time, I can spare four weeks. You'll have full co-operation from the instructors. There's a lot that goes on in preparing for the next wave. We have a videotape library of training and there are medical rollbacks you can talk to. We have several with minor injuries waiting for the next cycle. Take it or leave it,'' he dared her, knowing the victory was his.

''What choice do I have? Of course I'll take it.''

For the first time Marc saw vulnerability in her green eyes and it unnerved him. All his instincts were honed to protect and defend. Pitting himself against the weaker sex mocked everything he stood for.

''Then it's settled.'' The Admiral tucked her handout into his briefcase and rose to his feet.

Tabitha and Marc did the same.

''Miller,'' Admiral Dann gripped his extended hand. ''I'll trust you two to work out the details. If you need to reach me I'll be just up the road at Miramar Naval Air Station through next weekend. My daughter's graduating from Fighter Weapons School.''

''Top Gun?'' Marc asked.

''What can I say? The face of the Navy is changing.'' The Admiral looked pointedly at Tabitha.

Marc's gaze followed. *Not the face of SEALs.*

Under orders he'd conceded to the study. But he refused to give up the fight. What had she said? She knew which battles were worth winning. So did he.

''Say hello to Michelle. And Zach,'' Tabitha added.

"Tabby's brother is in the same class," Admiral Dann explained. "Now there's someone who would be an asset to the SEALs."

Marc watched Tabitha bristle. "Zach gets his thrills from carrier landings."

"Maybe you can put me in touch with your brother, Lieutenant," he taunted. "SEALs can always use a good *man*. Especially a pilot."

"I'm aware of that, Commander." She gave him a scathing look.

"That's my cue to leave." Picking up his walking stick, the Admiral headed to the door. "Miller." The older man nodded. "Tabby, I'll see you this weekend if you can make it to the graduation. If not, I'll give the family your best."

"I'd appreciate it if you didn't say anything to my father just yet. I'd like to break the news myself."

"All right," Admiral Dann agreed. "But don't wait too long. Word has a way of getting around."

So Prince didn't know. And Dann wasn't going to tell him. Marc noted the look of affection that passed between godfather and goddaughter. He craved equal attention. When this was over, the Admiral would retain his hero status and *he* would be resigned to knight in tarnished armor.

Somewhere deep in his gut that thought sat uneasily.

The Admiral paused in the doorway. "I suppose these words are unnecessary, but... No more dancing, you two."

TABBY FELT A BLUSH tinge her cheeks. Miller closed the door, and it was like waiting for a bomb to explode and Fourth of July fireworks all rolled into one.

Dread and anticipation.

He'd given in.

But she wasn't stupid. Uncle Mitch had everything to do with her small victory. She'd been put out by their early meeting; now she wasn't so sure she should be.

"Talking about me again?" she goaded. Protocol be damned. If he got mad, at least it would break the tension.

"You weren't the only topic of discussion, Lieutenant. The man *is* my boss." His gaze traveled the length of her body. "And now I'm yours."

In the face of that pronouncement Tabby pushed aside the unexplored feelings she'd struggled with all weekend. She didn't know what to make of his car being in the BOQ parking lot Saturday morning. And she'd found herself thinking of the man all too often.

But today was different.

It was easy to put on a facade with the uniform. She could wear a professional demeanor like the gold braid on her epaulets. And he had even more gold to hide behind.

She only had to put up with him for four weeks. A sorry compromise for what she'd been after. But a full year in his company? She was better off with less.

"So, *boss,* where do I hang my hat?" she asked, searching for his playful side, afraid it was already out of reach.

His blue gaze darkened, then narrowed. "We have to set some boundaries, Lieutenant. *A… tennn…hut!*" He sounded off in what could only be described as a drill instructor's bellow. Walls shook and windows rattled. "I said *attention*, Lieutenant."

Tabby was too Navy not to respond. She knew an order when she heard one. Like a caged predator with raw meat, he circled while she waited for him to tear into her, piece by piece.

"Let's go over the rules. You're here for four weeks and four weeks only. While here you'll follow Miller Regs to the letter, which includes any rule I make up on a whim. Rule number one." He held up his index finger. "You'll address me by rank in public, by name in private, and by sir when I have you at attention. Is that understood, Lieutenant?"

"Yes, sir." With him yelling just inches from her face how could it not be?

"Rule number two." Up popped his middle finger. "We wear our skirts three inches below the knee around here. And we're not going to have this discussion again. Where does the uniform hemline fall, Lieutenant?"

Tabby decided he was having too much fun. She'd like to see him in a skirt! But she didn't relax her bearing. "Three inches below the knee, sir."

Not according to Navy Regs.

She could think it. She just didn't dare say it.

"Lower the hemline. That's an order! Rule number three." His ring finger rose to the call. "There'll be no fraternization while under my command. No SEALs, officer or enlisted. Past, present, or future."

Now he sounded like her father. She couldn't date the married men, that was a given—and a court-martial offense. She couldn't date the enlisted men. Though enlisted and officer marriages had been known to take place, and she didn't think they met at the chapel door.

Miller was way off-limits because he was her CO.

But any other officer or civilian should be fair game! Hugh, for example. Or even Alan.

She listened for any hint of his steps as he circled behind her. She felt his breath on her neck. Shivers raced the length of her spine.

"Have I made myself clear?"

You don't have to win all the time, Chapel.

So she wouldn't date. "Yes, sir," she said tightly, focusing on the paneled wall in front of her. If it wasn't for the study, she'd date any eligible SEAL that asked just to spite him.

A series of awards and pictures hung in neat patterns and she concentrated on those. Was that Miller shaking hands with the President? It looked like the top brass in Washington did know about this guy.

"Four." Pinkie. "When addressing a superior officer in the presence of another officer or officers, *ask.* Don't demand. Even if he's your godfather."

Ouch! She almost winced visibly at that one.

"And five," Thumb up. "Knock when entering my domain, and I'll give you the same courtesy."

He stood somewhere behind her. The silence went on so long she wondered whether he'd left the room.

"Will that be all, sir?"

"I knew it! Sooner or later you had to open your mouth." Smugness underlined each word. "I should mention rule number six.'' She couldn't see if he held up another digit. ''The man on top *always* gets the last word.''

Damn! He'd tricked her!

''In the line of duty I've gone hours, even days without speaking. Trainees learn to give me quiet or noise on demand. Let me hear the SEAL victory cry, Lieutenant.''

''Hoo-yah, sir!''

''Louder,'' he demanded.

''Yes, sir! Hoo-yah!''

''I can't hear you.''

She answered every time. And still he wanted more. It became a game to prove her incapable. ''Hoo-yah!'' She croaked a hoarse response.

''Hoo-yah!'' he answered with a resounding bellow. And then he didn't ask again.

Breathing fast and shallow, she inhaled deeply and tried to regain control.

''Your jacket's unbuttoned.'' He stepped into her line of vision again and dropped his voice to a low rumble. ''Permission to touch.''

Her heart skipped a beat. She met his request with direct eye contact. Satisfaction spread across his features, lighting his eyes and curving his mouth as she broke bearing. He'd meant to do that.

Shifting her gaze, Tabby concentrated on setting his mouth out of focus. The soft blur became an unwelcome reminder of how often since meeting the man she'd thought about kissing him.

''Lieutenant,'' he prompted.

He had to ask. And he could only correct the

problem. No more. To keep him from touching all she had to say was *permission denied*.

"Permission granted."

He reached for her gaping jacket and buttoned it. She sucked in her breath.

"If your uniform's too tight have it let out." With a tug he smoothed the jacket over her skirt and dropped his hands away.

Was he calling her fat? Instead of being grateful he'd misinterpreted her reaction, indignation boiled her blood. All her uniforms were tailored to fit perfectly! Unbuttoning her jacket kept it from wrinkling when she sat down.

Locking her knees, she held her back ramrod straight.

He circled behind her again. "Unlock your knees. You'll pass out."

Tabby bent them slightly only because he was right. The last thing she needed was to faint. As if he'd catch her.

Marc positioned himself to catch Tabitha if she fell. Shouting took oxygen and locked knees cut off circulation. Not a good combination. Add a little sun and sweat, and he'd seen whole lines of trainees drop.

He'd had his fun. Maybe too much. It was time to get on with the inspection and get her settled in. Strawberry blond hair brushed her collar well within regulation. For women, hair couldn't fall *below* the collar or it had to be pinned up. Different standards for different sexes.

He didn't have a problem with that. Women had their place in support, not in combat. The problem was women who changed the standards so they could fit the requirements.

The problem was Tabitha Chapel.

"Your hair's below your collar," he snapped. Why had he said that? She had beautiful hair. Now he'd be forced to make her cut it. Reaching up, he touched a strand. Just as soft as he'd imagined.

She twisted out of his grasp. "I didn't give you permission." Moving past him to the couch, she picked up her briefcase.

His hand stilled, midair. Feeling comical, he dropped it to his side. *Hoo-yah. Big trouble, boy.* "Where do you think you're going, Lieutenant? You're not dismissed."

She turned on him. "I won't be harassed."

"It was an accident." He fisted his hands at his sides.

"Accidents are involuntary. I call it a mistake." She held up her index finger. "You're allowed *one.*"

"I guess you wouldn't understand uncontrollable urges." He couldn't resist. But that was Friday. This was Monday. and a whole new set of rules.

She dropped her hard-sided briefcase.

It landed on his foot. He hopped backward, cursing under his breath.

"Oops, sorry. It was an accident," she said, retrieving the briefcase, all the while smiling at him.

Marc scowled as she stared back with innocent eyes. "You're allowed one." Hobbling to the door, he opened it and said, "Preach, show the Lieutenant to her office."

He always had the last word and the last laugh.

0959 Monday: Temporary Office of Lt. T. Chapel
NAVAL SPECIAL WARFARE CENTER,
Coronado, CA

HE HAD TO BE KIDDING. It was little more than a
storage closet with more shelves than space. A single window with grime thicker than the pane didn't
even allow in any light.

One Navy issue haze-gray desk and one wobbly
chair completed the inventory.

Tabby tossed her hat to the desktop, then removed
her jacket, before hanging it on the back of the par-
tially opened door and rolling up her sleeves.

She heard a light rap and turned to find Miller
filling the frame with his attitude. Apparently he'd
recovered from the briefcase incident.

"Comfy?" he asked.

She wished she'd recovered so easily. "Yes,
thanks." She forced a demure smile.

He surveyed the closet. "I see you've found the
videotapes." He pointed to the shelves behind her.

"And enough toilet paper for any emergency,"
she mocked.

He chuckled. "It'll be nice having you around,
Chapel."

For a moment she let herself believe he really
meant it.

Then he reached outside the door and produced a
wastebasket. "Oh, I almost forgot..." he said,
dumping a pile of papers on her desk while she
stared dumbfounded.

"What—"

"The contents of my In box. If you want the inside scoop on SEALs you'll get through that by Friday.''

Tabby picked up the top sheet and skimmed the letter. Routine red tape. ''Some inside scoop.'' She put it back on the heap.

He left the room and reappeared a second later with a TV/VCR cart. ''For the tapes.''

His grin broadened and she knew he wasn't through yet. He started unloading binder after binder from the cart's bottom shelf. Ranging in size from one to three inches, they ended up in a teetering stack on her desk.

''Memorize and *comply*. By Friday.'' He pulled one off the top. ''Start with this. It's the SOP for training.''

Miller Regs, she read, Standard Operating Procedures for SEAL Training. If it covered hemlines, she'd bet the entry was new.

The man was definitely getting on her nerves. How was she supposed to cope with four weeks of his condescending manner, *and* keep her mouth shut in deference to his rank?

Next he uncovered her buried phone system. ''This button gets you Preach. This one my office. Training Officer. Classrooms by room number. SEAL barracks.'' He went down the list. ''Dial 0 for the base operator and 9 if you want an outside line. Any questions?''

About a million that had nothing to do with this joke he called orientation. She shook her head. Let him have his fun. She had a job to do.

''Good.''

As she sat in the desk chair, she said, ''Maybe just one—'' The seat collapsed. The rollers slipped.

And she flew backward, hitting her head on the shelf.

She ended up with her heels in the air, while rolls of toilet paper fell on her in a final humiliation.

''Are you all right?'' Concern clouded his handsome features as he leaned over her.

Of course she wasn't all right!

He braced her forearm and pulled her up to a sitting position. She tugged down the hem of her skirt. From now on she wore pants.

He ran his hand along the back of her head. She winced when he found the lump.

''That's a nasty bump. Let's get you over to sick bay.''

''I'm fine,'' she insisted. Why didn't he laugh so she could get mad? Instead he showed genuine concern. Reminding her he was a nice guy. If he was any other man aside from her Commanding Officer, she'd welcome his touch.

''You sure?''

No. Kiss it and make it better. Not just the lump on her head, but the whole out-of-control situation. ''Yes, I'm sure.''

''What was it you wanted to ask me?''

A last roll of toilet paper bounced off her head and hit the floor. There was an apologetic glint in his blue eyes as he covered his smile.

''Where's the ladies' room?''

1300 Monday
NAVAL SPECIAL WARFARE CENTER,
Coronado, CA

HAIR DAMP FROM his recent run, Marc strode toward his office. Dry cleaning in one hand, deli lunch in the other, he dropped the sack on his desk and continued through the paneled door to his private locker room.

RHIP. Rank Had Its Privilege. A far cry from his enlisted days. But then not everyone took the hard road. Some like Lieutenant Chapel with her Academy appointment and background of wealth had it made.

At eighteen he'd been too eager to be his own man to stay at home. And too impatient for college. His grades were another matter. And of course there was his family situation.

Not to mention his record full of criminal misdemeanors. Joyriding—in a borrowed car at fifteen. Shoplifting—a can of spray paint. Vandalism—because the spray paint was too tempting. Underage drinking—his share of a six-pack with the guys. And a B&E that almost landed him in jail when he was really only climbing *out* of Carol's bedroom window.

The judge had given him a choice. The Navy had seemed like the right one at the time.

Streetwise and with a chip on his shoulder, boot camp was a breeze. SEALs struck him as a challenge worth meeting. Then Seaman Miller came face to face with the Toad. SEAL instructor, Captain Tad Prince.

Hanging his uniforms in the first of four oversize lockers, he picked up his laundry from the bottom.

He sniffed a T-shirt just to make sure it was dirty. "Whew." No question there.

He tossed it and a couple of stray socks to the rack along the opposite wall. Complete with Navy issue cotton sheets and wool blanket it often served as his bed during the long hours of indoctrinating trainees. A chair at the foot was the only other piece of furniture in the room.

His home away from home. Hell, it was home from predawn to postdusk five days a week and more often than not on weekends. He'd come this far just to prove himself to one man. A Toad who took perverse pleasure in knocking that chip off his shoulder every day for twenty-five weeks. A Toad who'd proved that at nineteen, Seaman Miller was a far cry from a man.

It was the Toad who'd dared him to do more. To be more. Marc scoffed at the distant memory. Night school and a little Brasso could turn even the toughest street thug into an officer.

But apparently not a gentleman.

His behavior toward Lieutenant Chapel was reprehensible at best, felonious at worst, definitely beneath a Naval officer.

What was it about the woman that made him forget all he'd learned? Her father? Her ambition?

Whatever it was, she was fast becoming his obsession.

Marc grabbed his shaving kit. As an afterthought he turned to the door that led to the passageway. Opening it, he turned around the hand-printed sign that read Ladies' Room. Funny he'd never noticed the whole damn building didn't have one.

He headed to the shower. Stripping, he cranked up the warm spray and stepped beneath it. He soaped his body and lathered his hair. What had he been thinking when he'd reached out and touched spun gold?

That it was as soft as silk.

"You weren't thinking, Miller. That's the problem." He closed his eyes against the sting of shampoo. He couldn't help himself. There was something about her that sent the blood rushing from his brain to his nether region.

Was he finally becoming the thing he despised most?

God help him.

During the inspection he'd felt a surge of power that had nothing to do with rank and position. And everything to do with control. He was powerful. And he held her powerless. Marc turned up the cold water until the icy spray pelted away the image, and all he remembered was that damn briefcase she'd dropped on his foot.

He grinned. She was a tough cookie.

Cookies crumbled.

Why did he feel this overpowering need to break her or take her? If he didn't do one or the other—

"Commander?" He'd recognize that voice anywhere. Had it only been five days since he'd met her?

"Damn!" He wasn't in the habit of closing the door adjoining his office. There'd been no need for privacy, until now. Grabbing a towel, he wrapped it around his waist.

His office door was wide open, and she stood on the threshold.

"Back here, Lieutenant." He ran a hand over his

dripping hair. Two hundred and twenty soaking wet pounds in nothing but a towel and dog tags. He'd teach her to knock.

"Perry wasn't at his desk. The door was…" She stopped midexplanation and midstride, shielding her gaze with a stack of manila folders.

"I thought every Midshipman learned to knock his first week at the Academy."

"I knocked. You didn't hear me."

He stared until she peeked over the folders.

"I'll wait outside."

"That would be a good idea."

Red-faced, she gripped the door handle in passing and pulled it toward her.

"They usually faint," he teased, when it was almost shut.

She poked her head back in. "Get real. I have two brothers." She looked him over in what could only be considered a very *un*sisterly fashion.

"Go before I decide to drop my towel."

She bowed out gracefully, leaving him so hot, he forgot he'd taken a cold shower. Where was his resolve? It was painfully obvious. He had to get himself under control.

He had the upper hand. For the next four weeks she was in his territory, playing by his rules.

Yeah, but for the next four weeks *he* was in trouble.

Hell Week was a cakewalk compared to this.

Marc dressed in fatigues. He left the uniform shirt on the hanger in favor of the puke-green T-shirt worn underneath. He took his time lacing his combat boots.

"Enter," he called when he finished, closing the locker room door behind him.

Tabitha stopped just inside his office, hugging the stack of folders. The blush was still in evidence, giving her that "girl next door" look. It contrasted with the uniform. And both contrasted with her sassy tongue.

"Approach the desk, Lieutenant. I don't feel like shouting across the room." Sitting, he pulled a Tootsie Pop from his stash. He didn't offer her one. He hoarded them jealously.

She laid the stack of open file folders on his desk. "These need your signature, Commander."

"What—?"

"That pile of paperwork you dumped on me this morning."

Rolling the grape-flavored sucker over his tongue, he skimmed the first one as she explained what it was and pointed to a brightly flagged signature block with her neatly trimmed and buffed fingernails.

As she went through the similarly marked stack, he found himself paying more attention to her manicured hands than to what he was signing. While making love, would she rake her nails across a man's back? Or dig them into his flesh? Maybe she wasn't a scratcher and a biter, but drove a man crazy with her hands kneading his buttocks. Or maybe she ran featherlight caresses down his spine.

He wanted to know. He *needed* to know.

He didn't have a preference. As long as they were *her* hands and *his* back.

"Commander?"

"Huh?"

She tapped the signature block on the letter and he lowered the suspended pen to scribble his name.

"I was reading," he muttered.

She'd pared down what had to be a week's worth of paperwork to one neat pile that dwindled to nothing in a matter of minutes. He noticed mailing envelopes with some and base routing envelopes with others.

"This is a supply request. For my new chair," she explained as he signed that form, too.

"Of course," he answered indulgently, feeling magnanimous in even giving her a chair.

"And these are worksheets for enlisted evals. They don't need your signature until finished form. E-5s are due at the end of the month. I put them on top. Underneath is a typed schedule showing when the rest are due."

She pushed aside the pile when he was done and set two stacks of note cards in front of him. "These are invitations that require an RSVP. And these are the ones you've already missed. I sent your regrets and flowers to the hostesses. I paid with my credit card. I'm assuming you'll reimburse me when the bill comes."

He removed the sucker from his mouth. "Of course," he said, meeting her gaze. Her generosity surprised him, considering how demanding she could be when she wanted something. It made him feel stingy.

Why should he begrudge her a damn chair? It was only government issue office furniture. It didn't mean she was going to become a permanent fixture at SEAL Training HQ.

But the chair would be.

He should request an impact study. From the moment she'd walked in the door things had changed. When she left things would never be the same.

At least not for him.

Tabitha looked away and Marc realized he'd been staring. Recovering, he stuck the Tootsie Pop back in his mouth and picked up a gilt-edged invitation from the pile that still required answers.

"You should go," she advised. "It's from the base Commanding Officer's wife. This Saturday. Their residence. Black tie. The Captain made the cut. He's on the short list for promotion to Admiral. There'll be a lot of brass there to check him out. Gromley will be there," she tempted. "It's good PR. And *good* for your career."

How did she know all that? It was on the tip of his tongue to ask her to go with him. But it would be totally inappropriate.

No dancing. And no anything else.

"Shall I let the CO's wife know you'll be there?"

He nodded automatically, committing himself in the process. Then he touched another invitation and she shook her head. They went through the rest of the stack that way.

"I'll send your regrets to the others. And don't forget to take your formal dress uniform to the cleaners. I don't do personal errands."

As if he couldn't handle picking up his own uniforms. He'd been doing it for years. Just because his

In box was a mess didn't mean his life was. "Is that all?" he asked in his most dismissive tone.

"Well—" she cleared her throat "—I'd like to leave early Friday to attend my brother's graduation."

"Have you memorized those manuals?" Resentment underlined his words. He couldn't help it. She was good at her job, and he didn't want her to be.

Even if it made his a hell of a lot easier.

Too bad she couldn't help him out on his *other* project. She had one of her own to worry about, and all the extra work he could pile on her.

She leveled a reproachful glare at him. "You gave me until Friday. But I did get far enough to know Miller Regs doesn't cover hemlines. Or whims."

"I still gave you an order." He waved the sucker. "I'll think about graduation."

She heaved a sigh. "Can I be frank with you, Commander?"

"No. But you can be Tabitha."

"Funny."

"Spill your guts," he invited, chewing the chocolate center.

Bracing her hands on his desk, she leaned forward. "If you think tucking me into an obscure little closet and piling a mountain of paperwork on me will make me forget why I'm really here you're mistaken."

That's exactly what he'd hoped.

She straightened, crossing her arms. "While I'm happy to help, I'm doing it only to free up your time. So you'll have no excuse not to spend it with me."

"Pretty speech, Lieutenant." He tossed the sucker stick to the trash. "If you want to find out what SEALs are all about be here tomorrow at 0500. And not a minute later."

"All right," she said, accepting his challenge. "Will that be all, Commander? I have tapes to review and manuals to memorize."

"For the record, I'm not impressed."

"Yes, you are. And you're dying to know how I got through all that paperwork." She smiled. "I sorted. And delegated. Your yeoman has a stack of typing on his desk this big." She pinched an inch of air. "And a stack of filing this big." She doubled her pinch.

Delegating or not, she'd worked straight through lunch. On impulse he picked up the deli sack and handed it to her. "Turkey on whole wheat, mustard, lettuce and tomato. There's cola or bottled water." He moved to the small refrigerator to dig out her preference.

Giving her the bottled water, his fingers barely brushed hers, but it was enough, and not enough. He wanted more.

"Thanks. But you didn't have to." She gripped the bottle of water and offered one of her demure smiles that meant she was up to something. "By the way, can I have a Tootsie Pop?"

"Dismissed, Lieutenant!"

Before I start licking your tootsies and work my way up from there.

Inflating his cheeks, Marc listened to her high heels fading down the passageway. He expelled his breath in a huff, then grabbed another sucker.

"Holy shit!" Perry's exclamation drew his attention to the open door. The yeoman stormed in waving a Post-it note. "The Lieutenant—"

"Posted pink sticky notes all over my office," Hugh finished, pushing his way past Perry.

"She left me a stack of typing," Perry added his complaint. "How am I supposed to get through all that by the end of the day?"

A sharp rap sounded on his open door interrupting further tirades. A group of non-rates in dungaree work uniforms hesitated outside his office.

"Excuse me, sirs," a timid Seaman found the nerve to speak up. "The Officer of the Day sent us over. You requested a work detail? Something about cleaning an office?"

Marc hid his surprise. He hadn't ordered a cleaning detail. But he could guess who had. "That would be down the hall on the right. Lieutenant Chapel. You can't miss her."

"What's with her?" Hugh asked.

"She left me a stack of filing this big." Perry exaggerated, spreading his arms. At least Marc credited the yeoman with exaggerating and Tabitha with telling the truth.

Wasn't she something? Marc started laughing. Though he doubted Hugh and Perry found anything comical about the situation, he didn't stop until his side ached and tears streamed from his eyes.

"Get used to it, Preach. She's in your chain of command now."

"What about mine?" Hugh demanded.

"'Fraid so."

"I'm the Training Officer. She's TDY. What's her title?"

Marc made one up. "Protocol. We're all going to learn how to conduct ourselves like gentlemen." He knew he, at least, needed to. And just as soon as he got a chance he'd unearth those workbooks on sexual harassment in the workplace and brush up on the rules.

Hugh rolled his eyes.

"She's a D.C. paper pusher." He should have realized that before. A pile of paper wasn't going to scare her off. "Get used to it. Things will settle down in a few days."

His stomach grumbled, reminding him he'd given away his lunch and candy wasn't going to fill him up. On Monday nights he had a regular commitment at the base Recreation Center that didn't leave time for dinner. "Preach, if you're flying, I'm buying." He pulled out his wallet and handed over a twenty. "Burgers for three."

"Can I borrow your car?" Perry asked sheepishly.

"Hell no!" No one drove his Viper.

"Hey, just thought since you were in such a generous mood…" Perry shrugged. "It's a little hard to carry drinks on my hog."

"Here." Hugh fished out his keys. "It's a rental, be careful. The dark blue Cutlass." Hugh plopped down on the couch when the petty officer left. "Man, at least my girlfriends leave love notes, not training schedules."

"Your car still in the shop?" Marc asked, leaning back in his desk chair.

"Yup. Another week at least. The garage is behind."

"Any particular reason you were hanging around the BOQ Friday night when you live off base?"

"What's with the third degree?" Hugh snapped. "I should be asking you the same question."

"I asked first."

"I was watching your back." Hugh stood and moved toward the door. "You can thank me later."

CHAPTER FIVE

A HAND CLAMPED over her mouth, holding back her scream while pushing her against the pillow. Through a sleep-clouded haze of interrupted dreams, Tabby stared at the shadowed image of a man dressed in black from hood to boots.

He stood over her to the right of her bed. Her heart pounded, echoing in her head. *What was going on?*

She struggled. But her efforts met with firm resistance.

He put his finger to his obscured lips. ''Shh.''

His eyes sparkled in the moonlight. She recognized those eyes, blue in the daylight.

But not morning-glory-blue.

She couldn't quite place them. But she bet they belonged to a SEAL.

It only took a moment for Tabby to assess the danger. The unidentified man had her at a disadvantage. But her hands and legs were still free.

A calm settled over her. She could handle this. She hit his wrist with the flat of her palm. With her other arm, she blocked him from trying again and followed through with a blow to his rib cage.

"Ugh!" he grunted, jumping back.

She sprang to her feet in the middle of her bed. Breathing heavily, she held off the intruder with an aggressive stance.

Shadows moved along the wall behind him, heading toward the window. One...two...three others. The arrogant Night Crawler blew her a kiss and followed the rest, leaving her confused.

What had just happened?

She scrambled from the bed, but they were already gone.

The curtains billowed in her open third-story window. Sticking her head out she looked down. Then up. The end of a rope disappeared over the roof.

"Security check my—eye." So that was why he'd wormed his way into her room. It hadn't been the Commander, but she was sure he had everything to do with this. "Ha! Ha!" she shouted in the general direction of the disappearing SEALs. "Very funny, guys." She slammed the window shut. "Okay, I'll get it fixed."

All that trouble to prove a point?

Did he have to send his men to scare the pants off her? She wasn't even wearing any beneath the thin T-shirt. Well, she would from now on. Feeling self-conscious, Tabby wrapped her arms around herself and only then realized she was shaking. Taking deep breaths, she managed to slow her rapid heartbeat.

She had no delusions about being able to defend herself against a group of SEALs. Not even with her

martial arts training. If they'd wanted to hurt her...
Well, they hadn't. But she was fooling herself if she
thought that had been about an unsecured window.

She was lucky she hadn't experienced a blanket
party. Or worse. No. The visit had been about getting rid of her. Now there was no doubt in her mind
that they didn't want her here. That *he* didn't want
her here. You'd think the man could at least do his
own dirty work.

He didn't have anything to do with this.

Or maybe she just didn't want to *believe* he had
anything to do with this. Exhaustion washed over
her and she leaned back against the wall for support.
She'd stayed up late, working on the study. She felt
tired. And very alone.

She looked around her stuffy little room and
sighed. No more open windows. No more day-
dreams about a certain handsome Navy SEAL Commander. She couldn't help it if he crept into her
dreams at night, but she could keep him—and the
others out of here.

Okay, back to her present dilemma. If he *was* responsible, where was he? And if he *wasn't,* well,
where was he? They *were* his men.

What did she expect? A champion riding in on
his trusty white steed. *No, just a Naval officer in his
black Dodge Viper.*

In all her childhood fantasies, she'd been the
sword-wielding knight-to-the-rescue. She didn't
need or want a man rescuing her.

Except sometimes...

Enough nonsense! She could take care of herself.
She just had to remember to watch her back. *Watch*

her heart. And scare the snakes from the bushes by making a lot of noise.

The alarm clock buzzed. Tabby jumped.

Hand on her heaving chest, she hurried to the nightstand and shut it off. Then she headed to the bathroom determined to face down all her dragons.

Alone, if she had to.

He'd challenged her to join him at 0500. She had half an hour to comply.

Switching on the bathroom light, she glared at her reflection in the mirror through a scrawled red heart. The words *Get Lost* were printed in the middle. She capped the discarded lipstick in disgust—her best shade—and chucked it in the wastebasket.

"Very funny," she repeated. Funny, she didn't feel much like laughing. But she didn't have time to dwell on the prank. It *was* only a prank after all. Meant to drive her away. She wasn't going anywhere except to HQ. And if she was going to make it on time, she needed to hit the shower.

Stripping, she turned on the spray and stepped beneath the tepid water. The shower slowed, then sputtered. She played with the handles.

A burst of red heat hit her.

Tabby screamed and jumped back. Too late.

Red dye tinted her skin. Tainted water streamed down her body and pooled in the bottom of the stall before disappearing in a scarlet swirl.

Tabby held up her hands in horror.

She stuck them under the now clear water and scrubbed, rubbing soap along her skin. Her breasts. Her belly. The entire front of her body was red. She felt it on her face and in her hair.

It wouldn't come off. Panic increased with her desperate attempts.

She heard pounding on her door. *Were they back to gloat?*

"Tabby, open up. It's Nydia. Is everything okay?"

Turning off the water, she grabbed a towel and ran for the door, dripping trails of red onto the carpet along the way. After peeking through the crack, she let Nydia in.

"Oh my God! What happened?"

"Those—those—Creepy Night Crawlers."

"Worms?"

"That's right. Belly crawling, low-life SEALs!" Tabby ran a hand through her hair.

Nydia's expression confirmed the worst. "That's some nasty dye job. It's really red, girlfriend."

Tabby caught a glimpse of herself in the full-length mirror. Clown-red hair stuck straight out from her head in uneven tufts. "What am I going to do?" she wailed.

She looked at Nydia. Nydia looked at her.

"Get even!" they answered in unison.

1313 Tuesday
NAVAL SPECIAL WARFARE CENTER,
Coronado, CA

MARC STOPPED PACING and stood in the middle of his office, arms akimbo. "Preach!" he bellowed, ignoring the intercom and letting his voice carry to the outer office. "Is she here yet?"

"No, sir."

"Did you call over to the BOQ like I asked?"

"Every hour on the hour, Commander."

Marc checked his watch. *Where in the hell was she?*

Lieutenant Chapel hadn't just missed meeting his challenge. She'd missed morning muster. It was afternoon and still no sign of her.

Marc stormed out of his office. "If she comes in, she sits her butt in *that* chair and doesn't move." He pointed to a chair in the reception area.

"Got it...sir," Perry added, retreating before him.

"She's lucky I don't write her up as UA," Marc muttered, giving vent to his anger. Directing it at the missing Lieutenant Chapel wouldn't help matters. There was a good reason he didn't write her up as an Unauthorized Absence. More than likely she was Missing In Action. And his men had something to do with it.

They could be very creative when they wanted to be.

Like introducing the new Executive Officer to Super Glue. Though it had happened to Lieutenant Commander Kyle, Marc shuddered at the memory of the new Exec's initiation less than one month ago, which had involved surgically removing a toilet seat. The man was still on leave, recovering.

He hadn't allowed himself to think about it earlier. But now he suspected the worst. Though he doubted she was in any real danger, even pranks could get out of hand. In the back of his mind a niggling suspicion formed and he couldn't let it go. The SEALs were daring her to stay.

The men had never bothered initiating him when

he'd transferred from Team One three months ago. He'd worked with some of these guys before, trained with others. SEALs worked as closely knit units. His appointment as Commanding Officer created a new dynamic.

Had he somehow set himself apart from his men?

What had Lieutenant Chapel done to ingratiate herself? They were all pissed at her yesterday. Was he reading too much into her absence? Maybe it was a female thing.

He'd start by personally checking her room. If his search didn't turn up anything, he'd grill every man within a breath of his life until one of them talked, beginning with Hugh.

Having a plan of action made him feel somewhat better. At least he was doing something aside from pacing a hole in his rug. As he strode along the passageway, Marc heard laughter coming from the men's locker room. That wasn't unusual, but he decided to start there, cornering them all at once.

"Have a nice workout?" he asked in general, stepping to the middle of the room.

Complete silence and covert glances followed his question. Most covered the need to keep their mouths shut by continuing to strip out of workout gear.

The man who made all the decisions was an outsider. He could accept that. But he wouldn't accept being ignored.

Hugh strutted past naked, toothbrush in his mouth. Marc noticed a fresh bruise along his rib cage.

"Where is she?" he demanded.

"Back in D.C., I hope." Hugh didn't even pretend not to know what Marc was talking about.

A chorus of raucous laughter and comments followed. It sure didn't sound like they'd dared her to stay. Marc frowned his displeasure at the inappropriate remarks, and several of the men moved toward the showers.

"Come on, Marc," Hugh said, foaming at the mouth. "It was just a little harmless dye in her showerhead."

"If it's so harmless why isn't she here?"

"You know women." Hugh spat toothpaste toward the floor drain. "She's probably holed up in her room because she doesn't want anyone to see her."

Marc had his answer. The question was what was he going to do about it?

Hugh tossed his toothbrush in a sink and stepped into the nearest shower stall. He turned the spray and when nothing happened, he fiddled with the taps to increase the water pressure. "What the—" Green dye exploded in his face and ran the length of his body.

Several green bodies emerged from the showers muttering obscenities. Before Marc could say anything, firecrackers sounded in the locker room bay like gunfire. Men trained to react crouched in ready positions in their various stages of undress.

Heavy metal music blared over the intercom system. Lights flickered. Smoke bombs billowed into green clouds.

"Female on deck!" The acoustics of the tiled

room allowed Tabitha's voice to carry above the smoke-filled confusion.

Marc turned just in time to see her slipping in through the smokescreen.

She wore black knit from top to bottom. Sunglasses shielded her eyes. Gloves covered her hands. A scarf draped her head Grace Kelly style. She looked every bit the proud princess.

Awe struck Marc like lightning, fast and furious, leaving him breathless and electrically charged.

Toting a Supersoaker filled with who knew what, she stared him down.

"Back!" she ordered, though no one threatened to move. Marc could only assume it was because they were all stunned into immobility. Any one of his men could put her out of commission without even trying.

She kept a watchful eye on her backside, making her way to the row of sinks. Using lipstick, she scribbled the message "I don't get lost, I get even" on the mirror above.

Then she pulled sunglasses down her nose and boldly appraised the men crowding the open bay.

"Lieutenant Chapel, my office!" Marc roared, remembering not a moment too soon he was the man in charge. "Hugh, you too. Get dressed first," he said over his shoulder, shoving Tabitha toward the door on his way out.

To think he'd wasted his concern on her.

· "Are you crazy? What were you thinking?" he demanded, dragging her down the passageway.

"I was—"

"That's right, you weren't *thinking*. Give me that." He snatched the squirt gun from her.

A green-faced Hugh caught up with them. In uniform and out of breath.

"Park it." Marc pointed her toward a chair outside his office, then ushered Hugh inside and slammed the door.

Tabby sat. Why was he all bent out of shape? She was the injured party. Righteous indignation surged through her. Too bad she hadn't rigged his shower. But she'd only had enough time to install the dye packets in half a dozen of the showerheads before the instructors returned from their afternoon run.

Within seconds her vocabulary increased with words she never knew existed coming through the solid door. Her heart hammered. And she couldn't stop fidgeting on the hard seat.

She darted a glance at Petty Officer Perry, who continued to type away, pretending not to hear the Commander's tirade. But when the door opened, they both ducked as if expecting Lieutenant Leighton to come flying out.

He did. But under his own power. There was a sickly cast to his already green face and an apologetic glint in his eye as he walked past.

Marc stood in the doorway staring at her, his face as red as her own.

Dread filled Tabby, making her want to heave the uneasy contents of her stomach. If she'd bothered with breakfast she probably would have.

"Come in." The calmness clashed with his angry color.

Tabby stood, caught the pity in Perry's eyes, and

skulked into the Commander's office. Heart beating as if she'd just completed a hundred yard dash, she thought seriously about turning around and running from the room.

He closed the door and started pacing.

Tabby stood at attention. Waiting. And waiting…

The silence grew. She expected the tongue-lashing to start any moment and forced herself to hold her own tongue. Even though she really wanted to give him a piece of her mind for the role he played in rigging her shower.

Words will never hurt me. She repeated a portion of the silly childhood rhyme. She'd used it often enough when boys teased her about her gawky size. Despite the fact she was a better ball player, or because of it, they'd taunted her mercilessly every at bat she'd had as the only girl on the Little League team.

Her father had made her tough it out.

She'd never cried. Even though the words did wound the little girl inside.

And she knew the Commander's criticisms would hurt. They'd made a grown man run from the room. Still, it went deeper. She didn't want him thinking badly of her, although she knew he already did. And not because she'd gotten back at his men. Simply because her presence threatened his peace of mind.

Just like those boys of summers past, the Commander was unable to accept a girl on the playing field. Equality and ability meant nothing. Her study meant nothing. He wanted her out of the ballpark.

"At ease," he said at last, settling into his seat. "And take off that ridiculous getup."

Without thought of disobeying, she removed her gloves, then her sunglasses, and slowly unwound the scarf. She heard the sharp intake of his breath and met his gaze across the desk. Running a hand through her hair, she felt its unnatural stiffness. Who knew what he was thinking. Probably how ugly she was. He already thought her uniform needed to be let out.

What did it matter what he thought?

She dropped her gaze to the items in her hands, forcing herself not to think about the horrific color.

"Are you crying?" he asked, his tone a quiet contrast to the gruffness of a moment ago.

"No," she snapped, glaring at him through red-rimmed eyes. The dye covered her lashes and irritated her pupils. But she wasn't crying.

"I can't tell." He sighed wearily, running a hand through his own hair. "I apologize for my men, Lieutenant."

Tabby felt moisture pooling and blinked. It was only the chemical irritation. Then a lump formed in her throat.

Why wasn't he yelling at her? That she could handle.

He plucked a tissue from the box on his desk and stood to give it to her.

She held herself rigid, rejecting the hand out.

He slipped it into her hand. "A little damage control."

She fisted the tissue by her side, refusing to use it.

"Speaking of which…" He reached into his back pocket for his wallet. Producing a credit card and a business card, he offered them. "It'll take more than tissue for this operation. Take the rest of the day off, Lieutenant."

"I don't need your money."

"I'm aware of that. Take it. I owe you." He forced her to accept it. "Then you can keep the card for all those flowers and gifts you order in my name."

Tabby looked at the second item in her hand, the business card. *Curl Up and Dye.* That sounded about right.

"I prefer the barber on base," he said sheepishly. "But I think it's just what you need. I'll call ahead. Once I explain the emergency, they'll take you as a walk-in."

"I'll take the afternoon off, but if you're trying to get rid of me, it's not that easy."

"Is that what you think?"

"Aren't you?" The harshness of her words made it an accusation.

"No."

"You knew about my window."

"Yes."

"And you spent Friday night in the BOQ parking lot."

He was slower to confirm or deny. Her gaze held his.

She felt her heart sink to her stomach.

"Yes." He turned from her, rubbing a hand along his jaw. "I had my suspicions about Hugh," he continued. "I take full responsibility for the actions of my men." He faced her again. "But I didn't order them to your room. And I sure as hell didn't tell them about the window.''

"I want to believe you."

"Then do." There was a hint of pleading in his voice.

Her spirit lifted, soared, then landed back somewhere in reality. "I'll think about it."

In many respects the shower incident had served to calm her fears about predawn visitors. They were serious about getting rid of her. But they wouldn't seriously hurt her. It was all just fun and games. No harm, no foul. The best part was, she'd gotten even.

"Female on deck?" he asked.

"It was fair warning for them to get covered." She slipped on her sunglasses. "And Commander, expect a *very* large credit card bill."

1410 Tuesday
CURL UP AND DYE,
Chula Vista, CA

STILL COVERED by her black camouflage, Tabby splurged on a taxi to a strip mall where the driver dropped her off in front of the salon. It had a catchy name, a trendy look…and a pricey feel, she realized when she walked through the door.

The scarf and gloves hid her features, but drew attention, making her feel like a movie star traveling incognito. Without removing her sunglasses, she gave the girl behind the counter her name.

Miller had said he'd call ahead and set up the appointment. How ironic the man's reach should extend to beauty salons. Of course the name that appeared on the business card could belong to a woman he knew intimately. That wasn't something she wanted to dwell on.

The receptionist used a pencil to punch in a series of numbers on the intercom system because the length of her blue-and-purple nails made them less than functional. They did, however, match the streaks in her otherwise jet-black hair. "She'll be right with you."

"Thank you."

"Tabby, welcome." Carol Bailey, wearing a stylist's black smock with the salon's logo, greeted her with a bright smile.

"Carol...you work here?" Tabby hoped she wasn't gaping.

"Marc didn't tell you? Isn't that just like a man?" Carol clicked her tongue. "Anyway, it's just us girls today. I've freed up my whole afternoon."

"If that's a problem—"

"No, not at all," Carol insisted. "Tuesday's usually my day off, but with Brad gone—" she shrugged "—I decided to put in the extra hours. My schedule's really not that full. Nothing the other girls can't cover."

Tabby followed the woman to a row of sinks where Carol waved off the shampoo girl. "Well, let's have a look at you."

Tabby removed her disguise, revealing the garish red dye job. "Men will be boys," she said.

To her credit, Carol didn't even blink. She simply draped Tabby in towels and guided her to the chair. "It's going to take a two-step process to match your natural highlights. But I'd like to start by taking the color out of your hair and skin...

"Marc said to treat you like a princess. We'll let him put his money where his mouth is," she whispered in a conspiratorial tone.

"Just promise me I won't make the same fashion statement as the girl out front."

"You mean, the owner's daughter? I promise." Carol laughed as she poured on shampoo. "We'll have you back to your old self in no time."

Tabby wasn't the pampered princess type. But the lather being massaged into her hair felt so good she decided to relax and enjoy the afternoon. As long as she didn't make a habit of taking time off, why not?

The feasibility study would proceed on schedule. She'd spent much of last night condensing the timeline from one year to one month. The SEALs were not going to get rid of her, or even distract her from her mission that easily. But they'd try. And she'd be prepared.

They'd test her; they'd push her. But how they'd treat her depended on how she reacted. The best course of action was no reaction, and that's how she intended to handle them from now on. She'd learned that through a lifetime of experience with two brothers.

But it had felt *so-o-o-o* good to get even just once.

After the wash and bleaching process, they moved on to Carol's cutting station. Tabby's hair and skin were pale, but at least the reflection she saw in the mirror resembled something closer to normal.

"Better take an inch off." Tabby tugged at a damp curl. "The Commander sets his standards a little higher than the Navy." Or in the case of hemlines, lower.

"I know. He likes that high and tight military look. He even prefers the barber on base. But I like to cut his hair, it's so soft and thick... I love running my fingers through—" Carol stopped midsnip and met Tabby's gaze in the mirror. "I just meant he has nice hair..."

Tabby grew increasingly uncomfortable with the explanation and finally asked herself the question she'd been avoiding. Were Carol and Marc having an affair? "It's none of my business."

"Oh, but I don't want you to think— I mean, I was hoping you and I could be friends."

Tabby saw the other woman's pleading expression and didn't know how that would be possible when she carried around these ugly suspicions.

Not to mention the even uglier emotion she was feeling. Was she really jealous of Carol because she thought the woman was having an affair with Marc? But were they really? Carol's eyes lit up whenever she talked about Brad. There was more of a distant fondness when she mentioned Marc.

A friend's reach across the table, a stylist admiring a healthy head of hair, those things didn't mean anything. Except Tabby found herself wanting to hold Miller's hand, to know the strength and gentleness of his touch. And she wanted to run her fingers through his hair, to get lost in the texture and explore...

"You've got color back in your cheeks," Carol commented, running a comb through Tabby's damp curls.

"I was just thinking—" at least that much was true "—that I would like to be friends." Miller wore his uniform with too much pride and integrity to carry on an illicit affair. Carol was off limits, and so was she. They had that much in common at least. "Actually," Tabby admitted as Carol took the first snip. "I was thinking you and Miller had a past."

"Doesn't everybody?" Carol relieved the tension by laughing it off. "But you're right. We sort of dated in high school. And we almost got married...twice."

Sort of, almost? Twice!

What the heck did that mean?

"Twice?" She couldn't stop herself from asking.

"Uh-huh, once right out of high school and again a couple of years ago. It broke my heart to say no to him, both times." Carol worked comb and scissors as they talked.

"Then why did you?" It felt like prying, but she had to ask. That type of information wouldn't be listed in a service record. Besides Carol had every right to stop the conversation before it infringed on his or her privacy.

"I was just someone to come back to. We grew up in the same small town. Harmony, Colorado. Ever hear of it?"

Tabby shook her head.

"Hold still," Carol reminded her. "Marc's been searching for something for a long time. I think that's why he likes the sort of rootless existence the Navy provides. He's really never had any..." Carol paused. "Um, I don't feel comfortable talking about Marc behind his back. He's been very good to me.

He introduced me to Brad." Her eyes took on that sparkle and she sighed. "It was love at first sight. We married before his leave was up."

"Sounds romantic." Tabby found herself warming to the change in subject and Carol. But her mind wandered back to Miller. *He's really never had any*...roots? Family? She could think of a multitude of ways to end that sentence.

"You know what it's like," Carol continued in the new direction, "I moved from Colorado to California, where I don't have any family or friends. Brad's gone half the time. It's been a long first year."

"You may grow to love it. An extended family wherever you go. A change of pace with every new duty station. I actually missed it after my father retired and before I attended the Academy. But while we lived it—" Tabby shook her head at the memory "—I understand how you feel."

"Really?" Carol's mood had grown darker with their revealing conversation, but lightened again. "I keep myself busy with work. And since Brad's promotion to CO of Team One I've been trying to start a Navy Wives' Club for the team." She finished cutting and fluffed Tabby's hair with her fingers. "We're expecting our first baby at the end of October."

"Wow! Congratulations. I'd have never guessed, you're not showing at all."

"I'm only two months. Not ready for maternity clothes yet. I guess that's when it will feel real. Do you want children?"

"I think kids are great. I just don't think they fit

my life-style,'' Tabby hedged. Children were something she didn't allow herself to think about very often.

''Is that because you want to be a SEAL?'' She shrugged apologetically. Information passed both ways. ''Brad told me. Marc told him.'' Finished with the cut, Carol rested her chin on Tabby's shoulder so they were side by side in the mirror. ''Frankly, I wouldn't want someone as gorgeous as you going off with my husband to wherever it is he goes. I'll just have to get you married off so the rest of us Navy wives can feel safe. You know, Marc's a nice guy—''

''He's not my type,'' Tabby cut her off with a laugh. ''And according to him neither is any SEAL that breathes.'' Just in case Carol had any other ideas.

''Hmm, that's interesting. That's the same exact thing he said about you. Let's get some color back in your hair. It would be a shame to shave it all off for SEAL Training.''

''It's just hair.''

''Now I know you're a brave woman.'' Carol smiled at her.

As they moved from station to station and process to process, the pleasant cha-ching of a cash register rang in Tabby's ears. Her makeover was costing Miller a fortune. And sooner or later she'd be bald anyway.

Wearing a salon robe, with foil wrapping tufts of her hair, Tabby ignored the fashion magazine in her lap and closed her eyes.

''Daddy, Daddy, look what I found,'' Tabby ran

up to her father holding a boxed G.I. Joe. They were in the Navy Exchange. Her pretty and petite mother was pushing the shopping cart. Bowie was sleeping in the cart's baby carrier, and Zach was riding in the back. "He looks just like you, Daddy. See he even has a scar and everything. And he comes with all this stuff. Can I get him?"

Her dad squatted to eye level. "Well, if he looks just like me and comes will all that stuff, we'd better."

"I thought you picked out the Barbie," her mom said, holding out the box.

It was a tough choice for a five-, almost six-year-old. Barbie wore a wetsuit and came with a killer whale. Tabby loved her swimming lessons and the time they spent on the boat. But G.I. Joe looked just like Dad... "Daddy, can I have them both?"

"I don't see why not, Tigger." He mussed her hair.

"Tad Prince—" her mother started to protest.

"Come on, princess, I've been gone a month. And who knows when I'll be leaving again."

"You're spoiling her rotten and I'm the one who has to deal with it when you're gone."

"Let me spoil you both," he said, coaxing his wife with kisses. "Only six more years to retirement, and then you're going to be sick of having me around, I promise."

CHAPTER SIX

"HEY, SHORT TIMER." Clipboard in hand, Marc joined Master Chief Murphy poolside. Both wore the uniform of the day, ball caps, T-shirts and shorts. "How many days to retirement, Smurf?"

From his lounge chair, Jack Murphy, affectionately known as Papa Smurf, took a long draw from his stogie. "For me or for you, kid?" He exhaled the words with a puff of smoke.

Marc removed his ball cap and used it to swipe his forehead, then dropped it on the clipboard between his legs. "For you, Chief. I'm not ready to retire yet."

"One hundred and sixty-nine," Murphy bragged. The Master Chief had been counting down his last year in the Navy since day three hundred and sixty-five. Murphy acted like he couldn't wait, but Marc knew better.

Murphy lifted the lid of a nearby cooler and pulled out two soft drinks, tossing one over to Marc. "Used to be you could pull the tabs off these things.

We made short timer chains out of beer tabs. Yes, sir, everything changes.''

Marc popped the top of his soda can and contemplated the Chief's words. There'd been several changes to SPECWAR, since the arrival of Lieutenant Chapel. Over at the pool house, another male locker room bit the dust. At this very minute she was using it to change into a swimsuit.

Yesterday they'd toured the Special Warfare compound while she furiously scribbled notes for modifications to barracks, locker rooms, heads and anything else she could think of that could be converted into female facilities. Hell, if he had that kind of renovation budget, he wouldn't be spending it to remove urinals from the heads.

The SPECWAR tour included Team One and IN-TEL. Not much to see with the team gone. But at the intelligence units he'd touted the use of women as support personnel. He even offered to push through a transfer for her. She'd fall under the purview of his immediate superior, Commander Naval Special Warfare Group One, but out of *his* chain of command.

She'd turned him down flat. But for about ten seconds he'd considered it the perfect solution. Had even daydreamed about her moving from the District of Columbia to California to be his Friday- *and* Saturday-night girl.

''Swabby, you missed a spot!'' the Master Chief hollered at the petty officers swabbing the deck and reclaimed his attention. The sailor with the hose aimed at the one with the broom and a water fight ensued. ''He got it that time.'' Murphy nodded his approval. "You look beat, kid. I'd ask if you were up all night howling at the moon, but I know better. How many hours you put in yesterday?"

Marc shrugged. "Ten."

The Master Chief raised a pair of bushy brows.

"Okay, so it was closer to fifteen," Marc admitted. After the day-long tour, he'd still had his job to do, and his own observations to record. He'd researched the cost of every one of those damned renovations she'd proposed, then did a cost comparison to renovations that were actually needed.

"Learn to delegate. You carry too much weight on those shoulders when you don't have to." Murphy sounded a shrill whistle. "Don't forget to wash down the bleachers! Then go inside and swab around the belowdecks viewing area!"

"Actually, Lieutenant Chapel got to the bottom of my In box." Marc believed in giving credit where credit was due. And thanks to her the paper monster was under control. "It's a special assignment that's taking up all my free time."

"Baby-sitting," Murphy said. Teeth clenched around his stogie, he gave Marc his full attention now that the two enlisted men had moved inside.

"That, too." Marc took a gulp of soda. Basically that's what his time with Lieutenant Chapel amounted to.

The Master Chief pointed his cigar. "I don't think you mind the *baby-sitting* so much."

Marc met the other man's hawklike gaze. "I mind."

"Sure ya do. Eyes left."

Marc did as instructed. Lieutenant Chapel was rounding the bleachers in a one-piece bathing suit.

"I don't know whether to stand and salute or just keep looking," Murphy said. "I've never seen the old Stars and Stripes worn quite that way."

Marc stared and hoped his salute wasn't too noticeable. They'd spent the morning going over her tentative timetable for the month. He'd made a few adjustments and decided to start from the beginning to see if she could actually meet the entry requirements. She'd passed the run in boots this morning.

"Eyes back in your head, Commander."

Marc shifted his gaze from the Lieutenant to the Master Chief. "Where do you think they were?"

The Master Chief snorted. "Let's just say I've been around the block a few times." He tapped the ash end of his cigar into a sand-filled bucket and dropped the subject.

Marc took his Serengeti Aviators from his T-shirt pocket and put them on. Once again, he could look.

He just couldn't be *caught* looking.

"Lieutenant Chapel," Murphy acknowledged with the same belligerent air he reserved for all officers with more rank, and less experience than his thirty years.

"Master Chief." Instead of reprimanding the man, she greeted him with the respect he'd earned and Marc's opinion of her rose another notch. Chiefs were the backbone of the Navy. Too many officers didn't recognize that fact.

"Commander, am I early?" she asked, setting her towel and bag on one of the chairs.

Marc checked his watch. "You're right on time,

Lieutenant. Smurf, you're the timekeeper.'' Pushing to his feet, he removed his stopwatch and handed it to the Master Chief. Then he peeled off his T-shirt and tossed it to the chair. ''In the water,'' he said, peeping over the top of his sunglasses before he tossed them aside.

Tabby popped to attention and offered a mock salute. ''Aye, aye, Commander.'' She risked a glance at his chest. She envied his dog tags, lying against his bare skin.

Hmm, hmm, hmm. Please, make it a Speedo, she begged when he reached for his waistband.

While he finished, she went to dip her toes in the lap pool. The water was cool, but the afternoon promised to be a real scorcher.

She brushed back her hair, liking the feel of the shorter cut. Her hair had been returned to its natural color, meaning it would at least grow out unnoticed.

Since the dye incident he'd become protective, overprotective. He'd contacted the BOQ manager himself about her window, making sure it was fixed that same day. He also called every night about midnight just to check up on her. He started each call the same way, *Talk to me, Tabitha,* and she found herself looking forward to his words tucking her in at night. They talked for hours sometimes, about everything, and about nothing.

She'd shared the most intimate details about growing up in her family, but he'd shared nothing about his past.

''You'll never acclimate yourself that way.''

Dragging her toes from the pool, she turned. He wore plain black trunks. *Darn!*

''Race you,'' he challenged, diving in and splashing her in the process. Tabby didn't stop to cry foul, but jumped in intent on catching up. The cool blast of water stole her breath. She stroked and kicked until her stiff movements became fluid.

The Master Chief cheered her on, but the Commander was stronger. And he'd got a head start.

He touched the wall first.

She arrived breathless and second.

''Slowpoke.''

''Cheater.''

''Keep warming up,'' he suggested, rising out of the pool in one fluid movement. ''Then we'll time your laps.''

She pushed away from the wall. Drifting on her back, she prepared herself for the physical test that lay ahead.

The first requirement she had to meet was a 500-yard swim in under 12:30, using the breaststroke or sidestroke. After a ten-minute rest she had to perform a minimum of forty-two push-ups in two minutes. A two-minute rest, then fifty sit-ups in two minutes. Finally, at least six pull-ups with no time limit. She'd already completed a 1.5 mile run in 11:30 wearing boots and pants earlier that morning with seconds to spare.

She rolled over and warmed up her breaststroke. When she reached the end Miller and the Master Chief were waiting for her.

''Ready?'' Miller asked.

She nodded, pulling herself out of the pool and stretching. She poised, ready to start.

''Master Chief, you call it,'' Miller said.

"Set," the Master Chief warned. "Go!"

Tabby dived in. She was a natural in the water. And adrenaline aided her to an 11:03 finish according to the Master Chief.

"I did good!" she said, looking up at Miller.

He offered a hand up. "Cut several minutes. Build your endurance. You might make a mile in under an hour."

She tried not to notice the way her hand fit perfectly in his. "Might?" she scoffed. He was talking about the end of Phase I. Trainees had nine weeks to meet that requirement.

"Might."

"Nothing like a vote of confidence. I'll make it by the end of my four weeks here." Three, this week was almost over.

His blue eyes sparkled, reflecting the color of the water. "I don't make predictions. A trainee has to want it. I can't see what's in another man's heart. Or a woman's."

It was a good thing, considering the way she felt right now. She couldn't lose sight of her goal because of a pair of blue eyes. Too many other women fell in love and did.

"I want it."

"You have ten minutes to rest before push-ups. Spread your towel," he said, curtly and walked away.

"Do trainees use a towel?"

"Use the towel. You'll scrape your hands and knees raw without it."

She looked to the Master Chief. He shook his head. Trainees didn't use towels, and neither would she. Her hands and knees were raw and bleeding by the time she completed forty-five in two minutes, but she'd met the requirement with three to spare.

She'd have given anything to wipe the I-told-you-so look off Miller's face. The Master Chief produced a first-aid kit and she doctored her injuries during her two-minute rest. Then she breezed through ninety sit-ups in two minutes. Miller held her ankles, and they were face-to-face on every *up* with only her scraped knees between them.

Pull-ups were probably the hardest, but there was no time limit to complete the six. And she had his comments about the difference between men's and women's upper body strength to egg her on.

"How about that," the Master Chief said, recording her results.

Miller took the clipboard from him and examined it. "Passable," he pronounced. "But these are only entry requirements, Lieutenant. You have a long way to go. We can start with CPR and drownproofing."

"I'll get the ropes and Resuscitation Annie," the Master Chief offered, before heading toward the pool house.

"How are your knees?" Miller asked.

"They'll hold up."

Just then, with boom box blaring, Leighton, Perry and another instructor she learned was the XO Lieutenant Commander Harmon Kyle burst from the locker room at the end of the pool house. Leighton deposited the stereo on the bleachers and dove into the pool. *He* was wearing a Speedo.

"Looks like we have company," she commented to Miller.

Miller checked his watch. "When we're not in a training cycle I let them knock off early on Fridays. It makes up for the otherwise long hours. Go ahead and take a break, Lieutenant, we'll get back to CPR later this afternoon."

The Master Chief came back with a bucket of ropes and the life-size Annie tucked under his arm. He set the doll in one of the lounge chairs and placed the bucket beside it. Miller told him to take a break, too. So the Master Chief sat and lit up a cigar.

"Hey, Chief," Leighton called out. "Got a hot date with Annie?"

"You already have her calendar full."

The Master Chief's retort elicited chuckles from Perry and Kyle, who were busy setting up a net across the width of the pool. As soon as they finished, they began knocking the volleyball around.

"Marc! You in?" Leighton asked. "We need a fourth."

"I'm busy."

"You're always busy. Time for a little fun."

"Go ahead, kid." the Master Chief encouraged.

Marc shook his head and settled in next to Murphy with his clipboard. "I have training schedules I need to go over." It was an excuse. What kind of example would he set if he played around all the time?

Tabby shrugged and turned to the group in the pool. "I'm game."

"Not on my team, darlin', I play to win."

"Well, I don't play to lose."

"You can be on my side, Lieutenant," Perry invited.

Leighton served and the ball flew over the net before Tabitha even had a chance to get in the water. Perry dove for it and missed.

"One, nothing." Leighton gloated, setting up his next serve.

This time Tabitha and Perry were ready and a lively game of two-on-two water volleyball ensued. Marc found himself more interested in the game than the schedules. Leighton and Kyle cheated their way to victory in the first set. Admittedly, Leighton did all the cheating; Kyle just benefited. But Tabitha and Perry got the better of them the second time around.

"Break over, time to get back to work, Lieutenant Chapel." He called her out of the water before the winners could be determined with a tie-breaking game.

"You should have let us finish," Tabitha said, water cascading down her body as she emerged from the pool.

"We have work to do."

The guys clambered from the pool behind her and headed over to the cooler for cold drinks.

"I'd be happy to volunteer for basic CPR," Hugh said, joining them. Up close, his skin still held a sickly green pallor.

"I already know the basics," Tabitha countered.

"I could teach you advanced, darlin'."

Marc scowled. "Hugh, why don't you take the boats out for a maintenance run."

"Sure," he agreed readily. "Lieutenant Chapel—"

"Is leaving early today for her brother's graduation."

"If you don't need me anymore, Commander, I'll ride along," Murphy volunteered, rising from his chair.

Perry and Kyle also decided to go along for the test run of the boats. And that left him alone with Tabitha. And Annie.

"Thanks—for letting me go to Zach's graduation. I really appreciate it," she said once everyone was gone. "I thought you'd forgotten."

He had. He'd been distracted by her and by his own version of the study. And now he felt like a heel for not thinking of it sooner. "Tell him to give me a call," he said, getting the frown he deserved.

"Tell him yourself." She picked up two lengths of cord from the bucket. "I have my CPR certification, but do you have time for drownproofing before I head out?"

He had promised to show her the ropes, so to speak. He already regretted it. "Turn around."

Normally there were divers in the water, lifeguards around the rim, and an instructor or two in the observation deck watching the trainees from behind thick panes of glass. He trusted his skills enough to know the danger wasn't in drowning her. The danger was in her submitting to his control while they were alone.

She turned and placed her hands behind her back.

"You trust too easily," he scolded, binding her wrists. And once she found out he was playing both sides of her study, she'd have every reason never to trust him again. He tied her ankles without another word.

She tugged against the unnatural confinement.

He gave her a cocky grin. "A trainee only has to say *I quit* and he's out of the program. I'll make it easy on you. You cry uncle at any time, and I'll let you go. Otherwise you're mine."

He meant his to control. But he liked the other meaning better. There was significance to the word he'd chosen. He knew she wouldn't say it, but he'd given her the key to her chains.

"I don't know how, Lieutenant, but you've just escaped the enemy. Your hands and feet are bound. And you've made it to water."

"What do you mean you don't know how? I did it with wit and daring." She took a faltering hop backward.

He reached out to steady her. "Okay, Lieutenant. You outfoxed the bad guys. Now comes the scary part, letting go." He pushed her backward. With a splash she hit the water. "Bob. And keep bobbing."

He'd seen to it she barely had time to catch her breath before going under. Struggling against the ropes, she made a valiant effort to surface before sinking. She came up a second and third time, gasping for air.

"Don't fight it!" he instructed. "Push off the bottom. Bend at the knees."

She pushed and resurfaced above the twelve-foot depth, then settled into a rhythm of pushing and breathing for several minutes.

"Let the water do the work," he encouraged

when she showed signs of fatigue. He settled on the edge of the pool. "Keep it up."

"I don't exactly have a choice," she rasped out.

"Sure you do. *Uncle.*"

"No way." She sucked in water.

He slipped in and brought her to the surface. "Deep breaths, now," he said, supporting her and treading water for both of them. Two wet bodies, limbs entwined. There wasn't an inch of her he wasn't aware of. Long, water-spiked lashes framed sparkling green eyes, stealing what was left of his breath and replacing it with desire.

She'd impressed the hell out of him today. But her hope of becoming a SEAL was next to nil. Why couldn't she accept it?

"Tired yet?" he asked.

"No."

"Try doing it for hours."

"If I had to."

"You wouldn't make it one day. You're wet and cold. Tired and hungry all the damn time. That's what it's like to be a Navy SEAL." He continued to tread water. "It's all guts and no glory. And I can't figure out why the hell you want that."

"Why do you?"

His chest tightened. Damned if he knew. It had started out as something to do. Then something to prove. And along the way it became something he loved. Being a SEAL hadn't just made him a man. It had become a part of the man.

The man who wanted to kiss her so damn bad he could taste it. And there was only one way he could ever have her. "Quit, damn it!"

"No!" She looked deep into his eyes, as if gauging what was coming next. He let go.

She resurfaced, and he held her above water again.

"You shark," she sputtered. She'd put herself in his control. The game wouldn't end until he said so. Or she quit.

"Try a SEAL." He lifted her to the side of the pool. And climbed up after her. "I'm a sailor, not a Boy Scout."

Her shoulder strap slipped.

He reached over and pushed it back in place, his fingers lingering under the material. His hand ached to follow through by cupping her warm softness.

Game over, before he lost control. "That's enough drownproofing for today." He met her gaze and saw beyond the strength to the vulnerability she tried to hide. "Why do you want to be a Navy SEAL, Tabitha?"

"Because I never learned to take no for an answer," she said quietly, trusting him with the deepest part of herself. "I want the full Navy adventure, not the watered-down version. Most of all, I want to spend my life helping others. Like my father did."

Marc's throat tightened. He'd love to be the man who could give this woman everything she wanted. But she wanted the impossible.

"I've never had much use for Boy Scouts. How about untying this knot, Sailor?" She draped her feet across his lap. "I asked you the same question," she reminded him. "Why are you a SEAL? What is it you want?"

He worked the cord at her ankles, rubbing her

abused flesh, noticing how soft it was beneath his callused hands. He could only think of one thing he wanted right now. "Maybe I don't need a reason for being a SEAL. Maybe I just am what I am." He reached around to untie her hands. His arms encircled her and their bodies came within inches of being pressed together.

Maybe he just wanted to be a better man.

"It's my turn to tie you up and take you prisoner," she teased, taking his hands in hers.

It wasn't the physical restriction of the exercise that made him hesitate. He'd done it many times before. He could swim the length of the pool and back with hands and feet bound. It was something else that caused him to take the cord from her before she had the chance to use it.

Trust was all about believing in yourself or someone else, and the hardest part was giving up control. She trusted him enough to let him bind her hands and feet. She probably also trusted him not to go behind her back to make sure she never achieved her goals. He didn't want to play this game anymore, not when he'd already broken her trust.

Marc stood. "You'd better get going if you want to make your brother's graduation."

1355 Friday
MIRAMAR NAVAL AIR STATION,
Miramar, CA

TABBY HAD BORROWED Nydia's little red coupe for the day and took I-15 North several miles to Miramar Naval Air Station. Before leaving, she'd showered and changed into dress whites quickly, but was still pressed for time.

The drive gave her a few minutes to think about Miller's answer to her question. *Maybe I just am...* Did he mean he just existed? Or that he couldn't change who or what he was?

Arriving at the Miramar Officers' Club, she left the borrowed coupe and realized she should have been thinking about what she'd say to her father.

Flying an inverted V overhead, four F-14 Tomcats thundered past, emitting red, white, and blue jet streams from their tails. Then one pilot tipped his wings in a symbolic salute and dropped out. The others continued on in the *missing man* formation.

The sight never failed to tighten her throat.

She hurried around the building to the uncovered patio, then slipped into the last seat, in the last row, at the last possible minute. Tabby watched with pride as Zach received top honors, graduating first in his class. She also noticed that Michelle Dann was one of only two women in the graduating class. It was only a matter of time before one or two women were graduating with each class of SEALs.

The Prince and Dann families occupied the entire front row. After the formalities, Tabby made her way forward through the crowd. Chairs were taken out of their neat rows as soon as people stood and placed around tables being set up for the festivities to follow.

"And here she is, the prodigal daughter," Her twenty-three-year-old baby brother, Bowie said, moving toward her with the family camcorder. "How's it hanging, Tab?"

"That's *Lieutenant Tab* to you, Midshipman," she said with mock sternness, noting how handsome he looked in dress whites.

At almost six feet, he only topped her by an inch.

"We'd saved you a seat. Your hair's very pretty, dear. I like that new cut," her mother said. Lily Chapel-Prince was stunning in a cream-colored suit with her blond hair pinned neatly into a chignon. Seeing her, Tabby wished she'd opted for civilian clothes instead of her uniform.

"What happened to your hands, dear?"

"I, uh, fell and scraped them," Tabby said, locking her hands behind her back.

"Mitch said he wasn't sure the Commander would let you go," her mother continued in an undertone with the faintest hint of another meaning behind it.

"He'd have to answer to me if he didn't." Her father, impressive in his own dress whites, pulled her into the crook of his arm. "It's about damn time you showed up."

"I took a seat in the back," she admitted.

The graduating member of the family joined them, and her mother insisted on getting a picture of the four of them in uniform. The Captain served as the centerpiece, with a Lieutenant on one side and a Lieutenant Junior Grade with wings on the other. The Midshipman, soon to be commissioned Ensign, knelt down on one knee in front.

"Say cheese," Her mother refused to excuse them until she'd taken several snapshots. It was clear who outranked whom in this family. As a certified shipmaster, Lily Chapel-Prince was a captain in her own right, and the only one of them licensed to pilot a ship.

Before she'd become both Navy wife and mother, she'd been an explorer, searching for sunken treasure aboard the family-owned salvage tender, the SS *Lily Pad*. In more ways than one, her father was a rich man because of her mother.

What had her mother got in the bargain?

Her godparents stole her parents away for grown-up conversation and Tabby was left alone with her siblings. Zach sent Bowie to get them something to drink. Some things never changed.

"I can't believe he wore his uniform," Zach muttered once they were alone. She didn't have to ask, she knew he was talking about their father.

"Why not? He looks good." Except for the scar, Zach was the spitting image of their father, yet he didn't understand the man at all. "He wore it because he's proud of you."

"He wore it to show off his chest of medals."

"True. But he's still proud of you, and so am I." Of her two brothers, she felt closest to Zach, though it was often in a competitive sort of way. However, she was the only one competing. Everything came easy to Zach. She would have given anything to receive that same look of pride from her father.

"He only has two hands, Zach," Michelle Dann scolded as she joined them, carrying two beers in each of hers. "Bowie's bringing the food."

"I only sent him for drinks," Zach said in self-defense.

Michelle thrust one of the bottles at him and handed another to Tabby. Was it her imagination or was Zach standing up straighter? The two families had vacationed together every summer since forever. Michelle wasn't a conventional beauty—her brother's usual type. But her intense brown eyes gave her a bit of mystery.

"I'm glad you could make it, Tab."

"She came to see me."

"Grow up, Zach," Tabby and Michelle said, together.

"Did Zach tell you we've received orders to the same fighter squadron aboard the USS *Enterprise?*"

"No, he didn't." Tabby looked pointedly at her brother.

"It must have slipped my mind."

"Speaking of which," Michelle said. "I forgot, Dad wanted pictures of the two of us." Michelle and Zach left in search of Admiral Dann just as Bowie arrived balancing four plates loaded with food.

"I was hungry," he explained, setting them down at a nearby table, before accepting his beer from Tabby.

As the afternoon wore on, Tabby mingled, met new people, anything to avoid being alone with her parents. But the time came when the three of them were alone.

Questions about her TDY assignment to Coronado immediately came from her father. "What business does Gromley have throwing you into the snake pit? If she wants to study the feasibility of women SEALs, she should do it herself. You see what's going on here, don't you? The woman knows there's not a SEAL alive that would touch a hair on your head because you're my daughter.

"The next thing you know she'll have Congress believing you went down to SPECWAR and had a Sunday stroll in the park. Then bam—" he punched his hand to provide the proper sound effect "—there'll be women in SEAL Training."

Tabby took a deep breath. She'd only gotten as far as telling him there *was* a feasibility study. She caught the look of sympathy from her mother.

She had yet to tell him it was her idea, that she'd been working on it for years. And while she wasn't having a Sunday stroll, that she hoped Congress did approve women in SEAL Training because she'd be the first in line.

So why couldn't she just say it?

"With your physical conditioning," he continued, "I wouldn't be surprised if she tried to put you through the paces. I'm telling you, SEALs are like this—" he locked the fingers of both hands "—and they'll blackball any woman who does manage to make it through training."

This wasn't a surprise to Tabby. She knew training was only the first obstacle. SEALs more or less voted in their team members at the end of a six-month trial period. She could literally be blackballed, and never receive the Special Warfare Insignia of the SEAL Teams.

By the time her father finished, his hot temper made her long for Miller's cool disapproval, not that his temper hadn't flared on occasion. Strange that she hadn't noticed; their stature and strength of character were strikingly similar. You wouldn't ignore either of them when they walked in a room. She was relieved when a couple of her father's cronies finally pulled him away for some political debate.

Her mother brushed the hair from Tabby's forehead, making her feel about ten years old. "Just tell him, Tabitha."

"You know!"

"Of course, Mitch told me."

Uncle Mitch had agreed not to tell her father, but she'd never asked him not to tell her mother. In a way it was a relief. "I want to, but—"

"You know your father is all bark. I've never seen you afraid of him before."

"I'm not afraid of him, Mom," she said, putting her arms around her mother. "He taught me to believe in myself, but if I find out that when it comes to this, he doesn't believe in me—I'll have to take him off his pedestal." How could she believe in somebody who didn't believe in her?

"If he disappoints you, Tabitha, it doesn't mean he doesn't love you. You need to tell him how you feel."

Even with her mother's encouraging words, she knew she wouldn't be telling him today.

1900 Saturday
COMMANDER MILLER'S OFF-BASE RESIDENCE, Coronado, CA

MARC TUGGED AT THE TIE, releasing the bow. Staring at his reflection, he tried again. In his starched white tuxedo shirt with upturned collar, he measured the tie ends, adjusted them, but his normally nimble fingers refused to cooperate when he tried to make the bow.

The problem wasn't his fingers, it was the sixteen inches of material wrapped around his sixteen-and-a-half inch neck. He couldn't remember the last time he'd worn his formal dress uniform.

He yanked at the tie end again.

Whose bright idea was it to tie him up anyway?

It was all he'd been able to think about since yesterday morning at the lap pool. It should've been no big deal. He could swim like a seal with his hands and feet bound. A Navy SEAL to be exact. But she'd brought up the issue of trust and a trickle of conscience had broken through.

Hell, he couldn't even trust himself when she was around. Was it because of the way he'd started to feel about her? Or because he couldn't give up control in any area of his life?

Okay, so he wasn't a Boy Scout, he'd told her as much. But he did have his own code of ethics. Honesty, integrity and loyalty were the values he lived by. Lately, he wasn't measuring up to them.

He frowned at his reflection, but managed to get the bow tied. Turning down his collar, he checked his face in the mirror. If he'd been paying attention, he never would've cut himself. He removed the blood-spotted toilet paper and slapped on some aftershave, first cooling, then burning his abraded skin.

Why was he going to all this trouble for the CO's party? A party he didn't even want to attend. Because she'd rooked him into it. The woman should write a book on the guerrilla tactics necessary to manipulate your Commanding Officer. She'd certainly delivered him all trussed up and without the benefit of ropes.

1755 Saturday
CORONADO NAVAL AMPHIBIOUS BASE HOUSING,
Coronado, CA

"EVENING, SIR." The non-rate stuck with valet duty saluted though Marc had opted to park his own car.

Trotting up the steps, Marc returned the salute. Holding it a moment longer, he acknowledged another saluting non-rate posted at the front door.

Inside the foyer, he removed his white gloves and stuck them in his upturned hat, which he checked with yet another non-rate.

"Your saber, sir?" the wide-eyed Seaman asked.

"I'll keep it." Marc patted the sheathed sword dressed to the satin stripe on his tailored navy blue pants. "An officer never surrenders his weapon." It was probably a good thing the kid hadn't seen the holstered side arm he wore underneath his white dinner jacket.

"You're a Navy SEAL!" The Seaman could barely contain his excitement. It was then Marc realized it wasn't the saber holding the kid's interest.

Above the rows of service ribbons and medals pinned to his chest, he wore his pride and joy. The Navy Special Warfare Insignia, also known as the Navy SEAL Trident—an American Eagle gripping a machine gun in one claw and Neptune's trident in the other.

He'd earned it with his sweat and blood, even tears, when he was about the same age as the young man standing before him.

His chest swelled with pride at the memory. Before he remembered there was someone else who wanted one real bad—and who wasn't likely to get one.

"Begging your pardon, sir. My request chit was just approved for SEAL Training. I made the cut for the entrance requirements." He reddened in the face of his own boast. It was an impressive accomplishment, however, and the boy deserved to feel proud.

"What's your name, Seaman?" Marc asked, noting the name tag and rating badge at the same time as he spoke, but giving the kid the opportunity to answer.

"Armstrong, sir. Radioman Scott Armstrong."

"Armstrong, I'll see you in about a month. But do me a favor." He carefully modulated his tone to be encouraging without promoting too much familiarity. "Gain about ten pounds, because I'm going to sweat it off you. But put it on with bananas, not Big Macs."

"Sir! Yes, sir!"

With Armstrong's awed gaze still on him, Marc adjusted his satin cummerbund, checked the shine of his shoes and proceeded down the hall to join the party.

Stopping beneath the entry arch to the formal drawing room, Marc sized up the crowd.

First thing Monday, he'd kill Lieutenant Chapel.

He was overdressed.

Every other officer present wore dress whites.

Though the civilians were in black tie, he stood out like the proverbial sore thumb. His hostess spotted him, and he saw a hasty retreat was out of the question.

"Commander! Commander Miller, come in. Come in. My, how dashing you look this evening." Mrs. Peck latched on to his arm. "I can't tell you how surprised I was when your secretary called and said you'd be attending. I can barely get the married officers to my little soirees, let alone the bachelors." She smiled at him with genuine pleasure. "The flowers are absolutely beautiful. And so thoughtful."

Marc had to think about that for a moment. Flowers weren't very high on his agenda, but then he realized Tabitha must have sent something in his name. With his credit card.

After an hour or so Marc knew the reason Captain Peck's wife didn't get too many bachelors at her parties. The get-together was *boring* with a capital *B*.

He wasn't really very good at the kind of brownnosing required here. Wandering from room to room, he discovered one held dancing, another a buffet. In the latter, he stopped in front of a table of tiny bite-size food. He debated whether they were actually for eating.

Taking a plate, he calculated a polite departure time. He also decided to torture Lieutenant Chapel before killing her. And for the first time that evening his mouth turned up at the corners.

He'd half expected her to show up at Manny's last night, even though he knew it was unlikely

she'd make it back from graduation. But it didn't
stop him from looking for her then, and it didn't
stop him from searching the room for her now. Miramar was just up the road.

When had he become dependent on her presence
to lift his mood?

Marc bit into a barbecue cocktail wiener and
loaded more onto his plate. He passed on the pâté
and anything else he couldn't identify, though he'd
eaten worse *and* under artillery fire. Grabbing cheese
and crackers, he rounded out his meal with veggies
and fruit.

With his plate overflowing, he settled into an obscure corner of the drawing room and leaned against
the wall. He didn't know what drew his attention to
the archway, but suddenly the object of his musings
was walking in on her godfather's arm.

Tabitha wore a little black number that didn't
even remotely resemble a uniform. The hemline cut
across her thighs, the daring cleavage dipped low.

He met her gaze across the crowded room, and
he gave the belowdecks nuclear activity a warning
order: Do not launch the Trident Missile.

She turned to the Admiral and whispered something in his ear, then headed Marc's way. Ogden
entered behind the pair. The two men wore formal
dress, which made him stick out less. He smiled.
The Chief of SEALs' appearance had probably
made Seaman Armstrong's night.

Marc put down his plate and napkin and dusted
the crumbs from his fingers. Locking his hands behind his back, he set his scowl firmly in place. He

couldn't wait until Tabitha got her cute little butt over to him.

How dare she advise him on what to wear, then show up in a knock-down, drag-out, punch-in-the-gut civilian dress?

Several minutes passed with no sign of her. He'd thought she'd been headed his way. Five, ten, fifteen minutes passed. If she didn't want to talk to him, fine. He wasn't playing this game with her. He headed for a side door.

"Sneaking out early?"

CHAPTER SEVEN

TABITHA STOOD where he'd been. She looked out over the room instead of directly at him.

"I wasn't sneaking. If I had been you wouldn't have caught me. Sneaking is a SEAL speciality." He moved closer to her side, but still kept several feet between them and pretended to ignore her as well.

"But you weren't having a very good time?"

"No," he admitted.

"Maybe you should try coming out of your corner once in a while."

How'd she know? "Maybe you should've told me dress whites would do. Then I wouldn't feel so out of place."

"Out of place?"

From the corner of his eye he caught her giving him a once-over and smiled to himself.

"The reason I suggested formal dress," she continued, "was to make you stand out, and it worked. According to Mrs. Peck, you look very handsome this evening, Commander."

"The woman only thinks that because I sent her flowers."

"*Who* sent her flowers?"

The corners of his mouth turned up, but his eyes

remained fixed on the crowd. To the casual observer, they weren't engaged in conversation or any form of fraternization. He was not a Commanding Officer flirting with a Lieutenant in his command.

Inside, he knew better. And as long as she didn't seem to mind, he had no intention of stopping. "We're getting off the subject," he said.

"Which is?"

He managed to glimpse a mischievous glint in her eyes and forced his attention elsewhere. "Uniforms. You're at an official function, Lieutenant, and you're *out* of uniform."

"Your problem is you're stuck in that monkey suit. Read your regs, Commander, cocktail dresses are appropriate evening wear for female personnel. *Even* at official functions."

He liked the snap in her voice, and the fact he couldn't stump her with a regulation. "That hemline is at least six inches up your thigh," he grumbled. "Besides, I thought you said I looked handsome in this *monkey suit.*"

"I said *Mrs. Peck* thought you looked handsome."

He snorted.

"*I* think you look very sharp this evening, Commander."

He was about to return the compliment when an older gentleman stepped forward. "Ms. Chapel, so good to see you again, my dear. May I steal you away for a dance?" The problem with standing five feet apart was you couldn't claim to be together.

"Congressman, I'd be delighted," she answered,

taking his arm and leading the man to the adjoining room.

Marc decided right then and there the congressman was a tailor-made rather than self-made man. And he had no business dancing with a girl half his age.

He grimaced. He wasn't bitter because he *couldn't* ask Lieutenant Chapel to dance, was he? Deciding he didn't want to explore that thought, Marc wandered toward the room set aside for dancing where a four-piece Navy ensemble attempted a big band sound.

He couldn't take his eyes off Tabitha. Every pass tortured him with the memory of their dance. When she smiled at him over the congressman's shoulder, his collar tightened to a stranglehold.

Damn bow tie.

"Is that a saber in your pocket or are you just happy to see me, Sailor?" The gravelly voice intruded on his thoughts.

Marc knew he wasn't being *that* obvious. Adjusting the hilt of his sword, he turned to the woman at his side. She couldn't be more than five feet in the sensible pumps that peeked from beneath the floor-length skirt of her formal dress uniform. And yet, the woman was a powerhouse in D.C.

"Rear Admiral Gromley," he acknowledged.

"Armed and dangerous as per usual, Commander Miller?"

"Yes, ma'am."

"So are you expecting trouble this evening?"

"No." But she'd still walked in the door.

"And how are you getting along with my little protégée?"

"We don't exactly see eye to eye on the issue, ma'am."

"I don't expect you to, Commander. But I do expect your full cooperation. You may not like the idea of training women to be Navy SEALs, but if Congress approves, you had better do a damn good job of it. Understood?"

"Understood, ma'am. As long as you understand I'm not going to lower my standards so a few women can make the grade." He kept his tone even and free of insubordination.

"I wouldn't want that either, Commander. We're talking about very special women, like Lieutenant Chapel—" she nodded toward the dance floor "—who are a cut above."

He continued to watch the Lieutenant in question. To his relief, she parted company with her dance partner. "All the more reason to keep her out of the line of fire," he said with sincerity.

"Shouldn't that be her choice?"

Any answer he gave would reveal too much about what he was feeling. He needed air. "Excuse me."

Marc left the Admiral's side and slipped outside through a pair of sliding glass doors. A warm breeze welcomed him, and he headed for a dark corner.

"What took you so long?" Tabitha spoke from the shadows.

He took a deep fortifying breath and moved toward the concrete balustrade she leaned against. "I didn't know you were waiting for me." He dropped his voice to an inviting rumble.

With nothing and no one keeping their flirting in check, an awkward silence fell between them, as if both sensed it was possible they were about to go too far.

But losing control was not an option for Marc.

He didn't give his car keys to valets, check his weapons at the door, or even delegate his workload. He controlled his craving for cigarettes with candy. And he controlled his other needs with abstinence.

This time, he controlled his desire to flirt by changing the subject. "I never asked about your brother's graduation."

"Still trying to recruit him?"

He shrugged. "Your father going to drop in anytime soon? Maybe I should be ready for a surprise inspection." Prince showing up for a visit had been in the back of his mind; he hadn't realized how possible it was until he spoke the words aloud.

"I don't think so. My mother's keeping a pretty tight rein on him. They just flew in for the graduation. They're leaving tomorrow, and Zach can keep them busy until then."

That was a relief. Figuring that was all the chitchat he could handle, Marc checked his watch. "I don't think even Mrs. Peck could complain if I took off now."

"Don't go yet. The night is young, as they say. Come on," she coaxed, tugging at his sleeve.

He'd follow her anywhere—except into combat. She led the way past a drained swimming pool to the pool house where she knocked—three short, three long, three short raps on the door. S.O.S. in

Morse code. The Navy still used it, but he wouldn't have guessed she knew it.

The door opened. "Come in," Captain Peck said, his weathered features attesting to a lifetime of surf and sun.

"Captain, I caught the Commander trying to sneak out of the party early and thought I'd take him where the real action is," Tabby explained.

"I don't blame you, Commander. Who wants all that brass breathing down their neck?" He raised his voice to be heard by the Admiral and several other officers who were already inside. "I wasn't talking about you, Dann."

A billiard table dominated the pool house, which had been converted into a rec room. A large-screen TV sat in the corner with the remote in easy reach on the coffee table.

"I put in two hours party duty," Captain Peck said. "Then escaped out here. This information is provided on a need to know basis only. The wife wouldn't be happy to learn I'm not working as hard as she is for this promotion."

Marc grinned. He'd always liked Captain Peck. He'd just never seen this side of him before, or, to be honest, taken the time to see it.

"Help yourselves to beer and sandwiches in the refrigerator behind the bar. You play, Miller?" Peck asked, taking up a cue stick.

"Oh, yeah." Removing his jacket, Marc rolled up his sleeves and loosened his tie. This was *his* kind of party. "I sure do."

"Pick your partner." He introduced a retired officer. "Lewis and I'll take you on."

"Then you're in trouble, Captain. I happen to know we have a pool sharp in our midst." He winked at Tabitha and she looked flattered. She shouldn't be. She was good, but he had an ulterior motive. He wanted to see her bend over the table in that short, backless dress.

"That so?" Peck cocked a graying brow. "Well, a good game of billiards calls for cigars and brandy." He poured a round from a crystal decanter, then produced a box of Cuban cigars from behind the bar and passed them around. "A sailor can always get his hands on the good stuff, even contraband."

Marc took one to be polite, then put it in his mouth and gnawed on the end.

"May I?" Tabitha asked.

"Be my guest," Peck offered with obvious surprise, holding out the box.

She sniffed the length as if it were the finest French perfume instead of tobacco.

"The head goes in your mouth. The foot, towards the floor," Marc instructed, around the stogie clenched between his teeth.

She rolled her eyes and reached for the clippers sitting on the bar as if she smoked a cigar every day of her life.

Marc moved closer when Captain Peck went to claim his cue and break. "You could just bite it off. Like a real man."

Without blinking, she bit off the end and shot it into the spittoon. "There are a lot of smoking rooms in D.C. You'd be surprised at the deals made there." She drew on the head as he lit the cigar, then blew the offending fumes in his direction. "Pardon me. Does the smoke bother you?"

She couldn't know *that* about him. Could she? "If you want to make deals, take up golf. It's healthier."

Cigar clenched between her teeth, she left his side to take her turn at the table. She leaned into her shot; her skirt inched up. She ran the table while his gaze ran all over her.

Between shots, she propped herself against the bar with her cigar in one hand and her brandy in the other. Marc observed her from a distance because she tended to blow the smoke in his face when he got near.

Smoking was *not* sexy. But Tabitha Chapel *was*. Kissing her would be like kissing an ashtray.

He'd kissed worse.

"I have you all figured out, Lieutenant," he said, sidling up beside her. Another pungent cloud came his way, and he waved a hand in front of his face.

Triumph lit her eyes.

"You think so?" She crossed her arms, mercifully holding the burning end away from him.

"I know so," he said smugly. "You just wanna be one of the boys." He picked up his cue stick. "Well, let me be the first to tell you, you're all woman."

She stared at him so long, ash from the burning stogie fell onto her dress. Starting, she brushed it away.

The evening progressed with a second, third and fourth game. And he found himself looking at Tabitha whenever she laughed, smiled, breathed. The only woman in a room full of men, and all she wanted was to be one of the guys. What a shame.

They were in the middle of a tie-breaking fifth game when Marc took his turn and cleared the table. When he turned around she was gone.

So much for showing off.

Excusing himself from a rematch, Marc shrugged back into his uniform jacket. Brandy snifter in hand, he slipped outside. He found Tabitha behind the pool house spraying Binaca into her mouth. He leaned against the wall, swirling his brandy.

She saw him and with a deep sigh, settled a few feet away, staring at the stars overhead.

Mrs. Peck's potted plants and trees were everywhere, providing cover from prying eyes. He breathed in the night air and sweet smells that surrounded him. The sweetest of which was the woman hiding out in the foliage—if he discounted the cigar smoke still clinging to her clothes. But even that lent an exotic air to her sultry scent.

He could hear the sounds of hearty male laughter coming from the pool house, while music from the main party drifted through open windows. Suddenly, he felt like dancing.

Marc swallowed back the rest of his brandy and placed the empty snifter on a wrought iron table. Ignoring the fact that he'd be fraternizing, not to mention Miller Regs, he held out his hand to Tabitha.

She searched his eyes, then slipped her hand in his.

She knew it was wrong. He knew it was wrong. But he wanted these few stolen moments. So he drew her into his arms. His one hand slid down the length of her bare back. The other held hers.

The only sounds were their breathing, the slight breeze stirring the leaves, and the music from a four-piece Navy band. They swayed in a small circle, much more slowly than the lively tempo demanded, their bodies creating a melody all their own. Her head rested against his shoulder, her hand against his Trident.

"Your father pinned me."

"I thought maybe you'd trained under him." She traced the eagle with reverence.

"He doesn't like me very much."

She raised her head and met his gaze, her eyes wide with curiosity. "How so?"

"I guess I didn't live up to his expectations." He pulled her closer. "I don't think he'd like me dancing with his daughter."

"*I* like dancing with you."

"Even though we're not supposed to?" Against his better judgment, he'd given her power over him. The power to destroy what he revered most.

His career. Could he trust her not to tell?

"*Especially* because we're not supposed to," she answered. She peeked at him through lowered lashes.

"A rule-breaker," he commented.

"And you're not?"

"Used to be."

"Not anymore?"

"I didn't go from enlisted ranks to Officer Candidate School without a lot of discipline." He'd done it because Prince had told him he'd never amount to anything. And now he was holding the man's daughter in his arms, still feeling as if he didn't measure up to her father's standards—though he hadn't seen him in ages.

"You're breaking the rules now, Commander," she reminded him.

Sometimes they were worth breaking. He pulled her closer to his chest. Closer to his heart.

"I'm going to break all the rules by becoming a Navy SEAL," she proclaimed.

Marc took one faltering step back to reality, then stopped dancing altogether. "It's not going to happen, Tabitha."

"It is. And you're going to pin me with a Trident." Her fingers brushed the symbol that meant so much to him.

He'd never seen anyone who wanted it as badly as she did—unless it was himself. But he couldn't let her believe he'd ever pin her when he'd be the first to blackball her, if she even made it through training. "No, I'm not."

She leaned into him. "I can make you change your mind." Her words were a husky whisper, easily taken out of context. But he didn't take them that way. She meant she'd show him—with a toughness to suck up anything he could throw at her.

Still, it was a good thing he was her Commanding Officer and not some scumbag who'd take advantage of her. And he could take advantage. She wouldn't even know what hit her.

He shook his head.

She'd know. She was too smart, too focused. He

had to wonder, though, if she'd put any limits to her ambition.

"Hypothetical question." He cleared his throat. "Just how far would you go to guarantee a slot in SEAL Training?"

"Is that an offer?"

"Where's your integrity, Lieutenant?"

"Where's yours? You asked." She looked taken aback.

"Hypothetically."

"Well, hypothetically, I'd like to sleep with you." She pulled away from him and crossed her arms. "And it has nothing to do with anything else. But let me ask you, would you sleep with me to keep me out of the SEAL program?"

In a heartbeat.

She raised both brows at his silence. "I guess we've established that *hypothetically* we'd each like to sleep with the other. Would sleeping with you—"

"Don't even go there."

"I wasn't! You propositioned me."

"I didn't proposition you. But I'd do just about anything to keep you out of SEAL Training and off the teams."

They stood facing each other. She looked a little bewildered, her eyes wide with both innocence and outrage. And for the life of him he couldn't figure out what had just happened either. One minute they were dancing, and the next...

Marc raked a hand through his hair. He was in hot water here, and he'd never be able to get out because the truth was he wanted her even though he was trying his best to ruin her life. "I said some things…and I apologize. I hope you know I'd never put you in that position.''

''There's no need to apologize, Commander. I…'' She dropped her gaze to his shoes and took a deep breath. Instead of finishing the sentence, she pushed past him and left him standing alone.

The line was drawn again. She was back to calling him Commander, not a good sign. He needed a minute to regain his bearing, but he didn't have that kind of time. The Chief of SEALs was rounding the corner of the pool house.

''Miller, walk me to my car. I need to speak with you before I go.'' The Admiral checked his watch. ''I have an early flight tomorrow so I'm heading out now.''

Marc nodded. Duty called. They took a path that led to the front of the house.

''Ogden's brought it to my attention he's behind on some of his SEAL quals. I'd like to leave him here so you can bring him up to speed.''

''No problem.''

''Good. Run him through the paces and send him back to D.C. as soon as possible.''

They reached the front of the house, and Radioman Armstrong scurried down the front steps with their hats and gloves. Marc put on his cover. Slapping his gloves distractedly against his palm, he looked around for Tabitha.

The Admiral's driver pulled to the curb, and Admiral Dann continued toward his waiting limo. Ogden got out on the passenger side and opened the rear door.

"Where's Tabby?" the Chief of SEALs inquired impatiently.

"She's coming right now, sir." Ogden nodded toward the door.

Marc turned just as she stepped outside.

"Good night, Commander," she said distantly, courteously. As if those moments in the garden had never happened. As if he hadn't made just about the biggest mistake of his military career.

"Good night, Lieutenant." He didn't take his eyes from her even though she didn't look at him again.

He stared after the disappearing taillights. "The black Dodge Viper." He handed his keys to the non-rate with valet duty before he realized what he'd done.

1159 Saturday
BACHELOR OFFICERS' QUARTERS,
Coronado, CA

CLOSING THE DOOR to her room, Tabby kicked off her heels and made a mad stumbling dash through the dark for the ringing telephone.

"Hello?" She flicked on the bedside lamp.

"Talk to me, Tabitha."

Her heart started beating again. "I wasn't sure you'd call tonight." But she'd been hoping. She sank to the bed with relief.

"I wasn't sure you'd pick up."

A long pause followed. She didn't know what to say about earlier. They never should have danced. But he'd looked incredible this evening—like Prince

Charming military style. And she'd been caught up in the attraction, with no thought of consequences—especially to him. Only a wall had separated them and the Chief of SEALs. "You apologized to me, but I never apologized to you." Instead she'd run.

To regroup, not escape.

"It's not necessary. You have every right to have me hung from the Navy's highest yardarm. I'm responsible for my own actions."

Responsible but not to blame.

"Door locked?" he asked, going through his nightly security check.

"Yes."

"Window?"

"They're both locked."

"Keep 'em that way."

And if she didn't? Would he rappel down the side of her building and into her room? If he wanted to get in a lock wouldn't stop him. Though maybe it would make him think twice.

Something they both needed to do.

"Good night, Tabitha." He paused, then said, "This isn't hypothetical. I want to know you in every way possible. But you have to understand—I'm caught between wanting you and wearing the uniform."

She waited for the click before letting out her breath and hanging up. Wrapping her arms around the pillow, she rolled onto her side.

The proverbial rock and hard place had them both trapped. Because she was caught between wanting to be a Navy SEAL and wanting him. Was wanting him enough? She ticked off his faults. Controlling, overbearing, sexist...though there was a part of him that wasn't any of those things.

Still too many women gave up their dreams for men, including her mother. She wasn't going to be one of those women.

But that didn't explain why she left her window unlocked when she went to bed.

"Hey, Tigger. What ya doin'?" Her father sank to the floor beside her.

She continued dressing Barbie in G.I. Joe's uniform. "Barbie's going off to war."

"She is? What about old Joe there?"

"Oh, he's going to stay home with the babies."

"I think he'd like that. I know I would. But I came to tell you, Daddy's got to go away again."

Tabby dropped Barbie and threw her arms around her father. "I don't want you to go, Daddy."

He hugged her to him. "I have to."

"But Mommy gets sad when you go."

"I know. Mom makes a lot of sacrifices to be with me. But that's what love is sometimes. When I retire, I'll make it up to her, to all of you. Now I gotta go. Be a big girl and don't cry, I need you to take care of your mom."

"I'm seven. I can take care of Bowie and Zach, too. I can walk Zach to school by myself, you know."

"Well, you've got your hands full, that's for sure. Just remember to take care of yourself." He squeezed her tighter. "And look both ways before crossing the street."

CHAPTER EIGHT

TABBY HIT THE GROUND running. The instructors were already on the beach for their afternoon run, which had become a regular part of her routine. She raced to catch up with the formation, falling in step with Perry.

She'd been at the laptop all morning and on the phone through lunch. Rear Admiral Gromley's secretary had finally faxed over the requested information from Miller's service record.

Tabby couldn't wait to get back to her desk and read it.

But for the past two weeks, she'd taken every opportunity to train with the SEALs whether it was in the gym or on the beach.

The study was progressing. She'd read all the manuals, interviewed all the rollbacks and watched several hours of videotapes. With free run of the SPECWAR compound, she observed, took notes, and at night put them into something comprehensive—something that would give women the right to train with men, to become the Navy's finest, Navy SEALs.

And while she typed, she waited for the phone to ring. He never said much, just checked to make sure her door and window were locked. But she looked forward to his calls, because the rest of the time he was as cool and aloof as the day she arrived.

Miller set a grueling pace for their twice-daily sand torture. And even though Tabby ran competitively, it was all she could do to keep up, but she'd be damned if she'd fall behind.

Tabby stole a glance at Miller running to the left of the formation in shorts and tank top with Go Navy, Beat Army blazoned across his back. His muscular thighs tensed and flexed with each powerful step.

SEALs were known for having the bodies of Olympic athletes. She easily imagined him competing in a decathlon. But she preferred to imagine him running naked, like the first Olympians. He fell in beside her and she pulled her thoughts back to the present century.

"Nice to see you could make it, Lieutenant. Did you forget? You and I are running ten miles this afternoon."

She hadn't forgotten.

They reached the two mile point. The rest of the formation turned as a unit and headed back to the compound. And the two of them continued on alone.

The first time since Peck's party.

Miller checked his watch and dropped the pace. Still pushing the limits of her endurance, she suspected it barely affected him. They continued for several minutes in silence.

Her calves ached from the sand. But she kept pumping her legs, and they were getting stronger by the mile. SEALs had running down to a science.

"Rest next week. Or at least cut back to your regular running routine. There's a high risk of stress fracture in the third week of sand torture."

Her third week of sand torture, her fourth and final week of the feasibility study. She'd have plenty to do as it was. And then she'd leave. "Okay." She breathed out.

Sweat beaded, trickled and dripped the length of her body. She preferred to run in sweats, but peeled off her sweat-soaked shirt and tied it around her waist without breaking stride.

"Ready to cry uncle?" he asked.

"In your dreams, Sailor." She gritted her teeth and pushed on. This had been personal right from the start. Every swim stroke, every footfall, he taunted her to give up.

Little did he know, *Go Navy* had become her silent mantra.

Minutes ticked past without words. Her breathing even, her footing sure, matched his. He ran so close beside her, she skimmed the water's edge. The occasional wave lapped her feet and she longed to dive into the surf as the afternoon sun beat down.

"That has to be ten miles," she said finally. "And we still haven't turned around."

"Eleven point three. Because that's my place right there. I was shooting for fourteen. But if you can't handle it..." He increased his speed.

"What!" She raced him until her lungs screamed for a reprieve. Gasping for air, she stopped and braced her hands on her knees.

"Walk it out."

Pressing a hand to her cramping side, she moved slowly forward as he circled.

"Was that *uncle* I heard?"

"Yes, and it was coming from you. Your shoe's untied." In the split second it took for him to look, she shoved him toward the water. He didn't budge. Instead he wrapped his arms around her legs and tackled her, sending them both crashing to the surf.

They played in the water like a couple of kids, splashing and dunking and roughhousing. Until Tabby broke free and ran toward the house he'd pointed out as his. He scrambled after her, once again tackling her to the ground. They fell together, laughing and breathless and covered in sand.

"I think it's in my underwear," she said, rolling onto her back and into him. She gazed into his eyes, and the laughter died with the awareness. His gaze traveled to her lips and stayed there.

She felt his hot heavy breath mingle with her own.

Water and sweat. Skin and sand. His lips a breath away from hers, she heard his muffled oath.

Marc's career flashed before his eyes. What the hell was he doing? He didn't want to go down the road of officers who'd taken advantage of the women in their command.

He'd reprimanded himself for those few moments they'd spent dancing in the moonlight. His self-imposed punishment had been to avoid being alone with her for the past two weeks.

"My apologies, Lieutenant," he said, getting to his feet. He offered her a hand up.

She put her hand in his, and he savored the physical contact. "No apology necessary, Commander." She dropped his hand and brushed the sand from her backside.

"You can clean up inside. Get the sand out of your pants," he said, trying to lighten the mood. He walked across the beach and up to his deck. She looked over his shoulder while he punched in his security code "Memorizing it?"

"Just curious. You know, to see if you picked your birthday or something."

"My mother's."

"Your mother?"

"I call her on Sundays like every dutiful, loving son. I make it a point to see her once a year. And I shower her with gifts on her birthday and Mother's Day." She was gaping like a blowfish. "What? You didn't think I had one?"

"Doesn't everybody? I'm just surprised. You never talk about your family."

"Let's see. Mom's a young sixty-five, living in a retirement community in Florida where she's acting out her second childhood by doing all the things she never had time to do while raising a family." He shook his head at the memory of his mother bungee jumping. But as long as she was happy.

She'd had so little happiness in her life.

She'd like Tabitha, he realized, she'd like her a lot. For her strength, her commitment and her ambition.

"You have brothers and sisters?" she asked. "And what about your father?"

He should have never opened up the subject. "Two brothers, both older. Mom was widowed three years ago, after forty years of marriage to Warren Miller. He wasn't my father." He saw the question forming. "I don't have a father. And I don't want to talk about it." He was sick to death of talking about it. Growing up there'd been psychiatrists, family counselors, social workers...enough psychobabble to last a lifetime. Not to mention all the whispering behind his back and even the cruel comments to his face. His one friend, his only friend, had been Carol. "Water?" He passed through the dining room to the kitchen.

"Please," she answered, looking around. "You have a nice place."

"The owner's putting it up for sale. I'm thinking about buying it." In fact, he'd just made up his mind. He opened the refrigerator and tossed her a bottle over the breakfast counter. She caught it and used it to brush the hair back from her damp forehead.

Grabbing one for himself, Marc twisted off the lid and gulped half the bottle in one swallow.

Tabitha leaned against the breakfast counter, drinking with leisurely sips. She looked him over carefully. "I won't pry. But if you ever want to talk about it...I'm a great listener."

"I won't." Dropping the subject, he moved to her side of the barrier, surveying her from the top of her strawberry-blond head to the tips of her sand-covered sneakers.

His gaze settled on a bead of moisture that started just below her mint-green sport bra and trickled past her navel, disappearing in the rolled band of her sweat pants.

He wanted to follow the salty trails with his tongue. He wanted to strip the sweaty, sand-covered clothes from her body and delve into deeper pleasures.

"Do you want to shower?" The words came without warning.

"What?" She looked startled by his question and he knew what she thought. Oh, he'd meant it that way all right. But he recovered quickly. "You can shower upstairs and I can run your clothes through the wash. I have some work to do here before we head back to base."

"Sure. Thanks."

He led the way to his bedroom and pointed out the bathroom. "There's a robe hanging on the back of the door. Leave your clothes outside the bathroom door and I'll get them."

He left her and stomped heavily downstairs, heading to the second bathroom, where a cold shower awaited him.

TABBY DRIED OFF, then stepped from the shower stall. Wrapping herself in Marc's terry robe, she buried her nose in the lapel and inhaled. His scent clung to the material. Like a sea breeze off a tropic island, he was a man of the elements—sea, air, land and fire. She wanted to touch that fire. But she didn't dare.

The repercussions could be serious.

Standing before the steamed vanity mirror, she traced a happy face while her face split into its own contented smile. There was something intimate about being in the man's bathroom.

It said a lot about him. He was meticulous, anal really, and she had fun moving things around on the counter. Out of curiosity she opened a bottle of cologne, Aqua Velva. She scrunched her nose. *Not him.*

She went through the rest, tipping bottles and dabbing some on her wrist. Brut, Old Spice, an array of cheap aftershave. Not one smelled *exactly* like him. Not even the combination.

Disappointed, she closed the lid on the last one.

Picking up his brush, she ran it through her hair, each stroke sending shivers down her spine. She didn't dare use his toothbrush, but she found several still in the package while rummaging through a drawer. She opened one and squeezed on toothpaste, then brushed. Either he changed his toothbrush often or he was prepared for overnight guests.

Women guests? One woman? She stopped brushing and spit. There was no evidence among the toiletries to support that assumption.

Since the one he used and all the packaged toothbrushes were blue, she opted for the explanation that he was obsessed with oral hygiene. But she couldn't escape her curiosity about the women in his life. Until now she'd thought of him as available. Certainly not for herself because after all, he was her boss. But available.

Though that didn't mean he'd always been.

She ruled out a steady relationship. Who'd put up

with him for long? That left love 'em and leave 'em
one-nighters. Rinsing, she spit again and wiped her
mouth. Putting her toothbrush next to his, she pulled
out a length of floss. Well, they could have him.

He was more trouble than he was worth. And too
damn sexy for his own good. And she'd have to
sacrifice everything in order to be the woman in his
life.

Of course, that didn't mean she couldn't day-
dream about it. To counter that she started to think
about all his faults, again.

Major ego topped the list. She stared at her reflection. Bright pink flushed her cheeks. Just how
big was that ego, anyway? She checked her smile,
running her tongue along her teeth.

She noted her clothes had disappeared from the
pile by the door. She'd dawdled over her shower,
but she knew they wouldn't be done yet. In the bedroom a mirrored closet ran the length of two walls.
The L shape was broken only by the door to the
hallway. She glanced at the ceiling. At least there
was none up there.

An incredibly large bed was centered along another wall.

Too curious for her own good, she opened the
larger of the two closets. Uniforms hung in neat
rows by length and in color order, whites, khakis,
greens, cammys, navy blues and blacks. Several
pairs of polished shoes and boots lined the closet
floor. *Anal.*

What had she hoped to find? Some clue to the
man, or the father he didn't want to talk about? Her
hand ran down the sleeve of a uniform jacket to the

gold braid. She sensed there was more to the story
than a woman who'd had an affair during her forty-
year marriage. It was Tabby's nature not to assume
anything. Still she couldn't help wondering. Adoption, maybe—a foster child—there were several possibilities.

A built-in dresser with a false front opened like a
door to reveal a selection of ties and belts hung to
one side on a spinning rack, which she tested by
giving it a whirl. On the other side, a shelf held a
tray filled with pocket change, and typical Navy
stuff—shoe polish, lighter fluid, Brasso and a neat
stack of clean rags. Beneath the shelf, slim drawers
lined in black velvet revealed ribbons, medals and
medallions.

For a long moment she stared at his Trident, remembering the last time he'd worn it before she shut
the drawer.

To the right was a dresser. White T-shirts and
briefs in the first drawer. Green and black T-shirts
and green and black boxers in the next two.

Tabby found civilian clothes in the smaller closet,
also hanging by color, blue being predominant. *Really anal.* But at least they ran the spectrum from
light to dark. This closet held two more dressers.
The top drawer of one again filled with underwear,
but alongside the plain white boxers were a stack of
silk boxers.

She lifted a pair of red ones and held them up.
Did she dare?

MARC SAT IN THE DEN in front of his computer
screen. He'd taken that ice-cold shower, rounding

up a clean T-shirt and shorts from the laundry room. Then he'd gone back to his bedroom.

Instead of finding a pile of clothes in front of the bathroom, he'd found the door ajar and the sandy pile of wet clothes just inside on the tile floor.

Consideration? Or invitation?

He'd heard the pulsing beat of the shower, and the soft sweet strains of her humming. He could have inched the door open and watched her silhouetted behind frosted glass.

The voyeur in him wanted to.

But the very idea repulsed him. Besides, he didn't need to, his fertile imagination had taken over and by the time he'd made it downstairs with the laundry he was thinking about a second cold shower.

Until his thoughts moved to both the man who'd fathered him and the man who'd raised him. He understood why Warren Miller hadn't been able to love him. But he didn't understand why Miller had needed to beat that fact into him. Or worse, his mother.

Those were Warren's alcoholic years. At least he'd blamed the liquor. After that were his recovering alcoholic years in which he'd tried to make amends. In many ways those years were worse. There was always someone crawling inside Marc's head trying to ensure he grew up healthy, normal, well adjusted. His mother had stayed through the bad years of her marriage. He'd stayed only until he was old enough to leave. His family was closer now that Warren Miller was dead. If he'd had another last name to take he would have.

But the man who'd fathered him was worse.

And he was never going to be like either of them.

He checked his watch again. "What in the hell is she doing up there?" The shower had stopped ages ago.

What in the hell was he doing? He literally sat on the edge of his seat waiting for her. Was he hoping to get caught?

He'd opened the file to his counter-study, one-hundred-plus pages, which he'd finished last night. He'd covered every aspect of a SEAL's physical and mental conditioning, comparing women to men. He'd even provided combat statistics from Allied Services that used female combatants. If combat stats didn't force the bureaucrats in D.C. to open their eyes, then his cost analysis for renovating the training facilities would.

By the time he set his computer to print, she still hadn't come downstairs. He got up from the chair and headed to the kitchen. The whirl of the washing machine in the final throes of the spin cycle caught his attention. He headed to the laundry room. The washer stopped and he tossed everything to the dryer, setting it for forty minutes.

Enough waiting! He took the stairs two at a time.

He didn't know what he'd expected to find, but it wasn't Goldilocks sleeping in his bed.

Marc stood in the doorway staring at the woman curled up in his white terry bathrobe. Her unusual hair tumbled across her face, drawing his attention to the delicate flush in her pink cheeks.

When his heart started beating again, he stepped into the room. He could have let her go on sleeping, but he squatted by the bed and softly called her name.

"Tigger, what's that behind your back?" Her dad asked from behind his Sunday paper.

How did he do that? "Nothing, Dad," she lied. He turned down the corner of The Post *and stared at her until she felt compelled to tell the truth.* "It's your hammer."

"Where are you going with it?"

"Zach and Bowie won't let me in the treehouse. They put up a No Girls Allowed sign and won't give me the secret password. I helped you build it, too. So now I'm going to go tear it apart."

"I see. Boys can be mean sometimes, can't they? But if you tear it apart there won't be a treehouse."

She stopped to think about that for a minute. "I'll build a new one."

"A lot of hard work went into that clubhouse. It's not going to be easy building one from scratch." He went back to reading his paper.

Shoulders slumped, she moved slowly toward the back door. He was right. They'd spent all that time picking out the perfect tree, drawing up the plans, cutting the wood and then building it.

"Tabitha—" her father lowered his paper *"—bust the door down."*

She skipped off to do just that and the next thing she knew she was lying on the ground looking up at the sky through leafy green branches.

Zach and Bowie were yelling. "Mom! Mom!"

"What happened?" Her mother asked, sounding anxious. "Tabitha? Tad! Get out here!"

"She fell out of the tree!" Zach said. *"And a board hit her on the head."*

"Zach pushed her," Bowie said.

"Did not!"

"Did too!"

"Did not, did not, did not…"

"Tabitha?"

"I busted the door down, Dad."

"Tabitha, wake up. Tiger…"

"What did you just call me?" She stretched her way to wakefulness, sitting up in the middle of his bed.

"Tiger," Marc said. "You stretch like a cat, but a house pet's too tame. Tabby doesn't fit."

She laughed and shook her head. "My Dad used to call me Tigger."

"You've grown up since then." He sniffed the air. "You smell like a men's locker room." He caught a glimpse of skin and a flash of red before she closed the gaping robe. "Are those my boxers?"

"You didn't expect me to walk around commando, did you? And I'm wearing whatever's in your bathroom," she confessed. "Do you mind?" She swung her feet over the side of the mattress and sat on the edge.

"Actually, I do," he teased. "They're birthday and Christmas presents from my niece and nephews. Like the boxers. I don't wear them."

"Oh."

He stared at her mouth as her kissable lips formed and held a perfect *O*.

"Didn't you ever hear, curiosity killed the cat?"

She looked at him with more than curiosity. Desire shone in her eyes, and he knew it was reflected in his.

"Are my clothes ready? I need to get dressed—"

One minute hot, the next cold. He called her bluff.

Nudging her knees apart, he knelt between them. His arms went around her waist and her arms went around his neck.

She dropped her forehead to his. "I wasn't..."

"What?" he said, running the pad of his thumb along her full lower lip. "What weren't you doing? I want you. And I can't have you. I'm only a man, Tabitha. How much temptation do you think I can handle?" He brushed the drying hair back from her face. "But in one week, after your orders are cut...after you're out of my command... Pass that mile swim and fourteen-mile run and I'll spring for dinner and a room at the Hotel del Coronado your last night in town."

Historic Hotel del Coronado where Tony Curtis and Marilyn Monroe had filmed *Some Like It Hot,* and where, judging from the look in her eyes, they'd set the night on fire. "I can get to know you. And you can have your way with me, or not. You lead and I'll follow wherever you want to take us. But right now we both need to act professional. The uniform matters."

Marc heard heavy steps on the stairs. He had just enough time to push to his feet before Preach, Houston and Papa Smurf crowded the open doorway to his bedroom.

Seeing the trio in his house was no real surprise, all the instructors had his security code. It was just a house, a place to crash. But being caught was a big problem.

"We came to give you two a ride back to base," Hugh said, looking over Marc's shoulder at Tabitha. "Want us to take a hike?"

Marc knew what they thought. A half-dressed woman on his bed. One that shouldn't even be there. That his men even knew where to find him said a lot.

"I'm going to get dressed." Tabitha excused herself, getting off the bed and drawing the ends of the robe together. She squeezed her way past the men in the doorway.

Marc made no apologies and no excuses. It looked like what it looked like. He'd have to trust his men to keep this to themselves. SEALs lived by a code of silence. But he wondered if he'd fallen a notch in their estimation. And he worried about Tabitha's reputation.

He deserved what he got. She didn't deserve to be slandered—nothing had happened after all.

The men followed her downstairs. The initial tension was broken when Perry raided the refrigerator for soft drinks. The petty officer passed them around while they sat in the living room waiting for Tabitha.

"I'd do her," Hugh finally said.

"I'd marry her," Perry added.

"Don't listen to either of those two boneheads, kid. That gal's a whole lot of trouble."

Though Marc didn't appreciate any of the advice, he took it with the humor intended.

If his fist actually connected with Hugh's jaw, it would seem as if he cared. If he denied wanting to marry her, the rumor would be he already had. And if he admitted she was trouble, they'd assume he had firsthand knowledge.

"Opinions noted, guys. End of discussion."

CHAPTER NINE

SEARCHING IN VAIN for her room key, Tabby realized too late that it had been in the pocket of her sweats and was probably in the bottom of Marc's washer or dryer. If it hadn't been for the untimely arrival of his men, she might have figured it out at the time.

As it was, all she could think about was how she'd jeopardized Marc's career. Or had she? SEALs were a close-knit group. They watched out for each other.

Tabby descended the three flights of stairs, heading for the BOQ office. Her stomach rumbled, reminding her she'd skipped lunch. Though starving when she got back to the office, the fax from Gromley was her first priority.

Most of the items from Miller's service record were inconsequential. She learned nothing more about his family than he and Carol had already told her. In the end, she'd felt guilty for reading it, but reminded herself he'd read hers cover to cover.

She'd discovered Master Chief Thomas and the

others had exaggerated about Marc's almost burning down the SEAL barracks. He'd simply burned a hole in his blanket. But he'd been brought before Captain's Mast for destruction of government property—her father, his Commanding Officer at the time, had fined him fifty dollars and restricted him to barracks for fifteen days.

The list of disciplinary actions went on and on, amounting to virtually nothing, until one serious infraction—an Unauthorized Absence at the end of his SEAL training. Her father's notes were cryptic, alluding to family problems. Miller had received the loss of one month's pay, restriction to barracks for thirty days, and reduction in rate, suspended for six months—which meant if he screwed up again within six months, he'd be busted.

What family problems could have made him go UA?

The disciplinary actions ended there. But the enlisted evaluation her father wrote at the end of SEAL Training was less than glowing, most often citing his opinion that Miller was not a team player.

How'd he get from *not a team player* to being their leader? From what she'd observed over the past several weeks he still held himself back.

She reached the office and collected a spare room key.

"Good evening, Ms. Chapel." Alan Ogden emerged from the main TV lounge.

"Hi, Alan." He was staying in another wing of the building and occasionally she ran into him.

"I was wondering if maybe you weren't busy this evening..."

Tabby scanned the lobby while her mind searched for an excuse. The Commander had forbidden fraternizing with SEALs while under his command. Okay, she'd already broken that rule, but it would still sound like a lame excuse. The man really had no control over her social life. She spotted Nydia at the wall of mailboxes and cast her friend a helpless look. "Oh, Alan—"

"Sorry, fella, we have plans." Nydia draped her arm around Tabby.

"Another time then," Alan said before backing away.

"Well, that was cruel." Tabby turned to Nydia. "But thanks."

Nydia shuffled through her mail. "To lead him on *is* cruel."

"I don't lead him on."

"You don't say *no* either. He's a creep."

"He's harmless. All *you* did was put him off. Same as I do. He'll ask again." He was always asking.

"Are you grateful or not?"

"That depends. What *are* our plans? I could use a girls' night out."

"Haven't a clue. I was hoping you'd take me to that bar where all those men with nice bods and nice cars hang out."

"You mean Manny's? You've got to be kidding."

"Please, please, please. You owe me big time. I got rid of your boyfriend, didn't I?"

"Let me get changed, then we can grab a bite to

eat before heading to Manny's. I guarantee you'll walk in and turn right back around.''

They didn't. Nydia didn't sit out one dance once Tabby had reluctantly introduced her to Hugh. The guy was a jerk; she didn't know what her friend saw in him.

Tabby sat through all the dancing and bought her own drinks. No one even asked. She wondered how much that had to do with Miller. And how much it had to do with her invading the SEALs' territory.

They'd been there for a couple of hours when Carol Bailey walked in, obviously looking for someone. Tabby waved her over to the booth. "I've been meaning to call you—"

Carol waved away her excuse. "I know, you've been busy." She didn't sit down, and she seemed distracted.

"Are you meeting Marc?" Tabby asked, still hopeful she'd bump into him tonight, yet dreading Carol's answer at the same time.

"No, I'm trying to find Elaine Coffman, J.C.'s wife. Do you know her? She left a message on my phone, saying she'd be here. I'm trying to stop her from doing something foolish. There she is." Carol spotted the woman coming out of the ladies' room.

Elaine literally fell into the arms of a man that Tabby knew wasn't J.C., the XO of Team One. Together the couple staggered their way toward the door.

Carol rushed over, with Tabby on her heels. She'd gotten to know quite a few of the SEALs in recent weeks. And occasionally, a curious wife would stop by to see her. Elaine had been one of those.

"Elaine!" Carol demanded the drunken woman's attention. "I came to take you home."

"She's goin' home wif me." The drunken sailor at her side urged Elaine forward.

"I'm going home with, with, what's your name?"

"You don't want to do this," Carol pleaded.

Elaine looked torn, but took a few faltering steps toward Carol. Seeing his prize slip away, the sailor lunged for the woman. With lightning reflexes, Tabby grabbed the man's wrist and stepped between the two.

"Why don't you go home and sleep it off, buddy?" But the guy decided the odds were in his favor and that even drunk he could take on one measly woman.

His mistake. Tabby let him have it right in the Adam's apple, and he dropped to the floor at her feet. "Manny, this drunk needs a taxi." Tabby stepped over his still breathing body.

"Can you show me that move?" Carol asked.

"Sure."

"I miss all the fun," Nydia said, joining them.

Elaine started to sob. The three women ushered her out the door, deciding Carol would take Elaine, Tabby would drive Elaine's car, and Nydia would follow in a convoy over to Elaine's house.

They arrived at base housing ten minutes later.

"J.C. cheated on me," Elaine sobbed, then hiccupped and staggered her way to the front door. "I want to get back at that bastard!" she screeched, setting the neighborhood dogs to barking. A porch light flicked on across the street, but they got her inside without further incident.

Carol put Elaine to bed and called Brad. "I don't want to leave her alone tonight," she explained to Tabby and Nydia when she hung up the phone. "She's pretty shaken up. She found out J.C. didn't come straight home from his last mission and kicked him out of the house. He's over at our place."

"I can stay, too." Tabby volunteered.

"Me, too," Nydia agreed. "Though I was having plenty of fun with that SEAL."

"You mean Leighton?" Tabby asked. "Oh, please."

"He was kind of obnoxious." All three laughed. "Remember the dye incident?"

"Wait, wait! I want details," Carol said. "But first I'll break out the ginger ale. And we can order a pizza."

They settled around Elaine's coffee table for girl talk, interrupted only by the arrival of two very large pizzas. They drank ginger ale out of wineglasses, toasted their sisterhood, proclaimed all men pond scum and ignored calories completely. Carol even scrounged a chocolate layer cake and chocolate ice cream for dessert.

Poor Elaine had been trying to eat away her pain with chocolate. Right now Tabby needed it more. Her reputation was probably being maligned this very minute over a round of beer at Manny's.

They were talking about favorite movie couples when Carol said, "I think you and Marc make a great couple. I know you've said he's not your type…"

Tabby almost gagged.

A couple? What would it cost her? What would

it cost him? She stuck the spoon in the ice cream carton the three of them were eating from. Her appetite was gone.

"What time is it?" Tabby asked, looking at her watch at the same time. 2245. "I have to go."

2302 Friday
NAVAL SPECIAL WARFARE CENTER,
Coronado, CA

GRAPE-FLAVORED Tootsie Pop in his mouth, Marc reached for the telephone, then stopped himself. Not tonight. He'd already done enough damage.

Kyle knocked on the open door. "I thought I'd find you here. Can I come in?"

Marc nodded to his Executive Officer, and second in command. He'd been expecting something like this. Kyle sat on the desk, unable to make direct eye contact.

Marc kept his seat and looked directly at the man. After a long wait in which nothing was being said, he removed the sucker. "What's on your mind, Harm?"

Harm took a deep breath. "The guys wanted me to talk to you about this afternoon…"

"I've got the situation under control." He tossed the sucker to the trash and scrubbed a hand over his well-past-five-o'clock shadow. "I'm removing myself from the picture. Team One has a training exercise coming up; I've arranged to go with them. Lieutenant Chapel is only here for another week. Until then she can be your responsibility."

"Great." Kyle tried to muster some enthusiasm

for the baby-sitting duties just assigned him. "But I think it's probably for the best." Kyle visibly relaxed. "Feel like a beer?" he asked. "I'm headed to Manny's."

The men were right to call him on his liaison with Lieutenant Chapel. Normally it was his job to worry about them. But he admired loyalty. It was right up there with honesty in his book. And integrity. He seemed to be the only one lacking those recently.

"I thought I'd finish up here, then head home."

"Okay." Kyle turned to leave. The XO had been here a month, but Marc had never really gotten to know him. If the men chose him for this, they must respect him.

He had a sudden urge for Manny's. "Hold up," Marc said, pushing to his feet and following Kyle out the door. "I think I'll have that beer. And you can tell me how the doctor removed that toilet seat from your Iowa-born-and-bred dairy air."

1730 Monday
NAVAL SPECIAL WARFARE CENTER,
Coronado, CA

TABBY GAVE UP writing actual sentences and began doodling on the legal pad in front of her. It was time to call it a day anyway.

The morning had been fairly busy with an unexpected stream of SEALs interrupting her work to hand in completed workbooks for a course on sexual harassment in the workplace. Miller had designated her office as the drop-off point.

Perry even brought her an apple. An apple for the

teacher? A teacher who had a lot to learn about appropriate and inappropriate behavior with her boss.

But not one SEAL had said a word about her indiscretion with Miller.

She'd scribbled the lead tip of the pencil down to nothing. And had a page full of nothing to show for it as well. She kept thinking about Miller's proposed tryst at the Hotel del Coronado. *You lead, and I'll follow…* Where did she want this to go? Was the invitation still open?

"Tiger?" Marc knocked on the door frame, startling her. "I'm picking you up at 1815, your room. Wear something comfortable."

And then he was gone.

She moved to the doorway. She was surprised to hear him call her by the nickname, but she tried not to read too much into it. The man hadn't called her once over the weekend, and she'd only seen him in passing today.

Puzzled, she called after him, "Is this a date?"

"I don't date women in my command." There was definitely a seriousness in his voice.

"Where are we going?"

"You'll see."

1815 Monday
CORONADO NAVAL AMPHIBIOUS BASE,
Coronado, CA

MILLER DROVE across base in silence. As he'd requested, she'd dressed comfortably in blue jeans and a yellow sweater. He hadn't changed from the uniform of the day.

When he pulled up in front of the base recreation center, she still didn't have a clue as to why they were there.

"This way." He ushered her to a room with a mat-covered floor. It was clearly meant for sparring, although curiously there were also rows of chairs facing a blackboard classroom style.

She took the chair he indicated, and the room filled up behind them. Women of various ages, shapes and sizes greeted him by name. All wore sweats, making her feel overdressed.

Well, this definitely wasn't a date.

An elderly woman sat beside her "Is this your first time?" The woman reached out and patted her hand.

Tabby nodded. Her first time at what, she didn't know.

Marc stood at the head of the class. He turned the freestanding blackboard over and she read the words: self-defense for women. Six-thirty to eight, Mondays.

He pulled a sheet of paper from his back pocket and began copying it. *A Rape Victim's Rights*. He underlined the words. As he wrote, he lectured. The women around her took copious notes. Tabby listened to the empowering message. Strong words from a strong man.

Anticipation amplified around her when Marc donned a Redi-man suit made of padded neoprene, followed by a helmet and face mask. Tabby sat on the edge of her seat, waiting for whatever was coming.

Some of the women seemed excited, some apprehensive. But they all took their turn beating the crap out of him. While the women hit and kicked and clawed, they screamed at the top of their lungs one word. "No!"

While everyone clapped for the seventy-year-old grandmother of ten and great-grandmother of three, Marc removed his helmet and offered the woman a hand up and said, "Nice job." Sweat trickled from his hair and he swiped at it with a padded arm.

His gaze shifted from the older woman to Tabby. He curled his finger. Tabby looked around and realized he wanted her.

"I brought a friend for a martial arts demonstration. So you can see how this might look like without the pads. She may need a little encouragement though. Lieutenant Chapel…" He held out his hand.

More applause filled the rec room. She'd look churlish, and Miller foolish, if she didn't cooperate. She unlaced her boots and took them off at the mattress.

He peeled out of his gear. "Hit me with your best shot."

"Are you sure you want to do this?"

"It's one way to work out our frustrations. I wish I'd come up with it sooner. It would have saved me a lot of cold showers."

She blushed at the thought. "I'm not going to work out anything except my muscles sparring with you." Though she always felt better mentally after working out, she didn't think she'd find it an adequate substitute for having sex with this man.

"Wanna bet?" He tripped her, sending her sprawling to the mat on her backside.

"You—!" Her moves were tentative at first, but as he became more aggressive, she fought back hard.

She kicked. He blocked. She kicked again. He came back for more, and she tripped his feet out from under him.

He bounced back, and she caught him with a roundhouse kick to the ribs. He dropped to one knee. And the women all cheered.

"Marc?" She raced to his side, offering him her hand.

"I'm okay." He let her help him up. "Was I right about the frustration?"

She laughed and hugged him tight, burying her face in his neck. She heard the sharp intake of his breath as she squeezed and pulled back. "Are you hurt?"

"No." He smiled. "Hug me again."

But the other women claimed his attention and Tabby contented herself with waiting. She could afford to be generous, she decided. Just so long as none of those grandmothers decided he was *available.*

Marc usually didn't mind talking to the women after class, but tonight he felt a little frustrated. While he listened and answered questions, his gaze kept darting over the silver heads to pick his strawberry out of the patch.

"Good night," he called, finally able to wave the women out the door. He turned to her. "Ready? I thought we could grab a bite at the Navy Exchange."

"Not a date, huh?"

"Nope," he denied. Not a date.

They walked the short distance, settling opposite each other in a booth with their fast-food order.

"Where do you put all those calories?" he asked, watching her bite into a double cheeseburger.

"Where do you think? I'm sitting on them."

"I'll have to check that out." He bit into his own burger, then laughed when they both pulled off their onions. He was more comfortable with her than anyone he knew, including Brad and Carol. "I'm glad you came tonight."

"You surprised me, that's for sure. A real multifaceted man of mystery. How long have you been teaching self-defense to women?"

"Going on three years. It's been a regular part of most Monday nights for me." He put down his burger. "It's more personal than you may think." He met her gaze across the table. Taking a deep breath, he plunged in. "My biological father is a serial rapist serving a life sentence. My mother was one of his victims."

He could see her struggling for the right words. "I didn't—"

"You don't have to say anything. I'm only telling you because I want you to listen. A female SEAL would be vulnerable in ways a man isn't. Even strong and capable ones, like yourself. And a team is only as strong as its weakest player.

"It's not about what you can or can't do. You've impressed the hell out of me since you've been at SPECWAR. I like you, Tabitha Chapel. I wouldn't want to see you get hurt. Or put your squad in jeopardy."

She pondered the honesty of his words, then put

her burger down, too. "I know I'd have to deal with that if it happened, but I don't think I should make my choices based on the fact that it might. Any woman on the street or in her own home could be a victim—"

"I just wanted you to know the reason I've been fighting you on this, and why I'm going to keep fighting." He paused to look out the window. "And maybe someday when you realize the lengths I'll go to keep women out of SEAL Training, you'll be able to understand, if not forgive me." He was asking for her forgiveness now, only she didn't realize it.

He'd sent his study to Washington today.

"And what if I win?" She picked up her drink. "What if women are allowed into the SEAL program?"

His beeper went off, and he paused to check the message before answering her. "I don't honestly know if I can handle that. At the very least there are consequences for every action..." The unfinished thought hung in the air between them.

She didn't know it, but he was saying goodbye.

CHAPTER TEN

TABBY MOVED AROUND the small storage closet that had become her office, packing up the last of her personal belongings. She shoved the chair under the desk and took one last look around.

If she came back...when she came back, she corrected, it wouldn't be to sit behind a desk. It would be as a trainee.

The morning after Miller left she'd found an envelope with Tiger scrawled boldly across the front. She'd torn into it eagerly, only to find her missing room key.

It reminded her of *that* day and his promise to spring for a room at the Hotel del Coronado.

A promise meant to be broken.

A promise that should have never been made.

But she'd kept her end of the bargain. Today she'd completed a one-mile swim in under an hour, following a fourteen-mile run. She was in the best physical shape of her life, and that was after a mere four weeks with the SEALs. More importantly, she had collected all the information she needed.

Tabby closed her briefcase on the seventy-two page feasibility study that would make it possible for her, and other women like her to come through the door as trainees.

But today she was leaving. With no sign of Miller anywhere. And there was nothing she could do about it. The orders had been cut the day he'd agreed to the study.

"Hi." Carol popped into her office. "Did you get the word yet? They're back!"

Tabby's heart leapt. "When?"

"The helo just landed. I ran into the wife of an airman at the Navy Exchange. You know, word travels fast through the Navy Wife grapevine. I made one call to another wife and I bet most of the wives will be here before the men finish debriefing." She plunked down her shopping bags on the desk.

"How long does the debriefing usually last?" Tabby asked, trying to recall from her father's SEAL days. Was this what her mother had gone through?

The waiting. The worrying. The wondering. The anticipation taking over her insides.

Marc was home. Safe and sound.

"Forty minutes to forever. And sometimes they shower first. Or at least you hope they do," Carol said, unintentionally bursting Tabby's bubble.

She checked her watch. Her cab would be here in thirty minutes to take her to the airport. And she was cutting it close as it was.

Carol sat down in the desk chair, spinning around like an excited child. Then she showed off the maternity clothes she'd just bought while chattering brightly and inanely for the next few minutes.

"This one's pretty," Tabby commented, holding a floral print dress against herself. "You know they actually make maternity uniforms." *Not that she'd look good in one.*

Carol's smile faded. "Marc never told you?"

"What?" Tabby met the other woman's gaze.

"I can't believe he's never told you," she said then cursed softly under her breath. "Marc can't have children. He had a vasectomy."

Tabby's chest constricted. Why? But she knew the answer. *Conceived in rape.* Mechanically, she folded the dress and placed it back in the box, along with the secret dream she'd been harboring. The dream of having it all. Which, as evidenced by her own mother, was a dream few women achieved. "Is that the reason you and Marc—"

"It's just one of them, Tabby. We were never meant to be."

Obviously his paternity weighed heavily on his mind. But hadn't Warren Miller set a better example for him? Marc hadn't really said much about the man except he *wasn't* his father. And what about his mother? Hadn't she tried to help him overcome the guilt he no doubt felt?

She would probably never know. With a sigh, Tabby looked at her watch. It was checkout time.

She hugged Carol, wished her well with her pregnancy and promised to e-mail often. Then walked down the hall to Miller's office.

"Preach." Tabby leaned over the yeoman's desk. "I need my service record and travel orders. And could you give this diskette to the CO when he gets back?'' It was a copy of her study.

Perry nodded toward the Commander's door.

Tabby turned.

''If you want you can give it to him yourself,'' Marc said, from the doorway to his office.

Pure joy filled her heart.

He held out his hand, and she gave him the diskette, then realized he was waiting to receive her service record from Perry.

''Checking out today, Lieutenant?''

It seemed to her he avoided direct eye contact.

''Yes,'' she managed as joy faded to confusion. He knew she was. He'd cut the orders.

Why wouldn't he look at her?

He opened her file. ''Everything's in order,'' he said, before handing it to her.

She saw a flicker of something elusive cross his face.

''I marked your Fitness Report as *unobserved.* It's appropriate for assignments under six months.''

What? No words about her performance? She'd been here four weeks. Certainly he'd *observed* her in one way or another. He was only here for three of them, she reminded herself. But what had happened during the last week to change him?

Surely he realized he wasn't her Commanding Officer now that her service record was back in her possession.

He turned the disk she'd given him over and over. ''Was there anything else, Lieutenant?''

She blinked in the face of his dismissal. There was a whole lot of *anything* else.

Starting with, she'd missed him. Had he missed her? Or how about her passing the swim and run? Was he going to spring for dinner and a room at the Hotel del Coronado the way he'd promised?

Oh, and by the way, the little snip you failed to mention, doesn't matter. Because I still want you.

I love you.

But then, we don't really have a future together, do we? So none of this matters. And all of it remained unsaid.

"Lieutenant," he prompted.

"No, sir. Nothing else." He stared at her for so long she thought she would break down right in front of him. But she was saving that for the privacy of a bathroom stall at the airport. She turned to leave.

"Goodbye, Lieutenant Tabitha Lilith Chapel-Prince." Marc cleared his throat.

There was no use thinking about what might have been. He was doing the right thing. He tapped the disk against the flat of his palm. His report had gone out Monday.

She wouldn't be looking at him like that when she got hold of it.

"Do you have a ride?" he asked.

She swung back around.

Hope lit her eyes, and he saw he'd made a mistake. "Because I can have Preach call the duty driver," he finished.

He watched the hope fade, then die in her eyes.

"I have a cab waiting." She marched off.

For the last time, he listened to the sound of high

heels in the passageway as strawberries, long legs and green cat eyes walked out of his life.

He deserved it. And more.

"Can you proof this for typos, Commander?" Perry asked, interrupting his thoughts.

"Yeah," he managed to rasp out, picking up a pencil from the petty officer's desk. He leaned over and scanned the page for errors. The ink blurred before his eyes.

Master Chief Murphy walked in and went over to the coffee mess to pour himself a cup. "How 'bout that gal," he said, "She ran fourteen miles this morning then followed it with a mile swim in 58:09."

The pencil in Marc's hand stilled. The pressure at the tip became so intense the lead point snapped. Crumbling the paper, he tossed it across the room.

2020 Friday
COMMANDER MILLER'S OFF-BASE RESIDENCE, Coronado, CA

NO ANSWER. Tabby knocked again, already resigned to the fact that Marc wasn't home. She watched the cab disappear around the corner.

She'd made it all the way to the United ticket counter at the San Diego airport before turning around. Her luggage was on its way to Washington, D.C.

But she wasn't just going to pretend the past four weeks hadn't happened. He could listen to what she had to say. He owed her that much at least.

Picking up her backpack, she walked to the back of the house where she dropped it to the patio deck. Removing her hat, she tossed it to the nearest deck chair and fluffed out her hair.

Then prepared to wait.

Leaning against the rail, she stared at the ocean.

As the fiery sun dipped low into the water, then disappeared in a red blaze of glory, she realized how foolish she'd been. There was no telling where he was, or when he'd return. What if he was gone all night?

Amethyst and sapphire streaked a ruby sky, then faded to cobalt blue. "Red sky at night, sailor's delight…" Tabby watched the last hint of color vanish along with her hope.

The wind picked up around 2200 hours and gooseflesh appeared on her skin. Rubbing her arms, she looked longingly toward the door. She knew his security code, but she didn't feel right entering the house without his permission.

Better to meet him on neutral ground.

But not too neutral, she hoped.

"What am I doing here, anyway?" She sank to the top step and rested her head against the post. If she left now, he'd never know. But then she'd never know why he'd been so cold this afternoon.

Maybe it was better that she just let it go.

She rose to her feet and reached for her backpack. Then froze.

A man emerged from the breakers, water sluicing from his body. She would have recognized the breadth of his shoulders anywhere. She stood in the shadows, where he couldn't see her, and watched him as he moved up the beach.

Toward her. Toward home.

His head hung with the effort of his ocean swim and he stared at his feet as he trudged along. After unzipping his knee-length wetsuit, he slicked back his hair. Then he spotted her.

She wanted to run to him, or from him, but she couldn't make her feet move in either direction. Instead, she gripped the rail.

"What are you doing here?"

She could hear the coldness of his tone.

"I came to tell you to go to hell." Pride kept her from admitting anything else.

Closing his eyes, he raked a hand through his hair, making the short dark tufts stand on end. "What am I going to do with you?" His voice cracked, sounding his surrender.

"Whatever you want. You're not my Commanding Officer anymore!"

He was at the foot of the stairs now, scowling up at her. "Don't you think I know that?" he snapped. "We still have the training issue between us. I tried to explain to you—"

It was too much for Tabitha. Running down the redwood planks, she pushed past him.

He grabbed her arm. "You didn't come here just to tell me to go to hell." Icy fingers held her with gentle pressure.

"This is where you're supposed to say, *Tabitha, wait. Don't go*. If you can't say it, let me go!" She jerked free.

"Tabitha, wait!"

She stopped, afraid to move. His arm wrapped around her from behind. It tightened, pulling her closer in a wet embrace. The dampness from his wetsuit seeped through her uniform, but the circle of his arms kept her safe and warm.

"Don't go," Marc murmured in her ear. It didn't cost him anything to say it, but that didn't mean a relationship with her wouldn't.

They still had so much standing between them. Her study, his counter-study, her father, his background. But one obstacle was gone.

He wasn't her Commanding Officer anymore.

He nestled his nose against her hair and inhaled. She sagged against him. Then turning her in his arms, he brushed away her hair and kissed the bridge of her nose.

He dropped his forehead to hers. "Tell me you won't regret this. If I make love to you, how am I supposed to let you go?"

"Don't," she said simply, touching his lips with the pad of her thumb. "Don't ever let me go." Then her lips traced the path of her thumb in light persuasion.

He didn't need persuading, but he gave her a final out. "Tabitha, you have to get back in D.C...."

"I know," she admitted in a husky whisper. "But I can catch a flight Sunday. I'm not going to regret this, Marc. There's nothing between us right now. And if a time comes when there is, I'd rather have this weekend with you than nothing."

Damn! This beautiful woman wanted him. *Him!* He should be falling down on his knees in gratitude. Not trying to send her away. He rained kisses along her face and neck, showing her just how much he wanted her.

He'd settle for a weekend. A day. An hour. If that's what she wanted. He wanted her. He'd given her the chance to be free of him. On Monday when she was back in D.C. and finding out what he'd done, he'd have this memory. That would have to be enough.

"Where were you?" she asked, clinging to him.

Her warmth seeped through to his cold bones. "I swam to Point Loma and watched the lights come on across the bay." It was miles. And dangerous. But what he'd been trained to do.

"The Hotel del?"

The pain of physical exertion and taxed lungs was nothing compared to staring at, and thinking about, what might have been. "I don't have reservations," he said sheepishly.

"It doesn't matter. How do we get from kisses to the bedroom?"

"Just take the stairs."

"I don't think my legs will carry me."

He swept her into his arms. "No problem. I do stairs." He headed up the steps. "Where's your luggage?"

"On its way to Dulles. I don't even have a toothbrush." She punched in his security code.

"I know where you left one."

Navigating the house in the dark, Marc took the stairs two at a time. They were still liplocked when he pushed through the bedroom door.

Tabby felt the awkwardness of the moment when he set her gently on her feet. They were in his bedroom. They were about to make love. How many times had she imagined it? But she'd never really believed they'd get this far.

"Music?" he asked, tuning the clock radio until he found a love song. "Wait for me. I have to rinse off the salt." He left her standing in the middle of the room and disappeared into the bathroom.

She sank down onto the bed. Realizing where she sat, she stood up and looked anywhere except the mirrors.

She heard the shower. Should she join him? She kicked off her shoes and stripped off her panty hose. But before she could make a decision, he emerged wrapped in a towel. Her heart skipped about three beats, then started up again on the double.

Toting condoms in one hand, a lit votive candle with a light vanilla scent in the other, he placed both on the nightstand. "Lights, music, protection." He talked to himself. "Shower, deodorant. What am I forgetting?"

He was being absolutely adorable.

"Me," Tabby said, softly.

"Never," he said, taking her hand. "I'm just nervous."

She took a deep breath. "Me too."

"Shave! I forgot to shave."

"I like it." She touched his beard-roughened jaw. Tentatively at first, then growing bolder.

Taking her hand, he kissed her palm. "I don't want to give you beard burn." He backed up toward the bathroom.

"Marc..." Tabby tugged on his hand, refusing to

give him up one more time. "Beard burn. Rug burn. I'll hold up. You're stalling."

She heard the sharp intake of breath before he let it out. "Yeah," he admitted. "I just want everything to be perfect." He stroked her hair. "I've waited all my life for you."

"Then why wait any longer?" she asked in a throaty whisper because her heart stuck there.

His mouth found hers again. Like champagne after the cork popped, all her emotions bubbled over into the kiss.

"Tabitha...I promised myself the next time would mean something. This does—"

She stole his next words with another kiss. "Are we through talking yet?"

"Yes, ma'am."

"Permission to touch."

CHAPTER ELEVEN

"PERMISSION GRANTED."

Tabby explored the heat of his skin. The breadth of his shoulders. The tautness of his muscles.

Nothing was off limits.

The towel became an obstacle. "You're out of uniform, Commander," she purred, getting rid of it with one tug. She examined the obvious evidence of his arousal. "But you pass muster."

"If the Uniform of the Day is naked, Lieutenant, you're overdressed."

Looking up, she saw that familiar control on his face. This was her chance to break it. Slowly she unzipped her skirt, then dropped it and kicked it aside. Excitement made her fingers clumsy. But she tortured him with deliberate slowness, taking her time over each button on her shirt. Looking at him though half-lidded eyes, she stopped on the last button.

"Don't even think *you* won't pass muster," he said in a husky voice. He brushed the shirt from her shoulders, trapping her arms and pulling her to him. "I can take it from here."

Large calloused hands guided the material down her arms, sending shivers through her. The shirt fell to the floor, leaving only her lacy white bra and panties.

At his indrawn breath, she felt the heady sense of power known to women since Eve in the garden of Eden.

He wanted her. He wanted her bad.

His hot hands traveled up her arms, over her shoulders, across her back. Fever spread wherever he touched, looked. Unhooking her bra, he coaxed the straps off her shoulders. The bit of lace joined the pile on the floor.

She arched into his touch, her budding nipples greedy for his attention. He cupped them fully, filling his hands and fulfilling her need to be touched. He lowered his mouth to suckle. But the time he spent on one was torture to the other.

He laid her back on his bed and removed her panties. Then he kissed her. Touched her. Everywhere.

She felt whole in his arms. Wanted. Loved. Safe. Secure.

She groaned when he initiated a more intimate kiss. Her knees became jelly. "No!" she cried out. Her mind screamed, *yes!* "No, please," she panted out the feeble protest. She needed him to cover her trembling body with his.

She needed him inside her.

Without conscious thought she pressed his head closer as her world rocked, then shook, then erupted in an explosion of pure pleasure.

Marc nipped the inside of her thigh, the curve of her hip, her flat stomach, her peaked nipple, then took her mouth in a deep probing kiss. His roaming hand wandered back to her warm wet center. He broke their kiss to look at her and his mouth curved into a self-assured smile. She was his for the taking.

"Why are you stopping?"

"Believe me, I'm not that chivalrous. I don't just want you. I need you." He needed to make her his in every sense of the word. He reached for a condom.

It wasn't really necessary. A pang of regret stabbed him. Then guilt. *Tell her.* "Tabitha..."

"Shh." She put her finger to his lips.

And he slipped inside her warm and welcoming body.

Later. He'd tell her later.

TABBY STRETCHED her hand across the bed to Marc's empty pillow and pulled the feathered comfort to her. She inhaled. It wasn't a dream.

She hadn't even been asleep that long.

But where was he?

Rising from the bed, she padded barefoot to the dresser, put on one of his T-shirts, then made her way through the dark house.

Everything was quiet. Too quiet. Her heartbeat quickened. Where was Marc? Why had he left her alone?

The French doors were open slightly and movement on the patio deck caught her attention.

Hugging her arms around herself, she joined him and stared out over the rail at the ocean beyond. She heard the lapping of the waves, felt the cooling breeze and sighed. "You're one of those deep thinkers, aren't you?"

She turned and he held out his hand. When she took it, he pulled her into his lap.

"Penny for them," she said.

"They're about you."

"I won't overstay my welcome," she reassured him past the lump forming in her throat, easing away a fraction. If he wasn't comfortable with what had happened, she could catch the next flight back to D.C.

Lacing his fingers through her hair he pulled her back against his chest. "What the hell are you talking about?" He spoke with his lips pressed against her temple.

"I don't know. I suppose I want you to kick me out of your bed because that's the only way I'm going to leave here." She let out a frustrated sigh. With his body her pillow, the stars overhead her blanket, she closed her eyes.

"Regrets?" he asked softly. "It's too late to turn back the clock."

"I want more time…" Her voice held a note of desperation.

"Would a lifetime be too long?"

Her eyes popped open in surprise.

"This weekend isn't going to last forever. And I think the only way I could survive a three-thousand-mile separation is if we were married." He paused. "There's always the chance the Navy would honor a transfer so you could be with your husband." His proposal was a strange mix of romance and crazy logic.

"I'm coming back as a SEAL trainee."

"But what if you're not? Or what if it takes longer than you think?"

"What if I am?"

"I don't know." His voice was low and serious, but his eyes sparkled with animation. "I just know that every morning I wake up at the same time, I eat the same breakfast, I go through the same routine. When I get dressed, I make sure all the hangers in my closet are two finger-widths apart. Tonight I woke up with you sleeping beside me and I like the change. Besides, the least you can do is make an honest man out of me."

"You're talking crazy."

"I'm feeling crazy."

"We barely know each other."

"I could spend a lifetime getting to know you."

For every objection he had an answer. Butterflies fluttered in her stomach. He was sweeping her off her feet. Isn't that what every girl wanted?

She wanted it all. And he was handing it to her. At least the parts that he could give her. The rest she had to fight for. But when she tried to imagine her life without him—she couldn't.

You love him. What else matters?

And it *was* love—right?—not lust that made her want him so bad.

"You want to…" She was afraid to say the words. Afraid they weren't real. Afraid she'd wake up. "…marry me?"

"I thought you'd never ask."

She kissed away his smug smile. "Make love to me again."

Marc shook his head. "Mexico's twenty minutes

away. Let's make a run for it. Once we're man and wife I promise you, I won't let you out of bed for the entire honeymoon.''

Not until he had to see her off at the airport.

He'd use every bit of pull he had to get her back to Coronado. There were plenty of support positions. She'd be mad as hell at him when she found out about his counter-study, but he wouldn't let her out of bed long enough to let her work up a really good head of steam. And he had a lifetime to make her fall in love with him.

He wasn't looking forward to breaking the news to her father. But nobody got along with their in-laws, right?

But there was another piece of unpleasant news. Now was the time to tell her there'd be no children. Knowing it had made a difference once with another woman, made the words that much harder to say. He didn't want to lose Tabitha, not when he was so close to winning her over, but he couldn't marry her without talking about this.

Differences like missing toothpaste caps and feasibility studies could be worked out. But to have or not to have children was a decision that both of them had to agree on.

''You should know, I don't want children. I can't have them, and adoption's not an option I want to pursue.'' He couldn't raise another man's child. He had firsthand experience with how impossible that was.

''And you should know, I already know.''

''How—''

''Carol let it slip today. She'd assumed you'd already told me. It doesn't matter. But you have to tell me why or we're not going anywhere.''

"The why should be obvious," but he continued anyway. She wanted the whole story and he'd give it to her. "I was nineteen going on twenty—too young to know any better, I suppose. At the end of SEAL Training I went home to ask Carol to marry me." He searched her eyes and liked the hint of jealousy he saw there. "I wanted to do it right. Ask her parents permission. The whole bit. Well, I got an earful. According to Carol's father I wasn't good enough for his little girl. I'd heard it all my life so it wasn't anything new. But usually it was whispered behind my back—"

Marc took a deep breath, remembering exactly how he'd felt. "I thought I'd left it all behind when I joined the Navy, but I'd only left. Instead of returning from liberty, I went UA—to see *him*. He was in San Quentin."

"You mean the man who fathered you?"

He nodded. "Rell, Ralph, no middle name." He could have recited the man's prison number if he'd wanted to. He'd memorized it and every detail concerning Rell. "It was the first time I'd ever seen him, but right away I noticed the similarities. Not just looks, but mannerisms. He was the last man in the world I wanted to be and seeing him was like seeing my future."

"I can't imagine you were *ever* like him."

"I thought I was. And the people back in Harmony thought I was. It's no wonder they hated me."

"What about Carol? She didn't—"

"After her father said no, we planned to elope. But by then your father had tracked me down."

"It sounds like something my father would do."

It wasn't typical for a CO, but the Toad lived by his own set of rules. "I still remember what he said once he caught up with me. 'There are no deserters on my watch. You got that, son?'" He'd yelled back, *I'm not your son! I'm not anybody's son!*

"Were you planning to desert?"

"I really wasn't thinking that far ahead." He chuckled to relieve some of the tension, or maybe because he was a little nervous about telling her the rest. "Anyway, your father hauled my butt back to Coronado. Then over to San Clemente Island. There's a camp there, complete with ramshackle huts and a bamboo prison. Instructors use it for the trainees during mission scenarios. You get caught, you get locked up.

"That's where he took me—just the two of us— said he didn't know if I was ready for a team. He tied me to a chair in a hut." Marc heard the sharp intake of her breath and felt her stiffen.

"Do you hate him?" she asked, her voice barely above a whisper.

"No. But I did then." And for a long time afterward. For a kid who'd been abused most of his life it was a pretty helpless feeling. But Prince never raised a hand to him. "I guess you'd call it deprogramming because for hours on end he reaffirmed everything I'd ever heard or believed about myself by repeating it and then showed me that I was making it a self-fulfilling prophecy."

Marc had seen a kinder, gentler side to the

Toad—one he hadn't revealed in twenty-five weeks of training. He'd become a father figure. Only he hadn't called Marc *son* when he'd given his departing advice. *Miller, you can't run away from yourself. So what are you going to do about it? Sit here? Or get on with the rest of your life?*

"He untied me and left. I went to Captain's Mast for the UA, but got my act together and the team assignment I'd earned," Marc said. "I accepted my paternity, but decided not to pass along my heritage. At the first opportunity I had a vasectomy courtesy of Uncle Sam. And when I went home on leave to see Carol she rejected me—or rather a childless marriage, which is pretty much the same thing."

Marc searched Tabitha's eyes. "I know what I'm asking—"

"Shh." She put her finger to his lips. "We have each other. That's enough."

As they went back inside, Marc silently vowed to make her so happy she'd never regret marrying him.

But he wasn't sure he could keep that promise.

1800 Sunday
HOTEL DEL MAR,
Tijuana, Mexico

ROLLING FROM HER stomach to her back, Tabby stretched her naked body with the languid movements of a contented cat. It wasn't the Hotel del Coronado. But they were husband and wife.

Marc got up from his side of the bed. "Look what you've done to me, woman."

Propping herself on her elbow, she did just that.

He had to-die-for legs and broad shoulders tapering to trim hips. The firm muscles of his butt bunched and beckoned as he hobbled away.

"Poor baby," she sympathized. "Used and abused."

She'd let him make it to the bathroom this time.

Plucking the last strawberry from the bowl of fruit, she bit into it with a sly smile. He'd been very creative with them earlier.

The rest of their breakfast tray lay forgotten on the table next to the window. Sheer curtains billowed inward on a sea breeze. The sun had made the air hot and heavy, stealing any cooling effect.

Tabby dropped the hull back into the bowl and settled against her pillow then brought her hand up to admire the gold band on the ring finger of her left hand.

"Mrs. Marc Miller." Fingering the unfamiliar weight of the ring, she was unable to regret their rush into marriage.

She heard the shower and climbed out of bed. Surprised by the weakness in her own legs, she padded to the bathroom. They'd married Saturday morning, and from that moment on they'd spent their time in bed, making love as husband and wife.

Sunday had come all too soon. Tabby tried not to think about leaving. Instead, she focused on returning.

"Trying to sneak up on me?"

She pushed aside the shower curtain and stepped into the tub behind him. "Just coming to do my wifely duty and soap your back."

He glanced over his shoulder. "I can't be fooled into thinking I married a dutiful bride."

She took the soap from him and worked it into a lather. Massaging him, she pressed her body close to his, kissing him between his shoulder blades as the water poured down on their heads. "We have a few minutes...."

"I couldn't if I tried."

"Liar."

Marc turned to meet the lips tracing his shoulder. Drawing his wife into his arms, he kissed her. He couldn't get enough of her not to feel the loss of her leaving.

Damn duty. The Navy. And the whole friggin' world.

"What about your flight? You're going to be late."

"I can catch the red-eye back to D.C." He stole her breath and she moaned. "As long as...I—I'm there by morning." Panting, she clung to him.

Oh, God, he didn't want to let go.

HAND IN HAND they raced through the airport terminal, pausing only once to check the overhead monitors for flight information. Tabby stretched her legs to keep up with Marc.

"We didn't leave you enough time," he said, looking at his watch. "I'll call Gromley's secretary when I get to the office. Maybe she can buy you some. If your layover's delayed—"

"I'll make it." She couldn't feel sorry considering the way they'd spent it.

"Do you have your ticket?"

"Yes," Tabby reassured him for at least the third time since she'd traded in her military travel voucher.

"And the marriage license?"

"Yes."

"Just as soon as you check in with Personnel get the yeoman to make a Page Two entry in your service record."

"I know how to change my marital status, Marc." Page Two recorded all personal information. It wasn't necessarily the second page or even a single page entry.

She squeezed his hand, acknowledging his concern. Their haste and the fact that she was leaving made her short-tempered. Him too. He brushed her forehead with his lips and didn't watch where he was going. Dodging a passenger at the end of a long ticket line, Marc pulled her out of the way, bumping the man's suitcase and knocking it over in the process. The gentleman glared at them.

Marc shrugged. Tabby burst into giggles.

"Sorry," they said in unison and kept going.

"I'll call your detailer this afternoon and try and get you back to Coronado, ASAP. San Diego, or anywhere in southern California would be close enough," he added. "There's got to be an admin job for you somewhere."

Tabby stopped, tugging on his hand to halt his progress. "I'm not coming back to fill some administration slot. I'm coming back as a SEAL trainee. Remember?"

"Don't be ridiculous."

"Ridiculous? What do you think I've been doing

for the last four weeks? Rear Admiral Gromley arranged a meeting with the congressional committee for next Monday. If they approve—''

''Reality check,'' he said tersely. ''Nobody in D.C. is going to take that feasibility study seriously, Tabitha.''

Mouth gaping, she stared at him. ''And why not?''

Because he didn't?

He dropped his gaze. ''Come on. We can't stop now, we'll miss your flight.'' He reached for her hand.

She pulled it from his grasp. Something about the way he wasn't meeting her eyes put her on red alert. ''Why not, Marc?''

''Because the SEALs, all the way up to *your* Admiral Dann are endorsing another study.''

''What other study? Who…'' A sudden chill crept along her spine. ''How could you?'' She started walking.

''Tabitha,'' he said sharply, catching up to her. ''How could I not?''

He'd told her up front he would do everything in his power to keep women out of SEAL Training. She just hadn't realized that meant betraying her trust.

''Leave me alone!'' She started running, trying to escape what she already knew. He'd done this and then he'd married her.

''Tabitha—''

"Don't touch me!" she screeched, pushing him away. She threw her backpack to the conveyer belt and dashed through the security checkpoint, picking it up on the other side.

Marc followed under the arch, setting the alarm off.

"Sir—"

"Tabitha!" he called as she disappeared down the corridor.

He emptied his pockets with very little patience and jumped through, setting the buzzers off for a second time.

"Step over to the side please, sir."

Marc sized up the burly female rent-a-cop. Two men with handheld metal detectors joined her. He did the unthinkable and gave up his side arm and *all* his concealed weapons, seeing it as the most expeditious way through the mess. Each revelation widened the eyes of the onlookers. Shit! Why hadn't he disarmed before getting here?

"Sir, you'll have to come with us." The tallest of the two men drew his gun.

"He was chasing a woman," the female security officer said.

"That woman is my *wife!*" He could see he was getting nowhere fast so he tried a different approach. "Look, Ms.—Gordon. We just got married and my wife's a little pissed right now. We're having our first fight. I don't want her leaving until I've had the chance to straighten out a few things."

"Honey, I don't give a rip. You come in here armed like Rambo, you go with Mike and Ike."

0909 Monday
PENTAGON—NAVY ANNEX,
Washington, D.C.

"YOU'RE LATE."

"I know. I know." Tabby strode past the desk of Rear Admiral Gromley's secretary, Irene.

"She's been asking for you. And a Commander Miller called. Several times." Irene looked at her over the top of horn-rimmed glasses. "I told the Admiral you were in central files. And the Commander you'd call back."

"Thanks, Irene." Taking a deep breath, Tabby knocked on the Admiral's door.

"You're late." The Admiral's gravelly voice greeted her. A thin, unlit cigar was clenched between Gromley's stained teeth.

"Sorry."

Rear Admiral Gromley's brows drew to a thin gray line. "Never apologize. Women do too much of that already. The report," she said, holding out her hand.

Tabby produced a copy of the study from her briefcase. The Admiral nodded as Tabby sat in a chair opposite the desk.

"Damn smoke-free buildings," The Admiral said, lighting up and moving to an open window. "You know, don't you, that sonofabitch Dann conducted his own study. Giving it his *SEAL* of approval. And he had the nerve to put it in the hands of the congressional committee last week."

Tabby stiffened in her seat. She knew all right.

"I want a copy of that study," the Admiral continued, looking pointedly at Tabby. "I've asked, of course. But he won't give it to me."

"I'll see what I can do."

CHAPTER TWELVE

0700 Friday
PENTAGON—NAVY ANNEX,
Washington, D.C.

"THESE ARE FOR YOU," Irene said, handing over a stack of phone messages.

Tabby checked the pink slips marked urgent and deep-sixed the ones from Marc.

"When are you going to put that poor man out of his misery—"

Tabby stopped the secretary with a look and headed over to her own desk. Irene was at her judgmental best today.

"It's none of my business," the woman said, holding up her hands in surrender.

Tabby knew she deserved that kick in the butt from Irene. Marc was trying. She was the one letting the resentment build like the pile of unanswered phone messages.

But why hadn't he told her about his study on their honeymoon? Before they were married? When he mailed it? Wrote it? Compiled it? He'd had four weeks!

And every day of those four weeks he'd told her she wasn't SEAL material. Why had she assumed he'd changed his mind? Because she'd wanted him to. Wanted him to believe in her. The way she believed in him.

She'd have to talk to him sometime. But not until after the congressional committee met on Monday.

The phone rang. Irene answered. ''She's standing right here.'' Irene held out the phone instead of transferring the call to Tabby's line.

Her throat closed. It could have been anyone, but she didn't need to guess to know who it was! She shook her head vigorously. Irene continued to hold out the phone. Tabby rose to her feet and went over to Irene's desk. ''I don't want to talk to him,'' she mouthed the words.

The woman put the receiver in her hand and left the room. Tabby's heart beat a frantic rhythm, urging her to escape.

Coward.

Her hand curled around the instrument. Taking a deep breath, she put the phone to her ear. ''Commander. What can I do for you, sir?'' She kept it formal. She needed more distance than the miles provided. Silence. She heard his breathing. Or was that her own?

''So that's the way it's going to be. Damn it, Tabitha, talk to me,'' he ground out. ''I've been worried sick about you. About us.''

''Really?'' She tried to keep her tone light. Inside, she felt like crying.

''Don't get flippant. I'd like nothing better than to turn you over my knee.'' She heard him sigh. ''Look, I know I've hurt you. And I fully intend to make it up to you, but why haven't you returned any of my calls?''

"Have you read my report?" She measured her words carefully, afraid to say anything that would reveal what she was feeling. "I haven't read yours."

"Tabby, I understand if you can't talk..." He didn't sound very understanding, impatience underlined every word.

"I'm glad you think so."

"I didn't call to fight. And I don't want to continue this discussion over the phone. I called to tell you I can fly out for the weekend."

Was it her imagination, or did he sound hopeful? She twisted the cord around her finger, searching for the strength to stay distant. "I'll be reading your report this weekend. That is if you want to download the file to me."

"If I'm there, we can go over it together," Marc offered. "That way if you have any questions, I'd be available to answer them. And I can stay over on Monday for moral support."

Moral support! "That's kind of you to offer. I'll call if I have any questions." She thought about hanging up the phone in the drawn-out pause that followed.

"There was a time when a weekend wasn't enough."

No fair, her heart cried foul, wishing she'd ended the call when she'd had the chance. "I have to go," she lied, biting her lower lip to keep it from trembling.

"After this weekend I'll be caught up in a training cycle for weeks."

"Goodbye, Commander." Was that really her own cold voice? She bit down harder on her lip.

"I'll kiss it and make it better. I promise."

He was grasping.

Her throat tightened around a lump so big it threatened to choke her. That was exactly what she was afraid of. She could easily lose herself and her dreams in loving this man. Why hadn't she just kept that in mind to begin with?

"Goodbye," she repeated.

"Tabitha, don't hang—"

She did. Before *he* changed *her* mind. She was strong but not that strong.

0800 Friday
NAVAL SPECIAL WARFARE CENTER,
Coronado, CA

MARC EXCUSED THE MEN from morning muster. Nobody moved. "What?" he demanded, scowling at them.

Hugh looked at the men on either side of him. "Nobody's going to say it, so I will. Shit, Marc, you showed up on Monday wearing a gold band on your ring finger and never said a word. We'd like to know what's going on! As far as I know, no one here got an invitation to the wedding."

The resentment took him by surprise. Did they feel left out? Or at least put out? It was, after all, his personal life, but he supposed an announcement was in order.

"Lieutenant Chapel and I were married last weekend in Tijuana." A fairy-tale beginning that ended too soon. It didn't help that his bride was thousands of miles away and wasn't speaking to him.

Except for their very cryptic phone call very early this morning. At least he'd finally gotten through to her.

A collective gasp was followed by a chorus of best wishes and hearty pats on the back. His mood lifted for the first time in days.

"And why is nobody's business but my own."

That earned him a few ribald comments.

"How 'bout we throw you a bachelor party tonight at Manny's," Hugh suggested.

"I'm not exactly a bachelor anymore."

"Some of us are," Perry said. "And with the Lieutenant back East, that makes you a West Coast Widower, Commander."

God, he missed her. Marc didn't commit to the party. There was somewhere else he'd rather be. But it was decided that a party would be held in his honor with or without him.

Master Chief Murphy was the last one out. "You know, kid, usually you look before you leap."

It was true. His life had become so controlled, he rarely went with his gut now. And maybe that was how he knew he'd done the right thing.

Alone at last, Marc reached for the telephone as he had several times each day to check out flights to D.C., but he stopped himself from picking it up. Tabitha had made it clear she didn't want him there for the weekend. If ever.

He'd tried. Now it was up to her.

Had she forgotten so easily what it was like when they were together? They didn't even have to be making love. All they had to do was be in the same room and it was like a spark on gasoline.

Picking up the phone, he called for military hop information and found a supply plane leaving for Andrews within the hour. It was the last one headed that way for the day. Grabbing his cover from the rack on the way out the door, he bumped into Hugh.

"Marc, we have to go over these training schedules for next week."

He'd almost forgotten about the training schedules, even the trainees filtering in next week. Duty called. His marriage would have to wait.

0130 Saturday
MANNY'S DIVE,
Coronado, CA

MARC WAS half a dozen shots of tequila—and just as many beers—into a bender. His bachelor party was an excuse to drink himself under the table. And just as soon as it happened, he'd go home to that big empty bed and pass out.

Brad had already left. Along with most of the other married men, and some single guys who wouldn't be lonely tonight. Only the hard drinkers remained.

Maybe it was time he left. Marc staggered to his feet, bumped the table and made it about two steps.

"I got ya," Connie said, sliding into the crook of his arm and supporting most of his weight.

He leaned into her soft inviting curves and did his best to hold himself up. "I got ya," he repeated, the words finding their way through the fog in his brain.

But for the life of him, he didn't know what he was supposed to do with her. "I need my car keys."

Murphy stepped to Marc's other side. "I'll get 'em from Manny, kid, and drive you home."

"I've already got 'em," Connie said, dangling the keys. "I'll drive Marc home."

0520 Saturday
LIEUTENANT CHAPEL'S RESIDENCE,
Washington, D.C.

SHUTTING OFF THE bathroom light, Tabby grabbed her robe from the back of the door and put it on over her T-shirt and shorts. She'd been up all night reading Marc's report.

Damn the man! Why hadn't he told her?

There wasn't one thing in those hundred-plus pages that should keep her, or any other woman out of the SEAL training program. All he'd been was thorough and factual.

And he'd drawn conclusions from his own perspective.

She couldn't fault him for that.

Or was she letting him off the hook too easily?

She shuffled in sock-covered feet to the kitchen, opened the freezer, grabbed the unhealthiest breakfast she could find—a carton of ice cream—and dug in.

Leaning against the breakfast counter, she stared at the phone. A whole carton wouldn't fill the emptiness inside. She picked up the phone. One ring...six, seven...twenty-three. Where was he?

0800 Saturday
COMMANDER MILLER'S OFF-BASE RESIDENCE,
Coronado, CA

MARC AWOKE to the sound of rapid-fire drills exploding inside his head. Shutting his eyes tight against the morning light, he rolled over and buried his head beneath the pillow when he realized it was just the shower.

Just the shower! Naked, he clawed his way to the edge of the bed and swung his legs over the side, covering himself with the pillow.

No! Oh, God, no! Last night came back in slow degrees. Hanging his head, he covered his eyes with the heels of his palms. *"Connie!"*

If he was the point man and his marriage a minefield, he'd just stepped on a doozie. Nothing like blowing off your own damn foot. He didn't stand a chance in hell of salvaging his relationship with Tabitha now.

Nausea roiled through his stomach.

"What are you bellyachin' about, kid?" Murphy lumbered from the head with a towel wrapped around his waist and a cigar in his mouth. "That didn't sound like sweet talk to me. And if you're looking for another drink, the barmaid isn't here."

"Thank God," Marc breathed.

"Got ya!"

The room exploded with SEAL instructors. They came from the closets. The hall. The bathroom. The balcony. "Hoo-yah!" They sounded the victory cry. Someone snapped a Polaroid and handed it to him.

Marc groaned. He looked as bad as he felt. And he felt like shit.

Kyle put a wrapped present on his pillow-covered lap. Marc noted the birthday paper and tore off the lid. He supposed an initiation was like a birthday.

The box contained several well read copies of *Playboy*. A squeezed tube of K-Y Jelly with the lid missing. And a plastic ball and chain that looked like part of a Halloween costume.

Murphy ushered everyone out the bedroom door. "Hurry down, honey," he said, blowing Marc a kiss. "I make a mean western omelet."

When the men finally left, Marc collapsed against the mattress.

"You're welcome," Murphy said, peeking around the door. "SEALs look after their own and don't you forget it." The Master Chief flicked the ash end of the cigar at him. "I know you're lonely, kid. But I ruined three good marriages with that kind of lonely."

1630 Wednesday
PENTAGON—NAVY ANNEX,
Washington, D.C.

TABBY PACED RESTLESSLY outside the boardroom where for the past three days the congressional committee had convened to discuss the feasibility of female Navy SEALs.

With two reports in their hands.

The members of Congress had asked her some pointed questions two hours ago and then excused her from the room. Otherwise she'd been in there all three days.

She could only hope they'd make a decision, instead of tabling it for another day that might never come. If the decision was in her favor, how long would it be before she and other women could start training? Months? Years? She'd be the first in line. That is if the small problem of her birthday didn't come back to haunt her. But right now her age was the least of her worries.

The Chief of SEALs strode out the double wide doors. He didn't look happy. *Yes!* Or no? He gave her a half smile.

"And?" she prompted.

"Congress has ruled both reports inconclusive."

Her chest constricted. If they found her report lacking, that meant she hadn't done her job. And that meant she'd probably blown her last chance. She'd never got this far before.

Uncle Mitch looked her in the eye. "They want another study. And you're it. Pack your bags. You're going through SEAL Training. The official SEAL statement will be, we have no objections to a test program supporting the study." He shook his head. "What am I going to tell your father?"

"Let me tell him."

He checked his watch. "Better make it fast, I have a press conference in ten minutes. Do you want to come along? Or do you want to stay out of the limelight?"

"I'll pass thanks. What are you going to tell Commander Miller?"

Her heart stopped as she said the words.

What would *she*? What would happen right now if she told her godfather she was married to the man who was about to become her Commanding Officer for the second time?

Would they pull her from the study?

"Miller doesn't have a choice. But I imagine he isn't going to like it." The Admiral softened his smile to fatherly. "From here on out, you're on your own. And it isn't going to be easy."

"I never asked for easy."

0900 Thursday
NAVAL SPECIAL WARFARE CENTER,
Coronado, CA

"MARC!" HUGH CALLED, meeting him at the bottom step of the stairs leading to HQ and handing him the roster of trainees. "You're not going to believe this—"

Marc heard the warning in the Training Officer's voice. "Is she here?" He tacked his copy of the roster to the clipboard in his hand and turned to the *M*'s, scanning the page. No Miller.

"Did you know?"

It had been all over the news and the Chief of SEALs had called yesterday. She was coming in under congressional order and with Admiral Dann's blessing.

But that's not what Hugh meant.

"I didn't know it would get this far." He thought he'd have to spend his time consoling his wife about not being allowed to train with the Navy SEALs.

He waved in the instructors standing around on the blacktop grinder and they formed a loose huddle.

"How do you want to handle this?" Hugh asked.

All the instructors looked to Marc for guidance. "With kid gloves," he answered carefully. He went around the circle, looking each man in the eye. "It's our job to harass trainees, so we harass. That doesn't mean sexual harassment. If you don't know the difference, here's my definition—you don't do anything to my *wife* that you wouldn't do to your own *sister*. Other than that, I want her out of here *yesterday*."

Marc strode toward the formation of inductees, his men following. "Sunglasses," he hissed, putting his on. Instant intimidation. "Scowl." Instant anger. "Just add water..."

"Instant asshole," Hugh finished the little ritual.

"Come on, let's go meet the *boys*." He slapped Hugh on the back, then picked up his own pace to hurry them along.

The familiar sight of shaved heads lining the grinder in uneven rows met them. Marc moved to the front of the formation and tried to keep his gaze from drifting to the one trainee he knew intimately.

"Attention! Dress right, dress!" Hugh put the sailors in order.

"Armstrong!" Marc bellowed.

"Here, sir."

Marc pointed left and front. Keeping trainees in alphabetical order and giving them a number made things easier. "You're billet number one. Becker...Beeman..." he continued, repeating the process with each trainee. "Cha—" He choked on the name. His head snapped up.

She stood at the back of the crowd. Her beautiful hair gone. *It'll grow back.* It was a completely irrational thought. He should be wondering what the hell she thought she was doing. Not what in the hell happened to her hair. Or why in the hell she wasn't using his name.

"Chapel," he called her forward. She took her place beside Beeman. "Number four." He showed no outward emotion. It wouldn't do to let the other inductees see he wasn't in control. "For now."

Nervous laughter echoed around her after his comment. Marc read through the rest of the roster and launched into his welcome speech.

"I am *the Marquis!* Your royal pain in the butt for the next twenty-five weeks. Most of you won't last long enough to repeat my name. The rest of you will learn to hate me. And my name will become a curse on your lips…"

He'd never realized it before, but he'd adopted a speech amazingly similar to the Toad's. *I am the Toad Prince, your royal…* After the warm reception, he turned the trainees over to Hugh, who in turn, would hand them over to the Master Chief for buddy assignments.

"Make sure she gets Montgomery. Gummy Bear." He'd been through twice and hadn't made it past Hell Week.

"Chapel, my office." Marc summoned over his shoulder, heading to HQ. He didn't wait to see if she followed. But knew she did. He took the front steps two at a time. Strode down the passageway and through reception. "Preach, the Lieutenant's service record." He held out his hand in passing.

Perry stood motionless, then he started searching through the growing piles of service records on and around his desk. He handed Marc the appropriate file just as he reached the door to his own office. Marc stopped and ushered Tabitha in ahead of him.

"When Hugh comes in, ask him to wait," he instructed Perry, closing the door.

To Tabby, he said, "I'm sure this is going to be a good one. You can start any time." Rounding his desk, he flipped open her folder, ripped out the copy of her orders and read them.

She stood just inside the door at attention.

He looked up. "What? Nothing to say? Then why don't we drop this Commander-Lieutenant shit. After all, we are husband and wife. We should have *something* to say to each other."

At her silence, he continued. "Let me see, last week you were running from me in an airport. Then there was a single phone conversation. And now you're back here for SEAL Training. It seems as if I missed a whole hell of a lot between the honeymoon and today!" His face couldn't be any redder than his vision right now.

"You know why I ran—"

"But I don't know why you wouldn't talk. I don't even know when our marriage ended. Is it over?"

"That's not fair. And you know it. You deliberately kept your study from me, knowing how much—if you didn't know how much it would hurt me, Marc, you had no business marrying me."

"You're right." He'd known. He just hadn't wanted to admit it. "But I'm right about this—you need to quit. Right now." *For us.*

"No."

"Our marriage can't survive this." If she lasted one day, she'd hate him by the end of it. This was a test program, but the Navy didn't normally allow one spouse to be in charge of the other's training.

"Who did you marry, Marc?"

He knew a trick question when he heard one. The woman he'd married was standing in front of him, bald and in his face. But he wisely kept his mouth shut.

"Look at me, Marc. This is who I am. This is who I've always been. Maybe you married an image of the woman you wanted me to be."

No! Tabitha Chapel was not a bald and angry Navy SEAL. Tough was a part of the package, he knew that. But she was more. She was soft. And she was his.

"I can't be your instructor and your husband!" He scanned the Page Two entries in her file. "You never recorded our marriage?" She'd taken the marriage license just for that purpose. Otherwise he would have done it.

She wasn't even wearing his ring! Or his last name, he reminded himself.

"I know. I'm sorry, Marc..." her voice faded.

I want to be your husband. His throat constricted around the admission. She'd chosen. "Consider us legally separated."

Slipping off her dog tags, she removed her wedding band from the chain and gave it to him. He took off his and fisted them both. "You'll get your chance to prove yourself. And I'll get my chance to break you. I should've just screwed you and been done with it."

"You did, remember?"

CHAPTER THIRTEEN

1100 Thursday
NAVAL SPECIAL WARFARE CENTER,
Coronado, CA

"OFF YOUR KNEES. And on your toes."

He tapped her knee with his booted toe. Tabby's gaze drifted up the length of him, taking in combat boots, bare legs, T-shirt, sunglasses and cap.

Her husband.

Wearing men's swim trunks and a plain white T-shirt, she adjusted her position. He wasn't her husband, she reminded herself. He was her SEAL instructor. She'd made her choice. And it hurt worse than the pebbles digging into her palms from the cement pool deck.

"Seven...eight," he counted her push-ups. "Six... seven..." He subtracted, and she lost count.

She just kept pushing her aching muscles, lifting her body. She pushed and pushed until her arms shook and she couldn't push anymore.

"One more!"

She gritted her teeth and forced her shaking arms to extend. Then collapsed where she lay. Hell Week for Tabitha Chapel started the day she walked in the door.

2100 Sunday
SEAL BARRACKS,
Coronado, CA

AN HOUR BEFORE TAPS and lights out, Tabby sat on
her rack quietly writing letters to her family, which
carefully explained her extended study without saying she was an actual trainee. There'd never been
time for that phone call to her father. Thank good-
ness her parents had been out of the country for an
extended vacation during that press conference. The
media had soon lost interest but it was picking up
again.

They'd set her apart from the men in a big empty
bay all her own. To everyone's chagrin, especially
Marc's, she'd made it five weeks.

An explosion of artillery fire rocked the building.
She pushed aside paper and pen. Scrambling from
the room, she met up with Gummy outside. The
piercing sound of sirens filled the air. Confusion
reigned as trainees ran toward the blacktop grinder.

The Commander's voice, distorted by a bullhorn,
shouted, "Move it! Move it! Move it!"

Hell Week had begun.

Trainees arriving without swim buddies were reprimanded and sent back, learning the hard way
SEALs never left a man behind. Trainees arriving
in full fatigues were told to take off their shirts and
caps and deposit them back at the barracks.

The uniform of the day was boots, pants and
T-shirts. Those in proper dress were shoved to the
ground on their bellies in the mock battle zone.

A hand gripped Tabby's shoulder and pushed.

She fell forward on the blacktop, skinning the heels of both hands, Gummy lay beside her.

"On your backs, snakes!" the Commander screamed at them. "Hands behind your head. Ankles crossed."

She didn't even think to disobey. She just responded. Like everyone else. The piercing whistle of an incoming round sounded overhead as another simulator dropped into a sandbag-rigged barrel, serving as a grenade pit. An earsplitting explosion accompanied the ground-shaking detonation. Smoke billowed and curled.

Fog machines and glowing green chemical sticks lining the yard added an eerie surreal effect. Instructors fired blanks into the air. A shrill sound captured her attention. Tabby looked up at the man with the whistle.

The Commander blew twice. "Crawl!"

Crawling provided blessed relief from holding the same position for too long.

He blew three times. "On your feet!" Then, once. "On your backs!" The drill went on and on. One, two, three. Down, crawl, stand. "I can't hear you!"

"Hoo-yah!" Tabby sounded her part of the collective response. Trying to keep up with the whistle became impossible. She tried just the same. Fingernails broke to ragged stubs, hands and arms were scraped by the rough surface. Three whistles sounded. Tabby stood. Then the instructors herded the formation double time toward the beach for water torture.

Tabby sat shivering in the cold water, arms linked with Beeman and Gummy.

"I'm soooo cold." On Beeman's other side, Armstrong's teeth were chattering.

"Urinate," Tabby hissed under her breath so he'd shut up before they were caught talking. She didn't know what the penalty for talking was. But she sure didn't want to find out.

"You want him to piss his pants?" Beeman was incredulous.

"Everyone does sooner or later," Gummy whispered stoically. "It raises the water temperature. Temporarily."

Beeman broke from the line. They tried to pull him back. Five, ten, twenty trainees followed. Just like that, they quit. Tabby linked her free arm with Armstrong—who was looking lost without his swim buddy—and squeezed Gummy's arm, knowing how hard this was for him. His little brother had drowned in a mountain stream and Gummy had never made it past water torture before.

Tabby needed him to make it this time. *She* needed to make it. She looked up to see Marc staring at her.

Quitting was not an option.

"Follow the deserters! There's not one of you that's *man* enough to stay." Marc shouted through the bullhorn, then handed it off to Hugh.

They each had a role to play. Kyle was the ultimate good cop, befriending the unsuspecting. Hugh was the voice of reason, calmly instructing the trainees. Marc badgered them to quit and made them angry enough to stay. That's why he liked the part. But there was one woman he wanted to quit. How the hell she made it this far, he didn't know.

"Out of the water," Hugh ordered.

Marc walked down to the shoreline with the night shift doctor. "Pull her for hypothermia."

Doc Brown, also a SEAL, nodded his understanding. Shining his flashlight down the line, Marc stopped at each man, while the Doc checked for signs of overexposure.

They had this down to a science. Twenty minutes in the water. Five minutes out. Worse than freezing to death, which was relatively painless, water torture could drive a man crazy. But it was the only way to teach trainees what their bodies could handle and what to expect during cold water diving.

He shined the light in Tabitha's face. She blinked.

"Overexposure," Doc Brown said.

"Wh-what?" Tabitha barely got the word out. But the chill in her voice was nothing compared to the chill her eyes directed at him.

"Disoriented," Marc agreed, staring his wife down. "Pull—"

"Sorry I'm late," Nydia said, running up beside him. "We had a hard time finding you."

"What?" It was his turn to be disoriented.

"My nurses and I are here to volunteer, Commander. For the duration of Hell Week. We'll take shifts." She pointed to three other women, standing on top of a dune.

"That won't be necessary. Chapel's showing signs of hypothermia," Doc Brown supplied.

"Tabby, who am I?"

"N-Nydia."

"That's not hypothermia. That's *malpractice*." She stared down the doctor. "Women have a higher percentage of body fat. She could outlast every one of these guys. So unless you're ready to pull them all..." She let the threat hang.

"Dismissed." They didn't need Navy nurses hanging around. But Nydia was right. He couldn't pull her now. Although sometime during Hell Week he would.

"Which of your men is going to give Tabby hygiene inspections?" Nydia asked. "Or would that be you?"

During Hell Week trainees stripped daily for inspection. Medical personnel checked for any festering sores and broken bones the wannabes might be trying to hide. He couldn't humiliate his wife by checking her with the men. Or even alone. She'd be sore and bruised. Dirty and smelly. He hadn't planned on her getting that far. But... Marc scowled. "All right. You stay. But don't get in the way."

"You go, girl!" Nydia cheered, running back up the beach to the rest of Tabby's cheering section.

Now he was pissed off. Time for sugar cookie drills. Water torture and sand torture. Marc blew his whistle. Once, back. Twice, crawl. Three times, stand. Again, and again.

TABBY MADE IT to her fourth Hell Week breakfast, piling her plate with scrambled eggs and bacon, biscuits and gravy, hash browns and cinnamon rolls. Food meant energy and substituted sleep. They were fed four times a day, breakfast, lunch, dinner and midnight rations. But they were only given four hours of sleep during the week.

She wolfed down boxes of dry cereal in line, then

followed it with milk. "What? All your girlfriends eat salad?" she snapped at the guy standing behind her.

Gummy laughed and couldn't stop laughing. After four nights without sleep, trainees alternated between hysteria and aggression.

Their fourth and final one-hour rest period for the week came after breakfast. Tabby crawled into the mudpit with the others, resting head and shoulders on the bank while bullhorns blasted noises, simulating an air raid.

Marc watched as she fell into the jerky movements of instant REM. He didn't know how much more he could take. If she didn't break soon, he would. He couldn't stand to see her go through this. SEAL Training had been hard on him. He knew it wasn't easy on her, yet out of one hundred and twenty starting the class, sixty-three remained.

One of them his wife.

Rock portage came next—the most dangerous part of training. Trainees would practice landing a raft in the rocks and breakers just offshore near the Hotel del Coronado. Marc stood at the head of the classroom holding his breath against the stench of unwashed bodies.

"Listen up. Get the wax out of your ears and the fog out of your brains. A misstep on the rocks could mean a broken back when that hundred-and-fifty-pound raft comes hurling at you." He talked them through a proper landing. Made them repeat it back to him. Then showed footage.

The trainees filed out of the classroom. Marc watched his wife for a limp or any other excuse to pull her. She'd passed all her hygiene inspections, but that didn't mean she wasn't hiding something.

This was dangerous. It was the ranking officer's job to tie off the boat. And this time he did everything in his power to make the drill easy on her. He assigned a boat crew that rallied around her. Gummy, Armstrong and four others who seemed uncaring of the fact they were led by a woman.

Tabby tied off in front of the Hotel Del, just as Marc taught her. Tossing the rope. Working with the breakers. The landing went off without a hitch. And her crew cheered and whooped on the beach while curious spectators dining at the hotel's outdoor terrace observed.

The Commander gave the crowd the whole show, shouting at the crew, running them along the beach while they carried the raft on their heads. Tabby ran the sluggish pace of someone pushed too far. But she'd survived.

"Your crew is secure, Lieutenant."

It took Tabby a moment to realize he meant they'd passed Hell Week. In another life she would have been a spectator at the hotel, not the first female trainee. Her gaze drifted toward her husband. For the first time in six weeks she saw pride shining in his eyes.

Maybe they had a chance.

Armstrong grabbed her and hugged her. Followed by Gummy. She held on tight wishing it were another man she was holding. When she looked up, Marc was already moving down the beach.

1700 Friday
SEAL BARRACKS,
Coronado, CA

CARRYING FAST FOOD for two, Marc knocked softly on Tabitha's door. No answer. He calmed his rising panic by testing the knob. Finding it unlocked, he stepped inside.

She lay on her stomach, stretched across her rack. Still in fatigues and boots, she slept covered in five days' worth of dirt. Hell Week was over.

She was one of only thirty-six left.

He stared at her in amazement. *She'd made it.*

Pride warred with too many other conflicting emotions for Marc to allow himself to feel it. But it was there just the same, in the tiny part of his heart that hoarded the knowledge he was her husband and remembered how it had felt...once upon a time.

It wasn't unusual for trainees to sleep the next day away. And it was his policy to let them. Marc put down the food and checked her pulse anyway. The steady beat and warmth of her skin reassured him. He continued to hold her hand long after it was necessary.

He'd always react to her physically, he realized, laying her hand gently on her pillow. He almost didn't have the strength to let go. He brushed her cheek. Touched her hair. It was still beautiful, even shorn and covered in grime. She sighed in her sleep and he pulled back.

Moving to the end of the bed, he unlaced her boots and tugged them off, placing them side by side beneath her rack. Blood had seeped through one of her socks at the heel. It was already dry, and he pulled off the sock as gently as he could, knowing he'd start the bleeding again. She didn't so much as stir.

He managed to find an antiseptic swab and a bandage among her personal items and doctored her foot. Then he examined the other. There was visible bruising and swelling at her ankle. Marc poured out a soda in a nearby potted plant and used the ice to make a cold pack with her sock.

She jumped at the contact with the cold. "Leave me alone," she mumbled, kicking at him. Then she promptly fell back asleep. Marc finished and settled in a chair next to her rack with his half of the food.

For six weeks he'd stayed away.

He craved her company. Even if she slept through his visit. Thoughts of crawling in beside her and just holding her close crept into his head.

She'd chosen. Instructor over husband.

He couldn't be both. There were three more weeks in Phase One. Phase Two and Phase Three lay ahead. Failure was still possible. There'd be other tests of endurance, but none that required the same mental stamina as Hell Week.

Hell Week was meant to weed out the weak. And Tabitha had proved herself. Both mentally and physically. But the question most prevalent on his mind these days was not whether she would pass or fail. But how her passing or failing would affect their marriage.

The bite of burger lodged in his throat and he swallowed with difficulty, forcing down the food along with his feelings.

"Commander?" Perry's voice echoed through the barracks, followed by the sound of the screen door slamming closed behind him.

Putting down his burger, Marc rose to his feet and left the converted office that served as Tabitha's room. He spotted Perry walking up the aisle between two rows of empty bunk beds.

"A Captain Prince is waiting in your office," he said.

"Tad Prince? Facial scar?"

"Yes."

Tabitha's father. His father-in-law. Though he suspected the man didn't know it. *This should be interesting.*

Marc took a shortcut, cutting across the grinder to HQ, then through his locker room to his office. The move would put him immediately behind *his* desk. In *his* office. And in control.

"Captain," he said as he entered, capturing the attention of the man on the other side of the desk.

The Toad stopped pacing. "Do you always sneak into your own office, Miller?"

"Only when the visitor is unexpected," Marc replied, calling the retired frogman on his own sudden appearance. "Captain, it's been a while." He didn't bother to extend his hand.

Prince nodded. "I think you can guess why I'm here."

"Have a seat," Marc offered, sitting himself.

"I prefer to stand. Let me get straight to the point, Miller." The Toad leaned over the desk. "I would have been here sooner, but it seems I'm the last to know my daughter volunteered for the SEAL program. It's not bad enough no one bothered to tell me. No, I have to find out from the front page of a newspaper.'' He slapped the paper down, face up.

Hell and back. Marc read the headline. He remembered the interview. He just hadn't realized it was syndicated.

''I don't know who's crazier,'' the Toad continued. ''Congress, the Chief of SEALs, or *you* for not booting her butt right out the door.''

''I would've, if I could've.''

''I don't want my daughter rolling around in the mud with some dick-for-brains SEAL instructor. You got that? I want her out of here, now!''

Now was probably not the time to tell Prince he'd done more than roll in the mud with his daughter. It was obvious he didn't know Marc had married Tabitha. Marc was more than a little disappointed that she hadn't told her parents. He'd phoned his family.

While the man blew off steam, Marc realized the Toad didn't have the power to intimidate him anymore. He was still formidable. But Marc was all that and younger. And he didn't like *the man* in his face.

He stood and leaned across his desk, meeting Prince in the middle. ''I can't do that.''

''Don't give me shit, Miller! I *know* you can. Wave your magic pen across the page and write fail, and she's out of here. F-A-I-L, in case you forgot how to spell it.''

Marc barely contained his anger at the insult. ''Don't you think I would if I could? It's not that simple.''

''Of course it is.''

"It's just a matter of time. When she fails or quits, she's out of here." *If* she fails. Where had that thought come from? Of course Tabitha would quit or fail.

"If you can't or won't fail her, I know you sure as hell can make her quit!"

"I'm trying my damnedest!"

"Try harder!"

"Look I don't want her here any more than you—"

The locker room door opened behind him, and the Toad's face registered shock. Marc sucked in his breath. Slowly, he straightened and turned to face his bedraggled and barefoot wife.

Her mouth was a tight thin line. "I'm not going to fail. And I'm not going to quit," Tabitha said with quiet dignity. "Who the hell gave either of you the right to decide my future?"

She turned and headed back the direction she'd come.

"THE COMMANDER TOLD ME I'd find you out here." The Toad entered the barracks, letting the door slam behind him. He stood aggressively, hands on hips. It was a stance that might have intimidated a lesser man.

Tabby was used to it.

"I don't want to have this conversation," she said, gathering shower items and pulling clean civilian clothes from her locker.

"Then I'll do all the talking."

"That's the conversation I'm not having. The one where you lecture and I listen."

"I don't lecture."

Tabby laid her clothes on her bunk and turned to face him. "Trust me, Dad, you do."

"What good would it do me. You only pretend to listen, then do what you want anyway. Just like your mother."

"Don't blame stubborn on Mom. Those genes come directly from you." She crossed her arms. "And I do listen. That's why I'm here. I've listened to years of your Navy SEAL adventures. I put up with years of your being gone."

"Sea stories, glossed over to make suitable bedtime tales. You have no idea—"

"And I listened when you told me I could do anything." She raised her voice to be heard above him. "And the one time you told me I couldn't. Do you remember that? Why are you surprised I accepted the challenge? That's the way you raised me—to believe in myself.

"I always thought you believed in me too. But if it was Zach or Bowie you wouldn't be lecturing. You'd be patting him on the back. Bravo Zulu, son. Way to go.

"Well, guess what, I'm not one of your sons. I'm your daughter. I made it through Hell Week. And I want you to be proud of me! When the boys wouldn't give me the password to their clubhouse, who told me to break the door down? This conversation is over!"

"Like hell it is! You don't know what it is you're getting yourself into."

"I'll learn. Like you did. You weren't born a Navy SEAL."

"Look at my face! This isn't pretty. Do you think I want this to happen to you?"

Tabby had spent her entire life admiring that face. "I don't see the scar, Dad—" she reached out and touched it "—I see the badge of courage and the man underneath."

It was a rare thing to see her father all choked up. Tabby wrapped her arms around him and squeezed. "I may fail, especially if the Commander has anything to say about it. But you didn't raise a quitter."

"Are you sure those stubborn genes are mine and not your mother's?"

"I'm fairly sure."

"I am proud of you, Tabby. But no man likes to think of his little girl growing up. It's not just the job. It's the situations you'll be put in. The men."

"I know. But I am all grown up. I can handle the men. And I'll handle anything that comes up."

"Telling me you can handle men does not make me feel better," he chuckled. "You're to remain a virgin until your wedding night. And if you're not I don't want to know about it." Tabby stiffened in her father's embrace. She hadn't told him about Marc, and she couldn't bring herself to do it now.

"I have to shower. I'm meeting the guys at Manny's to celebrate." She pulled out of his arms.

"I'd almost forgotten how bad Hell Week smelled. You could use a little soap. And I have to get back to the hotel before your mother comes looking for me."

She threw a towel over her shoulder and headed to the shower.

"Tabby," he called after her. "Hell Week's only the beginning. Break the door down."

2000 Friday
RARE ROSE TATTOO PARLOR,
Coronado, CA

LAYING ON HER STOMACH with her jeans down around her hips, Tabby threw back another shot of tequila while the tattoo artist did her job. Well on her way to intoxication, Tabby had a hard time staying awake and even drifted off a couple of times. The past week had desensitized her. And the liquor didn't help much either.

Physically she was beyond pain. But emotionally was another matter. She knew Marc didn't want her to be a SEAL so why did hearing him side with her father hurt? Couldn't one of them be on her side? She thought she'd seen pride in Marc's eyes when he'd dismissed her from Hell Week, but it had been so fleeting, now she wasn't sure.

Having the SEAL Trident tattooed on her butt was the act of a rule-breaker, she knew that. But no matter what happened after this, no one could take away the fact she'd made it through Hell Week. She had a right to feel proud of herself, even if no one else did.

Besides, all the guys were getting tattooed.

2200 Friday
HOTEL DEL CORONADO, POINT LOMA,
Coronado, CA

BRIGHT WHITE LIGHTS dotted the terrace of the Hotel del Coronado where Marc lingered over his after-dinner Corona. He stared out at the black sky, listening to the waves as they swelled, then crashed against the rocks in a crescendo of salt spray.

"I used to celebrate the end of Hell Week the same way," Tad Prince said, pulling up a chair uninvited. A waiter immediately took his drink order. "I was out here this afternoon, watching Tabby's crew land their boat. Tell me, Miller, do you think she has what it takes?"

Marc leaned forward in his seat. "I think she's determined to prove she does."

The waiter reappeared with two beers, setting one in front of each of them. "Would you want to take her into combat with you?" Prince asked.

"No." Marc didn't even have to think about that answer.

"I don't like the idea either." He took a drink from his beer then pointed the bottle at Marc. "But I don't have a say in the matter. You teach my daughter what she needs to know to stay safe."

Marc nodded. "Will do." What he wanted slipped away as they spoke. Getting her to quit, was now secondary to keeping her safe.

"That's all I ask, son."

Son. Marc studied his father-in-law. Did he know? Had Tabby told her parents about their marriage? Their all-too-brief marriage. And current separation. He didn't think so. But he liked the sound of the word.

"I never thanked you for hauling my ass off to

the bamboo brig,'' Marc said, dredging up the past. ''You turned my life around.''

Prince looked him over long and hard. ''You're welcome. I knew you were trouble the day you walked in the door.''

''Sounds like me. You told me I'd never amount to anything.'' *But I love your daughter.*

''What makes you think I ever believed that? I know Tabby's in good hands.''

Marc tried to decide whether to tell the man he'd married his daughter. Tabby hadn't done it so it looked as if it was up to him.

Marc's cell phone rang. He picked up before the second ring, checking his watch, 2219. ''Miller.''

''You'd better get down here.'' Urgency marked Manny's normally carefree tone. ''Your wife's causing trouble.''

''I'll be right there.'' Marc disconnected and pushed to his feet. He'd have to break the news some other time.

''Trouble?''

''Yeah, nothing I can't handle.'' Marc headed for the door, grabbing his cover on the way. What had she gotten herself into this time?

He arrived at Manny's without any of the speeding tickets he deserved. Inside, the lights were all on. Chairs and tables were turned over. Broken glass was strewn across the floor. The place looked as if it had been hit by a hurricane. Marc knew better; he'd been in a couple of bar fights in this very room. He saw only a few patrons remained. His wife was not among them.

Peanut shells and glass crunched beneath his feet as he made his way to the bar.

Manny hung up the phone. "I was just calling you, again. The Shore Patrol hauled the entire training class off to the brig."

"What in the hell happened?"

"Tabby's a little drunk, I think."

Marc glared at him. "How'd she get that way?"

"Four beers. That's all I served her."

"That doesn't explain this mess."

"A dozen or so Marines walked in itching for a fight. Tabby hopped on a table to show off her new tattoo... Hell, Marc, there's no easy way to say this—she mooned them."

"Tattoo!"

"Everything after that happened too fast to recount. Needless to say Tabby has a wicked right hook. She threw the first punch and then it was every man for himself." Manny cleared his throat. "And woman. Afterwards, someone said she'd been tipping tequila before she got here."

Marc looked around at the mess left by Tornado Tabby. He pulled a couple of fifties from his wallet and handed them to Manny. "This won't come close to covering everything. Send me a bill."

The wheelchair-bound owner took the money. "They all blow off steam after Hell Week. Don't be too hard on her."

Marc's gaze narrowed at the advice. "Call Preach. Have him pick up a duty van and meet me at the brig."

It was well after 2300 by the time Marc drove up to the front of the brig.

Perry had just parked the van and walked over to meet him. "Typical Hell Week," he commented as they strode toward the two-story building surrounded by a twelve-foot fence topped with barbed wire.

Marc felt like leaving her here overnight. If she woke up hungover, staring at the barbed wire through barred windows, maybe next time she'd think twice before showing off a new tattoo. He frowned.

That Marine better never cross his path. Hell, the last time he'd seen his wife's bottom was six weeks ago and she hadn't even had a tattoo. He was hotter than hell mad at her. And hornier than the devil himself. It probably wasn't a good idea to spring her tonight.

They showed their ID and the gate guard let them pass.

"You have my trainees," Marc said to the guard behind the desk.

The Second Class Petty Officer smiled up at him. "Ah, the Hell Week brigade. Sign here, Commander."

Marc skimmed over the names on the list. "Where's Chapel?"

"She really one of yours? We didn't believe her. Even with the buzzed hair and all. We put her in a cell all her own." The petty officer dug out additional paperwork.

Marc signed and asked Perry to haul the rest back to the barracks. He followed the guard to a corner cell where he found Tabitha sleeping peacefully.

He dumped the rack over, just like he would for

any other trainee. No special treatment. She rolled to the cold floor and opened half-lidded eyes.

"Hi, Marc," she slurred, smiling at him. "D'you wanna see my tattoo?"

"No!"

"It's a really nice tattoo," the guard said.

Marc growled low in his throat, shutting the petty officer up. Just how many men had seen the damn thing?

His drunken wife had trouble navigating her way to the door. Tossing her over his shoulder, he exited the cell.

"Bye," she said happily to the shore patrol.

He didn't trust himself to speak even when they were alone in his car. Back at base he carried her through the empty bay. Eighty bunk beds cried, *take her, take her,* as he passed.

He went straight to the showers and turned on the cold spray, holding her under while she sputtered and screamed. When she looked more like a drowned rat than a woman and was sober enough to listen, he turned the knob so hard it came off in his hand. He threw it across the room, and it landed on the tile with a ping.

"Get a towel and meet me at your rack." He left her shivering in the bathroom. The smaller office seemed less overwhelming than the room with eighty empty beds. He pulled down the shades on the window and door.

Tabitha stepped in and he turned. "Close the door."

Towel around her neck, sober expression on her

face, she did. She circled him, keeping her back to the wall and her eyes on him.

''I want to see that tattoo.'' He stood in the center of the room with his arms folded. ''Why the sudden shyness? You already showed half the Navy and the Marine Corps.''

''I did not!''

He took one step, two steps toward her.

''You want to see it, fine!'' She turned her back on him.

He moved close in behind her. ''Don't,'' he said, putting his arms around her to still her hands on the zipper of her jeans. ''I just want to talk.'' He swallowed the lie; his body had something else in mind. Warmth from their body heat seeped through the wetness of their clothes. Did she still want him too? ''Put on something dry so you're comfortable.''

He let her go then turned around.

Tabby opened her locker and hid behind the door to put on a dry T-shirt. The whole thing seemed kind of awkward and sad for two people who were married. He was right. It was time to talk.

She didn't bother with more than a T-shirt and panties. He'd said comfortable and it was after lights-out. She switched on the bedside lamp and turned off the overhead light. She sat on her rack and invited Marc to sit beside her.

He sat down on the edge looking uncomfortable and wet. He didn't have much to say now that he had her attention. There'd been no private moments in the past six weeks. The communication gap had widened to a chasm neither of them seemed capable of crossing.

He just sat there looking sad and she wanted to reach out and touch him. She still loved him but love didn't seem to have much to do with making a marriage work.

"I didn't think you'd make it this far." He was the first to break the silence.

"I know you didn't."

"You proved you could. There's no shame in quit—"

"Marc, don't start. I'm not going to quit. You're afraid I'm going to succeed, aren't you?"

"Damn straight. I'm afraid *for you,* Tabitha. I wish you could see that."

"What about my fears? Are those any less real? You won't always be an instructor. In a few years you'll be back with a team." She wished her head didn't feel so thick from all the alcohol.

"You knew what you were getting into. You had to. Your father—"

"You knew, too. You didn't want a dutiful and complacent bride, remember? You wanted me. I wasn't aware that came with a 'no SEAL clause.' We can't be together until you accept who I really am."

"I can't," he said, pushing to his feet. "Accepting that goes against everything *I* am."

She hugged a pillow to her. "Why is it asking so much for you to believe in me?" *The way I believe in you.*

"What about you? You were just looking for someone like your father."

"You're crazy!"

"Crazy? I have the man's job! His same welcome

speech. Hell, I even have blue eyes.'' He paced the room. He couldn't help making the comparison after having spent some time with the man.

"You are so wrong!'' She threw the pillow at him.

He knocked it aside. "I'm not so sure. But I can tell you that I don't want to be somebody's surrogate daddy.''

"Well, you definitely went out of your way to make sure you'd never be a father, didn't you?'' The spiteful words just came out. She didn't really mean them.

He paled beneath his tan. "I would have had the vasectomy reversed for you.'' *Would have.*

She desperately wanted to take back the words but doubted she'd ever have the chance.

CHAPTER FOURTEEN

1100 Tuesday
San Clemente Island, CA

AFTER TABBY COMPLETED the nine weeks of Phase One, she moved on to Phase Two, diving. A natural in the water, she found the seven weeks to be as fun as they were challenging. She grew closer to her swim buddy. And further from her husband.

Phase Three started with four weeks of land warfare. In the fifth week they moved to San Clemente Island for five weeks to run mission scenarios in preparation for the real thing.

Tabby was less than two weeks from completing the course, and Marc still hadn't accepted the fact that she'd make it. She stood at parade rest while he glared at her over the heads of the other trainees.

"Listen up!" he said. "We're leaving here today to finish up our training with a live recovery op."

Excitement buzzed through the ranks.

"There's been a plane crash in Louisiana. No survivors. They need experienced divers, spotters and sharpshooters to recover bodies. This is not a pretty job. This is *our* job."

Tabby closed her eyes and lowered her head, saying a silent prayer for the passengers and crew.

"As trainees none of you will be diving. These are alligator-infested waters with zero visibility. It's too dangerous and you don't have the experience. You will, however, be shooters with *real* bullets. Your job is to shoot alligators. Not each other."

Nervous laughter escaped from the trainees.

"I think that's all I need to say on that subject. You'll be given your warning orders. Go get your gear. We leave within the hour!"

After the ride in a C-30 cargo plane, the trainees and the instructors boated into a bayou, where they were to meet up with Team One. At their campsite, Marc offered Tabby a hand out of the boat. She thought about ignoring it, since he hadn't extended the same courtesy to any of the others. But it had been so long since she'd even touched him. Her hand slipped into his and she squeezed as she found her foothold.

He let go abruptly. "There are no ladies' rooms here. Not even outhouses. Do you have a problem with that?" His tone told her he hoped she did. And that he didn't care.

"No, sir."

He turned to the men. "Stow your gear. We'll be relieving Team One ASAP." He indicated two large canvas tents lined with cots.

Tabby threw her gear over her shoulder.

"You'll be in the command tent. With the COs and XOs. Is that a problem?"

She didn't like being singled out for special treatment. "Maybe I should go with the rest of the men—"

"You're not sleeping with the *men*. And that's final!"

Heads turned at his raised voice. She held back a retort, knowing it was inappropriate to question his authority. She followed him to a smaller tent. Several interior flaps divided the tent down the middle. Four cots on one side. Two on the other.

Tabby stood in the four cot half, waiting for instructions. There were a couple of folding chairs, tables and lamps. Luxuries.

Marc headed for the side with two cots and put his gear under one of them. It was the closest they'd come to sleeping together since SEAL Training had begun twenty-three weeks ago. She felt a blush heat her cheeks and stole a glance at her husband's back.

Twenty-three weeks. Almost half a year as man and wife with no physical contact.

"Muster outside," he ordered.

The rest of their first day at camp was spent in biohazard suits, tagging bloody pieces sometimes identifiable as body parts and zipping them into body bags.

Afterward, Tabby refused her sea rations, deciding to brave the dangers they'd been warned about to find a semiprivate place to throw up the only meal she'd had all day.

She made her way back to the tent just as the sun dropped from the sky in a red-orange blaze of glory. The muggy heat remained and she spotted her washcloth with a few precious drops from her canteen. Sitting down on her cot, she wiped her neck and face.

Sensing rather than hearing him, Tabby looked up to find Marc staring at her.

Without stepping inside their shared space, he tossed her a can of peaches. "You'll be hungry later."

"Thanks," she said, but he was already gone.

Tabby curled up on the cot and promptly fell asleep. A while later she awoke to soft male voices coming from the other side of the flap. She identified the timbre of Marc's laughter as he responded to something Brad said and felt strangely comforted. They weren't talking about anything particularly interesting, but she lay in the dark listening, fading in and out of wakefulness.

"Make a wish," her mother said.

"I wish Dad was here."

"He would be if he could."

Tabby closed her eyes tight, wishing with all her might that her daddy would come home for her twelfth birthday.

"The Rockies are too young. I don't see them as a contender..."

Navy SEAL dads had a special job that took them places little girls weren't allowed.

"Walker's got the Gold Glove this year for sure..."

"Daddy!" She woke to find him standing over her bed.

"I was just leaving this." He took a new baseball glove from behind his back.

"I wished you home for my birthday."

"And here I am. Can't disappoint my little girl."

"Is it a scary place?"

He didn't answer for a long time. "The only thing I'm afraid of is losing my family."

"I won't let us get lost, Daddy."

He chuckled and pulled her into his strong arms. "I know you won't."

"Did you see Dipoto pull that game out in the ninth against the Cards..."

The place Daddy went wasn't scary. The job was hard. But there were other daddies, and they talked baseball.

"I'm going to be a Navy SEAL when I grow up."

Girls can't be SEALs. Under the covers now, and back to sleep.

"Good night, Tabitha. I love you," he said before kissing her forehead.

"Good night, Marc," she whispered. "I love you, too."

IN BLACK FATIGUES, wielding a Heckler & Koch MP5 semi-automatic, Tabby stood on one wing of the downed plane, Armstrong on the other. The rest of the trainees manned the fuselage and various other pieces of wreckage. Every so often someone would shoot a couple of rounds when an alligator moved toward a diver.

If anybody kept score it was Navy SEALs six, Gators zip. But the other team looked hungry.

Marc was one of the divers searching for the black box. Tabby had never felt so anxious as she did standing on the broken wing of the military craft. Each time he disappeared into the murky depths of the swamp, she'd catch herself holding her breath until he reappeared.

There were too many unresolved issues between them to lose him now. His diving experience gave her little reassurance when compared to the danger surrounding him. As a trainee it was her job to eliminate any threats to his safety. She watched a couple of alligators, then noticed a particularly large one zeroing in on a diver.

Marc!

She aimed. Fired. Then fired again. She was sure she'd hit her target both times, but the reptile was still heading his way.

Around her, men shouted warnings and fired more rounds. Tabby heard it all as if from a great distance; all five of her senses were focused on Marc.

Then man and alligator disappeared. Blood tinged the water. Other divers swam toward the spot they'd gone under. She held back the scream bubbling up inside her and tried to recall what she knew about alligators. Didn't they drag their prey to the bottom to drown them?

How long had it been? A few seconds? Minutes? *A lifetime.*

"Marc!" Shoving Gummy aside, she unsheathed her Bowie knife, but Brad Bailey caught her around the waist before she could jump in. "Let me go!"

"Tabby, he's in gear. You're not. Stay put and let the divers do their job."

She heard, but didn't listen. As soon as he let go, she clamped her Bowie knife between her teeth and dove in without even checking for gators. She didn't want to know the odds. All she wanted was to help Marc.

Tabby surfaced a few feet away from where he'd

gone under. A marker buoy bobbed to the surface, and Marc emerged a second after that. She sucked in big gulps of oxygen and would have thrown her arms around him, but he seemed less than receptive, as he pushed aside his goggles.

He yanked out his mouthpiece. "Oh, that's a really good look for you. Give me that." He took the knife from her clenched teeth. "Out of the water, now!"

The pontoon boat the divers used as a launchpad neared. Brad held out his hand and helped her in. Marc handed off the buoy and waited in the water while Brad hauled up the black box.

With that task completed, Marc pulled himself into the boat. Removing his hood, he directed a reptilian glare at her.

She wasted her efforts on the wrong creature.

The boat pulled alongside shore. She leaped off and marched to the tent with Marc on her heels.

"Lieutenant, your job is to provide cover. Not act like some Amazon Queen! I had the situation under control."

"Oh, I could see that!" she said, dropping the tent flap in his face.

He slapped it back and followed her inside to their twin bunks. "You hit him. I just had to wait for him to realize it!"

"You're welcome!" She untucked her wet shirt.

"I'd thank you if I had any reason to. You left your divers uncovered," he said as he unzipped his wetsuit.

She turned her back on him and removed her shirt. "My divers were covered!"

"By who?"

She glared over her shoulder and caught a glimpse of his bare back. She averted her gaze. "Gummy."

"You and Gummy!" he muttered.

"What about me and Gummy? Is that jealousy?" she demanded, unhooking her bra and throwing it on her bunk.

"I am not jealous!"

Tabby looked and found him staring at her. She quickly pulled on a dry T-shirt and green fatigue shorts over wet underwear, then ran from the tent and the hunger in her husband's eyes.

"I'm not through with you!" he shouted. Marc's hands were still shaking as he tugged a T-shirt over his head and followed her. He couldn't handle the thought of her being injured or killed in the line of duty. Especially if it happened because she was trying to save his sorry hide.

He didn't have to worry about not finding Tabitha. Every SEAL along the way pointed him in the right direction and he caught up with her in a matter of minutes.

"Tabitha—"

"Stay away from me," she threatened, stomping through the underbrush, each boot step taking her farther away from base camp.

He grabbed her arm and forced her to stop. "You're going to find yourself in quicksand."

"Let go!" Anger flushed her cheeks.

"Not until you listen. You could have been killed—"

"It didn't matter. I thought you were dead."

"What are you saying? That you give a damn about me?" He searched her eyes. She'd just tossed him a lifeline. It was the first indication in weeks that their marriage had a chance of surviving.

"You smell like a swamp," she said, trying to wrench her arm free.

"You smell worse." He pulled her to him.

"Don't you dare!"

"Why not? You need to come up with a reason or I'm going to kiss you. And then I'm—"

She kicked him hard in the shin and broke free.

"Damn it." He caught her again. And this time held on to his struggling captive. "I've waited long enough to see that tattoo."

"You can just keep waiting. Because you're not going to look at it."

"I sure as hell am!"

"Try asking and not ordering for a change."

"You left me no choice when you chose instructor over husband." Right now all he wanted was to be her husband. He had less than a week left as her instructor and he was afraid of being left with nothing. "I'm asking," he whispered, letting go.

She stopped fighting and showed him. "You said you wouldn't pin me, so I did it myself."

Marc dropped to his knees at her feet. He traced the eagle and their tags—*Tiger and The Marquis*—which were etched into a banner underneath. He pressed his lips to her skin.

"Let me make love to you, Tiger."

Hell, since he was already on his knees, he might as well beg.

0900 Friday
NAVAL SPECIAL WARFARE CENTER,
Coronado, CA

"COMMANDER, DO YOU HAVE a minute?" Perry stood in the doorway.

Marc slipped the postcard he'd been reading into his desk drawer and waved him in. "What's up, Preach?"

Perry entered the office and closed the door. "I thought you might want to see this." He handed over a sheet of paper with a note attached. "The Senior Chief in Personnel wants to know when you can sign the entry in your service record."

Marc read the copy of Lieutenant Chapel's Page Two documenting their marriage. "I'll take care of it at lunch." He dismissed Perry and pulled out the postcard again.

Sorry I missed your call. Tabitha.

Because Congress still considered her a test subject, she'd gone with the graduating class to Fort Bragg for the three weeks of paratrooper school that followed SEAL Training even though she'd missed out on the actual graduation ceremony.

With her usual bluntness she'd let him know what she thought of not being allowed to wear the Trident Insignia. It was a small enough victory for his side. She'd shown them all by being one of only a handful to make it through twenty-five weeks of the toughest training the Navy had to offer. Of course, the graduates couldn't actually claim the Special Warfare designation until they'd completed six months of probation with a SEAL Team. And there was always the chance that a probationer could be blackballed.

Tabitha definitely would be.

He hadn't wanted to train his wife to be a SEAL. And he sure as hell didn't want her to be one. He couldn't stand to think about the ugly things she'd have to see and do—the dangerous situations she'd be in.

When they'd made love in Louisiana, he'd regretted his vasectomy for the first time. It wasn't about Rell or anyone else. It was about wanting to give Tabitha a part of himself—to show her how much he loved her.

He didn't want her to save the world or even him. That was his job. It was sexist of him, but he wanted her safe at home taking care of their family— What family? He'd made sure there would never be a family. He'd even told her adoption wasn't a possibility.

Damn her for making him want her and so much more than he could ever have—and for throwing him a bone with the Page Two entry.

If they were really married, why had she sent him a postcard instead of returning his call? He ripped the card in half and tossed it to the trash.

1000 Friday
SEAL BARRACKS,
Coronado, CA

TABBY PACKED, LIMPING from locker to duffel bag and back again. The sprained ankle she'd received while at Fort Bragg for three weeks of paratrooper school with the Green Berets barely bothered her anymore, but she carefully kept her weight off it. She'd spent the weekend healing. And sulking.

Everyone else in her training group had been assigned to one of the teams where they'd still have to complete six months' probation before earning their Trident.

Marc had warned her. What had she expected?

For him to at least try to get her an assignment.

Now it looked as if she was headed back to D.C. The only offer she'd had was from a friend with the CIA who was so impressed with her SEAL training that he'd called and offered her a deep cover position. It meant she would have to resign her commission—lose her identity in the name of espionage.

At the moment, that didn't seem like such a bad idea.

1900 Friday
BACHELOR OFFICERS' QUARTERS,
Coronado, CA

"HE'S HOLDING UP my assignment to a team." Tabby said. Standing in front of her bedroom mirror, she held up the black dress she'd worn to the Pecks' party and a red one she'd bought earlier that day.

"I still like the black one better," Carol said, lounging on Tabby's rack among the remnants of their shopping spree. "I don't think Marc would do that on purpose."

"Umm." Tabby fingered the black dress. Too many memories. She hung it back in the closet. The red one followed. "I'm just going to wear my uniform. Of course it's on purpose,'' she said, taking her tuxedo shirt out of the dry cleaning bag.

"I wish Brad and I were going.''

"Why don't you? I bet you could still get tickets at the door.'' Tabby put on the shirt followed by the floor-length navy blue skirt.

"Are you kidding?'' Carol said, rubbing a hand across her extended belly. "What would I wear? My feet are too swollen for dancing anyway. I can't believe I still have three weeks to go. I'm ready to burst.''

"Brad taking any leave?'' Tabby wrapped the cummerbund around her waist, then slipped into the short white dinner jacket.

"Starting next week. A whole month. He promised me he wouldn't miss the birth because of a mission.'' Carol struggled to her feet. "Very elegant. Let me help you with your bow tie. I do Brad's all the time.''

Tabby stood still while Carol tied the bow.

"You should have let Marc escort you.''

Tabby snorted. "We'd look like a pair of bookends. Besides, the less time I spend in his company the better.''

"Why would you say that?'' Carol stood back, admiring her handiwork.

"We should have never gotten married. He's never believed in me.''

"The first year is always the hardest. But Brad and I worked things out.''

Tabby pushed aside the fleeting thought that this was her six-month wedding anniversary. Turning to the dresser, she rummaged for her ribbons and

pinned them on. Then she buttoned on her gold epaulets. "I'm not willing to compromise. He has to
accept the fact that I'm a Navy SEAL or else we'll
never work things out."

1930 Friday
MANNY'S DIVE,
Coronado, CA

A TYPICAL FRIDAY NIGHT at Manny's. And aside
from the fact that it was October 13, his six-month
wedding anniversary, and he was sitting across the
table from Brad instead of his bride, Marc had nothing to complain about.

After returning from paratrooper training, Tabitha
had moved out of the barracks and into the BOQ.
Not a good sign, considering he could count the
times he'd slept with his wife on one hand.

Their only recent contact had been her request for
a team assignment. This wasn't just about what
might happen to her in the field. Each was trying to
out-stubborn the other.

So he was going to do the right thing and give
in.

Except he was still a man who didn't want a Navy
SEAL for a wife, so he also had divorce papers
ready. He'd give her what she wanted most—the
freedom to make her own mistakes.

"Carol met Tabby this afternoon," Brad said,
making conversation. "They went shopping. Carol's
maxed out all our credit cards on baby stuff. She
calls it nesting. She even made me read a book on
the subject. Because how could I get mad at her

when a book says it's normal?'' Brad shook his head. ''I swear if this nesting phase lasts much longer, I'll be broke. And all she wants to talk about is breastfeeding.''

''That's all you talk about these days.''

''Well, if I was a kid I'd want a breast,'' Brad reasoned. ''Then I think about sharing, you know, and I don't like the idea so much. But lately she's not interested in, you know, *that,* either. I just wish she'd have the baby so we can get back to a normal sex life.'' Brad averted his gaze, avoiding Marc's. ''Sorry. Guess you'd rather not talk about married life.''

''Not really,'' Marc admitted, shifting in his seat, the hard surface growing increasingly uncomfortable. ''But I did bring you here for a reason.''

''Don't tell me. You want Team One to take on Tabby.''

CHAPTER FIFTEEN

2100 Friday: The Navy Ball
OFFICERS' CLUB,
Coronado, CA

"YOUR TICKET, COMMANDER?"

"I'm a gate-crasher," Marc said, tossing a couple of twenties at the petty officer and walking through the double doors at the entrance of Neptune's Ballroom.

With purpose he searched the fairy-tale setting. He had no idea what she wore, but assumed something short, black and showing a lot of leg.

He spied her in full dress uniform, standing among a group of officers on the patio. He paused for a moment just to watch her laughing with her friends.

She caught him staring and her laughter faded to a hesitant smile and a cautious nod. He strode toward her with single-minded intent.

"Lieutenant. May I speak with you in private?"

"Certainly, Commander."

It was time to make her choose—him or the SEALs.

He'd walk out of here with his wife. Or she'd walk out of here a free woman. Free to be the SEAL she longed to be. He couldn't handle it if anything happened to her in the line of duty. And he'd be damned if he would live his life worrying that something would.

She followed him to a secluded alcove containing a bench and potted plants. It reminded him of their night at Captain Peck's. "May I have this dance?" She must have taken pity on him because she put her hand in his.

Tabby's skin tingled where they touched. She loved dancing with Marc. Did it mean he was taking the step toward reconciliation that she so desperately wanted?

They danced, not one song, not three, but until she lost count and the last note died away. When they stopped, he let go, though she longed for him to keep holding her.

"I believe the last time we danced you mentioned my pinning you." His voice was strained, and she knew what it cost him to say those words.

She felt as if she was back in high school, talking about pinning and promise rings. She absently touched her naked finger, wanting that ring just as badly as the Trident. She forced herself to let out the breath she was holding and then take in another.

"On behalf of the elite, I'd like to recognize you as the first woman among the ranks of Navy SEALs." He removed his Trident and pinned it above her breast, close to her heart where she'd wear it forever.

He executed a salute. "Bravo Zulu, Lieutenant Tabitha Lilith Chapel-Prince. Well done."

"You gave me your Trident." Tears threatened

and she didn't try to hold them back. Let 'em fall. This was the happiest moment of her life.

"It'll mean more to me to have yours."

The lump in her throat was too large to swallow. It would be totally inappropriate to throw herself in his arms, but they were married. She'd even had the entry officially recorded. She opened her mouth to tell him and he surprised her into silence.

He pulled a pager from beneath his cummerbund. "You've been assigned Team One. Echo squad leader. I believe Gummy and Armstrong are part of your crew. Your time is no longer your own, Lieutenant. You're on twenty-four-hour call to your team and its mission."

She reached out to take the pager from him, but he held it back. "I've tagged you TIGER I. You have a locker full of equipment at Team One headquarters." He showed her the label on the pager, then gave it to her. "Don't let the men cocoon around you if you get hurt. Stats from Allied Services show men will spend more time with an injured female soldier. It just makes for a bigger target. The team medic, or the guy closest to you is responsible for taking care of your injuries. They'll get help if they need it. Take care of yourself, Tabitha. I'd be happy to take over that duty any time you want me to..."

Tabby couldn't believe it. He was saying goodbye. So much for the happiest day of her life.

"I just can't do this. I can't worry about your every move... Here are your walking papers, Lieutenant."

TABBY SAVED THE TEARS for her room. But she didn't have much time for them, because shortly before dawn her pager went off. She reached the hangar bay before she let herself pick up the phone.

She got Marc's answering machine and waited impatiently for the end of his message, looking over her shoulder as equipment was being loaded onto the helicopter.

"Pick up, Marc. Pick up."

"You got five!" Brad warned.

She wasn't the only one on her team making a last-minute phone call. But she didn't want to miss her ride.

Eventually, the stupid machine beeped. "Pick up if you're there, Marc. I'm not going to accept those divorce papers. I love you. I want you—I choose *you*. But give me a reason why I can't have both!"

She put down the phone and walked toward the life she'd always wanted to lead.

1909 Wednesday
ON-BASE FAMILY HOUSING,
Coronado, CA

MARC SPENT DAYS playing back that message. He'd been home. He'd even been tempted to pick up. But he hadn't. Because as soon as he'd heard the pain in her voice he had realized how cruel—to both of them—he'd been to make her choose.

He'd never told her he loved her. And five days later, he understood that he would always worry about her, whether they were married or not.

When he couldn't stand to be alone for another minute, he sought out Carol.

"Well, this is a surprise," Carol said, opening the door. Her protruding stomach greeted him first.

"Can I come in?" Marc was a little uncomfortable. He made it a point not to visit while Brad was gone.

"Sure," she said, stepping aside. "Excuse the mess. I can't see below my stomach anymore. So I never know what I miss with the vacuum."

The house was immaculate as always. She ushered him into the kitchen. A bowl of melting ice cream sat on the table.

"No pickles?" he teased.

"Care to join me?" she asked, already fishing out another bowl and spoon.

Marc went to the freezer to grab a container of ice cream. "You have any of those sprinkles?" he asked, searching the cupboards.

She found a bottle and they settled in at the kitchen table, neither saying anything for a long time.

"We haven't done this in a while," Carol said finally.

"I'm not sure Brad would like me meeting his wife while he's gone."

"Why not? Brad trusts you, Marc. I trust you. Does Tabby mind?"

Marc frowned. The truth was he didn't know. Maybe he should have thought about it before coming over. Not that it mattered. He'd signed the divorce papers before handing them to her. He stirred the melting ice cream in his bowl, mixing it with the colored sprinkles.

"I made Tabby choose between me and the SEALs." He let the spoon rest on the side of the bowl.

Carol smiled at him. He didn't see any reason for her to smile. He'd come looking for sympathy from someone who might understand what he was going through.

"Brad and I have those kinds of fights all the time. Almost every time he leaves."

She made it sound so easy. But it couldn't be normal to miss Tabby this much while, at the same time, being so angry he never wanted her back.

"I have a Navy Wife handbook if that would help," she offered with a wry laugh.

He rolled his eyes. "I don't think so."

"I borrowed it from a ship's wives' club. Actually, I'm going to put together a similar booklet for SEAL wives. I'll be sure to use nongender-specific language. So you husbands don't feel left out."

"I'm the only *husband,* Carol."

"You never know. Word gets out Tabby made it—"

"Congress hasn't made that determination yet. Tabitha's not even an official SEAL. Besides, she's one in a million..." His sentence trailed off.

"It's okay to miss her, Marc." Carol covered his hand with her own.

"What went wrong with us? I mean, besides the baby thing. I'm not trying to..." He didn't want her getting the wrong impression. "I just don't want to make the same mistake with Tabitha."

"What went wrong with us is that I'm not Tabby. I was just a habit. We weren't really in love. Once I met Brad I understood that. If Tabby had just been a D.C. desk jockey, would you have given her a second look?"

He'd never really thought about it that way before. The things he liked best about her scared him most.

"Marc!"

"I don't have an answer—"

"No, Marc, my water. It just broke."

He stared at her blankly. "Water?"

"The baby's coming!"

2400 Wednesday
LOCATION CLASSIFIED

THERE WAS A FIRST TIME for everything. Black fatigues blended into the dark hallways of a powerless building. Night vision goggles guided movements. Tabby stepped carefully and quietly on the tile floor of the apartment building, leading the six-man, one-woman Echo Squad on a *prowl and growl*—SEAL slang for kick ass and take names.

A balaclava covered her head and a bulletproof vest covered her chest, making it impossible for anyone—even her team—to see she was a woman.

H&K at the ready, she pushed aside her constant thoughts of Marc to concentrate on a game that wasn't a game. Three members of the squad were still designated BUD/S until they'd completed six months of real missions. Their job was to provide backup for the more experienced men of Brad's Alpha Squad.

Tabby nodded to Armstrong, indicating that he should move to the right side of the door frame. Her weapon pointed up and right, Armstrong's down and left, she counted to three and kicked in the door. It gave easily. Alpha had already done a top-to-bottom sweep of the building. Double checking was more or less just a little on-the-job training.

But nothing, not even twenty-five weeks of training had prepared her for the carnage in this building. It was hard to believe that people had recently lived here. Windows were blown out. Walls were gone.

On the basement level, there was a little more sanity. Fewer residential apartments. Storage. Generators. More places to look, but thankfully less to see. She and Armstrong coordinated their movements as they entered a storage room while two other squad members did the same across the hall. The remaining three men covered them in the passageway.

Her transmitter sounded. "Four, clear," Gummy said from the room across the hall.

About to voice an "all clear"—indicating the room and building were secure—Tabby heard something. She nodded to Armstrong. He shook his head. He didn't hear it. Switching her night vision goggles to infrared, she searched for hot spots. At first all she saw were rats scurrying across the floor, but then she found another, larger blot.

Armstrong indicated he saw it, too. Tabby went to investigate while he guarded their backs. Moving around upturned boxes, she was startled to discover a woman's body. It was clear that the woman had dragged herself into the room in a desperate attempt to survive.

Tabby checked for a pulse. Nothing. She'd died in her hiding place.

But the sound Tabby had heard persisted. She gently pushed aside the woman and the boxes, opened a steamer trunk and found the treasure the woman had been hiding.

Her child.

A little boy, maybe three years old, tried to hold back his tears.

"Navy SEALs. We're here to help," Tabby announced. Though he probably wouldn't understand her, she hoped her intent was clear.

"American?" he asked in accented English.

"Yes," she said with a smile.

"What's the holdup, Echo leader?" Brad asked through the transmitter. There was static, then he yelled, "Get out! Incoming."

"Go!" Tabby ordered her men as the first blast shook the building. Responsible for her squad, she counted heads as the men ran past. When they were all accounted for she grabbed the now screaming child and took up a position at the rear.

The exit remained clear, but an armored tank was approaching, strafing the building with fire. Alpha Squad provided cover while Echo hustled out the door and around the corner. Tabby cradled the frightened child as she ran. Brad was behind her when she heard the whistle of an incoming round.

"Cover!" Brad shouted, slamming her to the ground.

2400 Wednesday
NAVY HOSPITAL,
San Diego, CA

"PUSH!" MARC SHOUTED, caught up in the moment. Taking his cue from the doctor, he squeezed Carol's hand. "One more time."

"I can't. I can't," she panted, rolling her head from side to side.

"Yes, you can." Stilling her restless movements, he brushed her damp brow. "Breathe, Carol. For Brad."

"No," she moaned. "Something's happened to him, I know it. He's supposed to be here. We had his leave all planned!"

"Things change, sweetheart. This baby's coming now. Push!" He supported her while she bore down.

"It's a boy," the doctor announced.

Carol sobbed in his arms. "I hate him. I hate him for not being here."

"Shh. You don't hate him. You just miss him. He's doing what he has to do." The way the person he missed was doing what she had to do. The baby's cry filled the room and Marc pulled Carol closer. "Brad's going to kick himself in the behind until next Tuesday for missing this. And you can hang it over his head for the next twenty years."

The nurse handed him the swaddled infant, and his chest tightened. Counting fingers and toes with Carol, he knew this was what he wanted. *Brad, you lucky dog.*

He realized he had more than he deserved. How stupid he'd been not to have realized it before.

"We want you and Tabby to be the godparents."

"Thank you. I'd be honored. What's the little tyke's name?"

"We picked Duane for a boy. But I wanted Wesley."

"Stick with Duane."

"Wes is masculine," she defended her choice. "You macho types are all alike."

Marc called work to check in. Then at Carol's insistence, he made the first phone call to the XO's wife and started the Navy wives' grapevine rolling while Carol settled into her hospital room.

Navy wives were a strong breed.

They gave birth, cried and waited. Alone. Out of necessity they'd developed a strong support system for each other. If they were brave enough to send their husbands into danger, then, God help him, he'd do the same for Tabitha.

He could do this. Just as soon as she came home he'd show Tabitha how tough a Navy husband could be. Strong. Supportive. Loving.

It was nothing less than he expected from her.

They'd have dual Navy careers. Of course all his plans hinged on her giving him one last chance. His angry words came back to haunt him. How could he threaten her like that? Make her choose? He knew how important it was to have focus during a mission.

Marc pulled his dog tags from beneath his shirt. Their wedding bands dangled from the chain. "Forgive me?" he asked the air.

He had some serious butt kissing to do. He'd start at her sexy little tattoo and work his way from there.

He fueled up on coffee from a vending machine.

Passing the hospital florist, Marc stopped and ordered a roomful for Carol, carrying a simple bouquet with him. He bought other necessities in the gift shop. A camera, "It's a boy" cigars and a teddy bear with a blue ribbon. On his way back to the maternity ward, his step felt lighter than it had in months.

Being a godfather wasn't half bad.

He stopped by the nursery for a peek at Duane while he had his first diaper change. After a few snapshots, he wheeled the baby back to Mommy.

"Oh," Carol cooed when he brought her the baby and the gifts.

Marc's pager beeped. He read the message. *Choppers incoming. ETA 0645.* Fifteen minutes. Just enough time to stop by the florist again, before heading to the terminal. "They're back! Are you going to be okay, if I go meet the helicopters?"

"Of course." She bounced the bed in her excitement.

"Then I'll send Brad right over." He kissed her cheek, then the baby's and left.

It took him twenty minutes to get back to base. The first chopper was already on the ground, unloading, by the time he parked and stepped to the tarmac with an arm full of roses. The salesgirl had helped him decide on the color. *Yellow. For waiting.*

The team filed past, some of the lucky ones stealing kisses from their wives on the way to debriefing. He wouldn't be able to talk to her right away. But maybe he'd be able to steal a kiss.

He watched the men in passing. They were hanging their heads and avoiding eye contact with him.

Strange. He knew most of them intimately. He'd been their CO and Brad their XO before Marc had become the Commanding Officer of training. But even he wouldn't get information before they were debriefed.

The first chopper emptied. Neither Tabby nor Brad were on it. The hairs at the back of his neck rose. The second chopper landed and only a handful of men got off. As near as he could figure both Alpha and Echo squads were missing. He broke into a cold sweat.

In the history of the teams no SEAL had ever been left behind, dead or alive. The buddy system ensured every man came home. Every man *and* woman.

Flowers at his side, Marc strode over to J.C., the XO and leader of Bravo squad. "Where is she?" Marc demanded, grabbing the man by the arm.

"Hospital. In Greece."

"How bad?" Marc couldn't breathe because of the pain in his chest. He didn't know where he found the air to ask the question. He didn't know if he wanted to hear the answer.

"I don't know the extent of her injuries. We brought her in unconscious. Her squad stayed with her. If you hang around I could find out and fill you in after debriefing."

Marc nodded absently.

It was right that her squad had stayed with her. He needed to get to Greece.

"Brad stayed, too?"

J.C. sighed heavily and leveled his gaze. "Brad's

hurt too. And it's all her fault. If she hadn't been along in the first place—''

Marc closed in on the SEAL until the roses were crushed between them. Thorns pricked his skin. ''Whose fault was it when Manny got shot? Everyone on the team? There are risks to this job. You know it. I know it.''

''He was watching out for her.''

''And that's what I'd expect every CO to do for his BUDS. It's what I did for mine. Or don't you remember the bullet I took for you? Don't ever slander my wife again. I trained her. I know what she's capable of.'' He backed off. ''And I still want to know how she is doing,'' he said, softening his strained vocal cords.

''Sure, Marc,'' J.C. said quietly. Without another word, he walked toward the hangar.

''Have Elaine go sit with Carol,'' Marc called after the departing man. ''She just had the baby. Don't let anybody get her worked up. I'm going to take the first plane out of here.''

And he did. It probably wouldn't get him to Greece any faster than a commercial flight, but at least it put him in the air right away. He couldn't wait for the debriefing to end; he had to do something.

Crushed roses in his lap, he leaned back in his seat and listened to the hum of the C-30's engine. At Andrews Air Force base in Virginia, he switched to one of their larger crafts. Several untouched box lunches and windowless cargo planes later he was airlifted by a helicopter carrying mail and Naval personnel to an aircraft carrier in the Mediterranean.

All he had to do now was convince the USS *Enterprise*'s Commanding Officer to authorize the helicopter to leave once it unloaded, rather than the next day as scheduled. The pilots had already agreed for the price of a case of beer.

Stepping from the helicopter with his dead roses, Marc ducked under the whirring blades, thinking about what he could offer the CO in return for the favor. He stood by the elevator, waiting to go to the bridge, when the doors opened and several men got out.

A Lieutenant Junior Grade bumped into him, and Marc's eyes were drawn to the name tag on his flight suit. *Prince.* Could it be? Had to be. Except for the smile, he was a younger version of the Toad. "You wouldn't be Tabitha's brother, by chance?"

The junior officer sized him up. "By chance, I am." He flashed a cocky grin. "Miller... You would be my sister's pain in the—"

"Tabitha's in a hospital in Greece. What's the fastest way off this scow?"

Twenty minutes later with the Commanding Officer's permission, he was flying reel in an F-14 Tomcat with Prince at the controls. He hadn't liked flying before and he really hated it now after the takeoff from a football field instead of a runway.

He liked that Ltjg Prince was a man of few questions. If Tabitha's brother wondered what Marc was doing here he didn't ask.

When they finally got to the hospital, Marc discovered Brad had been discharged and that Tabitha was in the neurology wing. He headed there while Prince went to a bank of phones.

The waiting room outside of Neurology was filled with the SEALs. The two squads occupied every chair. Brad was among them.

As soon as he saw Marc, Brad, cast on his left arm, got to his feet. "That was fast." They gripped right arms.

"Don't ask. How is she?" he asked in hushed tones, pulling his friend aside.

"She's fine, Marc, really. A slight concussion, that's all. They're keeping her one more night for observation."

Thank God. "J.C.—"

"J.C.'s an asshole. You know it and I know it. She did good, Marc. Everything she was supposed to do. We're all proud of her. I can't even get the squad to leave. Maybe now that you're here—"

Marc looked around at her squad, Gummy, Armstrong and the others.

"They can stay," he said. "But do me a favor and get yourself home."

"I can stay with you. Carol won't mind."

"But little Wesley will."

"Wes— I'm a daddy! Wesley? We agreed on Duane!"

"Better hurry up then, 'cause Carol was about to sign his birth certificate into record," he teased, then gave Brad a quick rundown on the details of Duane's birth.

"Thanks for taking care of my wife."

"Ditto."

Brad was about to leave when Tad Prince and his wife walked in, demanding to see their daughter. Apparently, they had been yachting in the Mediterranean and Brad had sent word alerting them. Zach was with them.

Marc beat the Princes to the counter.

"Tabitha Chapel's room number?"

"I'm sorry," the station nurse said. "The doctor is limiting patient visitation to family only. Please, have a seat in the waiting room."

"For a *minor* concussion? How serious is this?"

"Serious enough." the nurse drawled. "Please have a seat with the men." She dismissed Marc and turned to the Princes.

"I'm her father…"

"I'm her husband." Marc looked his former Commanding Officer square in the eye. "That gives me priority."

Marc had started to turn. Otherwise, he would have seen the punch coming. It was the only explanation he could come up with from his vantage point on the floor. He sat up, checking his jaw.

"You denied me the chance to walk my daughter down the aisle. How are you going to rectify that, Sailor? You'd better see a Navy white wedding in your future complete with military arch."

"Yes, sir," he said without hesitation.

Tad Prince put out his hand and helped Marc to his feet. "I guess that makes you my son-in-law."

"I guess it does. If you don't mind, sir, I flew a long way to see my wife."

He thought he saw a glimmer of a smile on Prince's face.

"MOM! WHAT ARE you doing here?"

"I know I told you we'd be meeting the Thomases in Monte Carlo and spending the rest of October here. The Navy got a message to us.'' Lily Chapel-Prince stepped over to the bed and fussed with Tabby's sheets and pillows.

''Where's Dad?'' Tabby sat up in the hospital bed.

''I believe he's reacquainting himself with your husband,'' her mother answered.

Tabby moaned and pulled the covers over her head. ''My head hurts.'' She fumbled for the call button.

Her mother took it from her. ''Mind telling me when you decided to cut your family from your life? You should have told us.''

Tabby folded the covers to her waist. ''We eloped.''

''I gathered that.''

''Six months ago.'' She gave her attention to creasing the sheet.

''Six...''

''There's nothing to tell anyway. We haven't exactly been living as husband and wife. Marc's already filed for a divorce.'' Her voice broke as the full impact of the word hit her. She caught the sympathy in her mother's eyes. When her mother opened her arms, Tabby took comfort there and stopped trying to hold back her tears. ''He doesn't want me.''

''The man just flew halfway around the world. I'd say he wants you.''

''He hates my job.''

''I hated your father's job. The Commander just hates the idea of your leaving him.''

"I can't give it up, not even for him. I saved a little boy today. It's what I want to do with my life. I don't want to lose Marc. I love him, but I hate him for making me choose. Why do women have to make all the sacrifices? How did you stand it when you gave up the salvage business for Dad?"

"Tabitha!" Her mother pulled back. "What are you talking about? I didn't give up anything for your father that I didn't get tenfold in return. Besides we spend most of our time diving and yachting now. If you're not willing to compromise when it comes to your marriage you may as well go out there and tell your Commander to get back on that airplane. I chose a life on land rather than at sea so I could spend more time with your father and we could start a family. I wouldn't trade that for anything. He chose early retirement so we could raise you kids together. I know he wanted to stay in the Navy longer, but it was more important for him to be with us, and he'd already had his time as a SEAL. Just as I'd had my time as a sea captain. There are only so many child-bearing years in a lifetime…"

"What are you saying? I should give up the SEALs and have babies?"

"I'm not saying that—maybe this is your time to be a SEAL. All I'm saying is you have choices to make, you and your husband both. And if each of you wants the other in your life, you have to discuss them."

Tabby put her hand over her mother's. "Mom, Marc can't have kids."

"Don't tell me that. Between you and your brothers I'm never going to be a grandmother. Don't rush on my account, though. I can wait a few more years—I'm still a young fifty-nine.''

''A very beautiful fifty-nine.'' Tabby squeezed her mother's hand. ''Thanks, Mom, but I know Marc; he's going to want me to quit because of a little bump on the head. And I know I can't compromise about that.''

SEATED ACROSS FROM his father-in-law, with the rest of the squad scattered around them, Marc had to content himself with flipping through magazines in the waiting room because the nurse had threatened to call security and have them all removed if they didn't behave.

He also had to keep a keen eye on his brother-in-law who was hanging out at the nurses' station. If he wasn't mistaken, Ltjg Prince was flirting his way to being second in line to see Tabitha.

Marc had waited long enough to reassure himself she was all right—to tell her he loved her and broach her father's idea of another wedding with all the trappings. He just hoped he hadn't waited too long to work things out.

A small boy raced down the corridor yelling for his American mother.

''Hey, sport, what's the hurry?'' Marc saved the little rascal from running headlong into a magazine rack and received a grateful look from the nun pursuing him.

''Thank you,'' she said.

He smiled up at her, then turned his attention back to the squirming child in his arms.

''American?'' the boy asked.

"Yeah."

"I want American mother," the boy pleaded in stilted English.

Marc looked questioningly at the nun.

"The soldier who saved him from the rebels. I promised he could say goodbye before going to the orphanage."

"Not goodbye! American mother!"

"He's talking about Tabby," Gummy explained.

Marc had figured that out. He pushed to his feet and picked up the boy. He was a cute kid with mussed brown hair and a hint of mischief in his dark eyes. Why did Marc suddenly feel as if he'd come home? "I think I know where to find her. Let's go say hello."

The sister followed as he made his way to his wife's room. The thought of adoption—once not even an option—started to take hold as he held the boy. And maybe not just adoption. If he couldn't have his vasectomy reversed, there were other ways to make babies.

Tabitha's babies. His babies. Their babies.

In loving Tabby, he realized he had love to spare. It didn't matter who'd fathered the boy. What mattered was the character of the man who raised him.

He didn't have to repeat Warren Miller's mistakes.

The ones Marc made would be tempered with love. It was then he knew he could handle Tabitha's career choice. He'd been willing to give it a try before, but now that his worst fears were behind him, he knew he'd be the perfect Navy husband—and father.

He turned to the sister. "How hard would it be for an American family to adopt a refugee orphan?"

"Not hard." She smiled at him. "A lot of red tape. A lot of money. His name is Aaron."

"My wife is a wiz at cutting red tape." And they'd find a way to come up with the money.

Then he saw Tabitha standing in the doorway of her hospital room. A little bruised, but that was all.

He put Aaron down and savored the moment when the boy ran to her. She stooped and put her arm around him.

One step, two, three, and he was in the picture, too.

"I love you, Tabitha." He pulled her into his arms, as the boy watched. "I got your message. The one you left on my machine—and the one you've been trying to tell me all along. I came to give you this." He took off his dog tags and put her ring back on her finger where it belonged. "There's a big wedding in it for you this time around."

"How big? I want a small wedding."

"Small's okay. But it has to be white."

"A white wedding gown or dress whites?"

"I was thinking both. But I'm open to negotiation. Except your dad *has* to walk you down the aisle."

"Ahh, this is my dad's wedding you're talking about."

"Yeah, but the honeymoon is all ours."

She touched the silver leaf on his collar and peered at him through her lashes. "I'm open to negotiation, Commander."

He took a deep breath. "I'm used to giving orders. While it may be an appropriate way to handle a trainee, I think I've learned it doesn't quite work on a wife. If I ever back you into a corner again, let me have it right between the eyes.''

''I can do that,'' she said, wrapping her arms around his neck. ''I love you, too. You were always my first choice. But I still want to be a SEAL.''

''What was it you said about having it all? The more I think about it, the more I like it. Dual SEAL careers, a house on the beach and most important of all—kids.''

He picked up Aaron and included him in their embrace.

''You mean it? I'd like that—no, I'd love that.'' She smiled at Aaron and brushed back the boy's hair. ''I think you'll find we're more than you bargained for.''

''I'm counting on it.''

''And here I thought it would take NATO intervention for us to ever reach *détente*.''

''Not this time. The treaty is signed—now let's seal it with a kiss.''

IN UNIFORM

There's something special about a man in
uniform. Maybe because he's a man who takes
charge, a man you can count on, and yes,
maybe even love....

Superromance presents *In Uniform*, an occasional series that
features men who live up to your every fantasy—and then some!

Look for:
Mad About the Major
by Roz Denny Fox
Superromance #821
Coming in January 1999

An Officer and a Gentleman
by Elizabeth Ashtree
Superromance #828
Coming in March 1999

SEAL It with a Kiss
by Rogenna Brewer
Superromance #833
Coming in April 1999

Available wherever Harlequin books are sold.

HARLEQUIN®
Makes any time special ™

Look us up on-line at: http://www.romance.net

HSRIU

Coming in May 1999

Marriage FOR KEEPS

Three brand-new short stories by

Karen Young
Gina Wilkins
and
Margot Dalton

Sometimes you can stumble into
marriage for all the right reasons!

Available at your favorite retail outlet.

HARLEQUIN®
Makes any time special ™

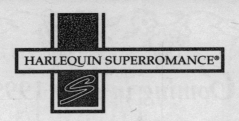

HARLEQUIN SUPERROMANCE®

From April to June 1999,
read about three women whose
New Millennium resolution is

By the Year 2000: *Satisfaction!*

April—*The Wrong Bride* by Judith Arnold.
Cassie Webster loves Phillip Keene and expected to marry
him—but it turns out he's marrying someone else. So
Cassie shows up at his wedding…to prove he's got
The Wrong Bride.

May—*Don't Mess with Texans* by Peggy Nicholson.
Susannah Mack Colton is out to get revenge on her
wealthy—and nasty—ex-husband. But in the process
she gets entangled with a handsome veterinarian,
complicating *his* life, too. Because that's what happens
when you ***"Mess with Texans"!***

June—*If He Could See Me Now* by Rebecca Winters.
The Rachel Maynard of today isn't the Rachel of ten
years ago. Now a lovely and accomplished woman,
she's looking for sweet revenge—and a chance to win
the love of the man who'd once rejected her.
If He Could See Me Now…

Available at your favorite retail outlet.

HARLEQUIN®
Makes any time special ™

Look us up on-line at: http://www.romance.net   HSR2000R2

COMING NEXT MONTH

#834 DON'T MESS WITH TEXANS • Peggy Nicholson
By the Year 2000: Satisfaction!
Veterinarian R. D. Taggart is the innocent bystander caught in the cross fire between
a blue-eyed Texas hellcat and her vindictive ex-husband. Susannah Mack Colton
inadvertently destroys Tag's reputation in what *appears* to be nothing but a vendetta
against her ex—and Tag intends to collect on his damages!

#835 THE DOCTOR'S DAUGHTER • Judith Bowen
Men of Glory
Lucas Yellowfly was always in love with Virginia Lake. More than a decade ago, the
half-Indian boy from the wrong side of town spent a memorable night with the
doctor's daughter. Now they're both back in Glory, Lucas as a successful lawyer and
Virginia as a single mother with a five-year-old son. Virginia's looking for a job—
and Lucas finds he needs someone with *exactly* her qualifications!

#836 HER SECRET, HIS CHILD • Tara Taylor Quinn
A Little Secret
Jamie Archer has a past she wants to keep hidden. She's created an entirely
new life for herself and four-year-old Ashley—a life that's threatened when
Kyle Radcliff reappears. Kyle doesn't immediately realize who she is, but
Jamie recognizes *him* right away. *Her child's father.*

#837 THE GUARDIAN • Bethany Campbell
Guaranteed Page-Turner
Kate Kanaday is a widow with a young son. Life is hard, but she manages—right
up until the day a stalker leaves his first message on her doorstep. Before long she's
forced to quit her job and run. And there's only one place to go—to the home of a
stranger who has promised to keep them safe whether he wants them there or not.
From the bestselling author of *See How They Run* and *Don't Talk to Strangers*.

#838 THE PULL OF THE MOON • Darlene Graham
9 Months Later
Danielle Goodlove has every reason to believe that marriage and family are not for
her. As a dedicated obstetrician, she's content to share her patients' happiness. Until
one moonlit night, when firefighter Matthew Creed is brought into the emergency
room. Now she wishes things could be different....

#839 HER BROTHER'S KEEPER • K.N. Casper
Family Man
Krisanne Blessing receives a call from her ex-lover, Drew Hadley, asking her to
come back to Coyote Springs, Texas. Drew is now a widower with a young son—
and he's also a close friend of her brother, Patrick. Krisanne is shocked to discover
that Patrick wants her and Drew to give romance another try. She's even more
shocked when she discovers *why* he's encouraging their relationship.